# MASTERS
# OF
# SEDUCTION

D1382395

# LARA ADRIAN
# DONNA GRANT
# LAURA WRIGHT
# ALEXANDRA IVY

ISBN: 0991647513
ISBN-13: 978-0-9916475-1-4

MASTERS OF SEDUCTION
© 2014 by Obsidian House Books, LLC
Cover design © 2014 by CrocoDesigns

MERCILESS: HOUSE OF GRAVORI
© 2014 by Lara Adrian, LLC

SOULLESS: HOUSE OF ROMERAC
© 2014 by Donna Grant

SHAMELESS: HOUSE OF VIPERA
© 2014 by Laura Wright

RUTHLESS: HOUSE OF XANTHE
© 2014 by Debbie Raleigh

**www.MastersOfSeductionAuthors.com**

Available in ebook and print. Unabridged audiobook edition forthcoming.

# CONTENTS

# MERCILESS
## House of Gravori

## Lara Adrian

# CHAPTER ONE

A gust of hot wind and fine, rust-colored sand twisted like a dervish in front of Devlin Gravori's hard-set face as the hatch of his private jet opened and he prepared to disembark from the long flight.

When he'd awoken that morning, he could not have guessed that before day's end he would find himself several hours away from his island citadel in the Adriatic sea, arriving at this small desert airport in a forbidding corner of the Middle East that had once—long, long ago—been known as Mesopotamia.

Then again, when he'd begun his day, Dev had no idea that his brother had been killed.

The shock of it, the piercing grief, clung to him as it had the first moment he'd learned the news.

Golden, charming Marius…dead.

Murdered.

Dev's fists clenched as the memory of what he saw earlier that day filled his vision. Marius and a human woman, both nude, sprawled together in tangled white sheets that were soaked with sweat and semen and a terrible pool of their combined blood.

The woman had been stabbed through the

heart—a certain, instant death for any mortal.

Marius would have been harder to kill.

Just shy of four hundred years old, he had been younger than Dev by several centuries, but no less formidable. They were Incubi, a demon race that fed on sexual energy and had existed for as long as Heaven and Hell had been at war over the souls of mankind.

Devlin and his brothers of the House of Gravori—and every Incubus in the nine other Houses of their race as well—were something ancient and dark, close to immortal.

There were few ways to slay one of their kind, and fewer individuals who would dare.

Whoever had sliced open Marius's throat in the midst of his sexual feeding last night had been aware of one of the surest methods.

If Dev had to guess, the slayer had taken advantage of Marius at his weakest moment, attacking from behind as the Incubus was having his carnal fill of his Thrall.

The human female had been slain with equal stealth and precision, no doubt while Marius was bleeding out. His big body slumped across her from the waist down, the woman had been pinned beneath his dead weight on the bed. A deep puncture wound had gaped at her breast, her fair skin sticky and dark with her life's blood.

The killings had been expert, and nothing if not thorough.

Except for one telling flaw.

Dev carried that evidence on him now, to an unannounced confrontation on what had forever been sacred, neutral ground.

Scraping a hand over his short black hair, he headed down the Gulfstream G650's stairs in his charcoal gray, custom-tailored Italian suit and gleaming leather shoes. He hadn't bothered to change into more appropriate attire for this meeting. If the trappings of the outside world offended, Dev didn't give a damn. He'd been called directly from his corporate office to the crime scene that morning, then had been en route to this swath of arid, heat-choked land within the hour.

Ironic that the lofty audience he sought now should be hidden in a place as hellish as this.

He muttered a curse. Nasty words, spoken in the ancient language of his demon ancestors.

"It's not too late to turn back, Dev."

The calm, deep voice belonged to Ramiel, the captain of the House of Gravori's Watchmen. The dark-haired bodyguard deplaned along with Dev, dressed in black pants and a fitted black T-shirt that clung to his broad chest and massive biceps. Elaborate tattoos declaring Ram's House affiliation and profession wrapped the Incubus guardian's forearms.

Ram shared Dev's bloodline; a distant cousin, but as loyal as any brother. And the Watchman was coolheaded and steady, where Gravori's Master was apt to strike hard and without warning at the first sign of attack.

Like the scorpion that had been the sigil of the Gravoris for eons, Dev's wrath was swift, blinding.

Utterly merciless.

It had earned him the nickname "Devil"

3

Gravori, a reputation that followed him in both his business dealings and in all other areas of his life.

Today, he was prepared to demonstrate the full force of that reputation in one of the most hallowed courts of the immortal realm.

"You don't have to do this," Ram went on. "Not like this."

"The hell I don't," Dev snarled.

The sight of Marius's killing was still raw in his mind. Every detail would be burned into his memory forever. Grief raked him, but it was fury that had put him on the plane and sent him here with a thirst for vengeance.

In the chest pocket of his suit coat, the errant object Dev had retrieved from beneath his brother's body felt like ice resting over his heart. "No one crosses the House of Gravori with impunity. Not even them."

He stared forward, refusing to slow his pace, let alone reconsider where he was heading.

Ramiel grimly strode alongside him, across the sunbaked dirt tarmac, where a local driver in an off-road SUV waited. The vehicle had been hired to take them deeper into the desert, toward a ridge of jagged, haze-shrouded mountains that loomed like a dragon's spine in the sweltering distance.

The driver wouldn't be able to deliver them the entire way. The place Dev needed to go would not be found on any map or road or shepherd's path.

For the last leg of his journey, to enter the neutral ground of the Nephilim court, Dev would need to rely on demon magic to transport him.

And hope to hell that same demon magic would

get him out again when it was over.

When they reached the idling SUV, Ram paused. The Watchman's face was grave, filled with dread and doubt. "Confronting the Three simply isn't done, Dev. You know that. They are the balance. They have the power to enforce Nephilim law. They have the ear of the Sovereign as well."

"The Sovereign." Dev grunted. "It's been more than five hundred years since the Council awarded the Obsidian Throne to the House of Marakel. Since then, things between the Nephilim and the other Incubi Houses have been anything but balanced. If you ask me, we'd all be better off if we cleared the decks and started over. Beginning with the Incubus seated on the Throne."

Ram exhaled an oath, low under his breath. "For fuck's sake, Dev. First you fly out here determined to demand an audience with the most powerful Nephilim in the realm, and now you stand here talking about treason."

Dev shrugged. "Change is coming, just not soon enough for my liking. The Three are due to step down in a handful of years, and if Marakel does not produce an Incubus heir before long, his House will die out the same way Akana's did."

Ram gave him a dubious look. "Yes, and in the meantime, the Three can—*and will*—do whatever they please, all in the name of peace. If you won't listen to reason, then at least let me stand with you in front of them today. As captain of Gravori's Watchmen, I'm sworn by blood and steel to ensure your neck stays intact."

"They wouldn't dare," Dev assured him.

Ram's answering gaze was sober. "Tell that to Marius."

Dev didn't appreciate the reminder, even though the warning wasn't without merit. But he wasn't about to let anyone stand between him and the trio of Nephilim priestesses whose hands, he was certain, were somehow stained with his brother's blood. Ram may have pledged his life to Devlin as the Master of the House of Gravori, but Dev's presence here was personal.

And if it turned into a battle, he'd be damned before he let anyone else fight it for him.

"There are worse things than death," Ram murmured. "Prison and torture in the Oubliette, for one."

Although the Watchman was right about that, Dev dismissed the thought of the infamous supernatural prison with a hissed curse.

"I can't let Marius's death go unchallenged, Ram," he said, his tone permitting no further argument. "Someone needs to answer for my brother's slaying. Someone needs to pay, blood for blood." Dev's hand came up to the place where the proof of his suspicion rested, cold against his heart. "I won't leave here without collecting on this debt."

# CHAPTER TWO

The audience with the Three was about to end in tears and disappointment.

Nahiri knew it, even before the Nephilim mother's chin began to quiver with emotion. The woman was on her knees in a reverent pose, her demure daughter beside her at the base of the broad marble stairs that led up to the elevated platform at the head of the temple's High Chamber.

At the top of the eight polished marble steps, seated behind a tall screen crafted of pierced sandalwood painted with gleaming gold leaf, the trio of Nephilim priestesses presided, unseen, over the temple and all within it.

Nahiri stood at the bottom right of the stairs. Like the mother and daughter seeking counsel, Nahiri was clothed especially for this chamber sanctuary, in an undyed linen tunic and pants, simple calfskin sandals on her feet. But strapped crisscross from shoulder to waist on both sides of her body were the woven leather sheaths that held the weapons of her station.

Nahiri was a Blade.

More specifically, she was a Temple Blade, one of less than a dozen Nephilim warriors responsible for guarding the High Chamber and protecting the Three.

Not that anyone had ever dreamed of doing them harm.

To Nahiri and the other Temple Blades—to all Nephilim, in fact—the exalted Three, being half human, half angel, were practically deities in their own right.

For nearly three hundred years, they had occupied this temple as supreme, sacred advisors. Like the Three who served before them, their lives were devoted in selfless counsel to the Sovereign on the Obsidian Throne, and to the larger Nephilim and Incubi populations that existed in secret alongside mankind in the outside world.

The decisions and edicts of the Three were intended to keep the ultimate peace, and to ensure harmony and balance between the Nephilim and the Incubi, above all things.

Unfortunately, for the mother petitioning the Three today on behalf of her daughter, those decisions did not always align with the whims and wishes of everyone who was granted an audience in the High Chamber.

Nahiri stood motionless at her post as the Nephilim mother attempted to persuade the Three to reconsider her request here today.

"Your Graces, please, I beseech you. Each generation of my family has been chosen to send one of our daughters to the Harem in her twentieth year. Why not this time? Why not my daughter? It is an honor we have always accepted most humbly—"

"As you should," said one of the Three, a mild but measured response drifting down from behind the obscuring screen. "Selection is an honor that cannot be requested or petitioned. It is a sacred duty that must be protected and preserved."

Although she respected the Nephilim way of life, Nahiri was relieved that as a Blade, she was ineligible for the Harem. The idea of being sent away to breed with the Incubi who visited the pleasure palace made her shudder inwardly. She'd heard enough tales of the Incubi's insatiable, unholy appetites and overwhelming sexual power.

She'd listened in appalled fascination to the stories some of the other Blades told in the temple dormitory late at night—stories they'd heard from Nephilim sisters and cousins on the outside about all of the things rumored to go on within the silk-draped walls of the Harem.

Wicked, deviant things that made Nahiri's cheeks flush and sent heat pooling between her legs, even now.

Awkwardly, she shifted on the soles of her feet, trying to ignore the unwanted stirring of her body. As she moved, she felt her long black braid swing against her spine.

Her perfect soldier's posture broken, Nahiri winced and hoped no one had noticed.

Naturally, someone had.

The shifting of her stance caught the attention of the Temple Blade posted on the other side of the High Chamber staircase. The tall blond Nephilim lifted a pale brow in Nahiri's direction, smugly noting the flaw.

Of course, Valina would enjoy seeing Nahiri squirm. The two had been in a silent competition with each other from the moment they both arrived at the temple to train as Blades at the age of eighteen. A decade later, they were still rivals.

Valina's stunning beauty won favors from everyone who looked at her, but the Blade was also a skilled fighter. Though she was not quite as skilled—nor as disciplined—as Nahiri. It was that slim difference that had won Nahiri the right side of the High Chamber stairs as captain of the Temple Blades, while Valina stood as her second on the left.

Even though pride was frowned upon in the temple, Nahiri couldn't help taking more than a little satisfaction in the position she had claimed through hard work and devotion to her duty.

Spine erect, expression placid, she stood at attention as the Nephilim mother and her daughter were dismissed by the Three and began to take their leave.

The pair had barely made it to the arched double doors when the fine hairs on Nahiri's nape started to prickle.

A stirring energy was gathering swiftly outside the Chamber.

The tall door swung open, admitting a startling burst of heat. It shot through the room, carrying with it a metallic punch of ozone that blasted into Nahiri's nostrils. Like the approach of a violent storm, the air turned electric.

Then it came alive in the form of a man.

A very large, menacing man.

*Incubus.*

Nahiri knew it even before the raven-haired demon materialized fully and lifted his dark head. His citrine gaze was narrowed, his stance aggressive, big hands fisted at his sides.

Alarm rushed over the room like a flash fire. Nervous whispers and anxious murmurs hissed through the ranks of the other Blades. One of the newer trainees let out a shriek.

Only the Three seemed unmoved by the intrusion.

Not that the Incubus seemed to notice.

Nor did he care.

His disregard was plain enough in the way he'd arrived, rudely disrupting the Chamber. But his attire added further insult. Instead of dressing appropriately for an appearance on sacred ground, he wore clothing from the outside, from the world of man. Modern, sophisticated clothing that somehow made him seem even more foreign and savage in this place.

The coal-gray suit he wore outlined every broad line and muscled inch of his body. At his throat, a patch of smooth, tanned skin showed beneath the unbuttoned collar of his crisp white shirt, hinting at lazy days spent under the sun.

*Decadent,* Nahiri thought disapprovingly. It didn't take much to imagine what she guessed to be a pampered, debauched lifestyle of sloth and pointless indulgence.

She tried not to imagine anything more about the sex-feeding demon, least of all how he and his kind were gifted with the power to seduce even the most unwilling soul.

She felt the depth of that power crackling in the air all around her as the Incubus stepped forward, neither waiting for, nor seeking, permission from the Three to approach.

Nahiri settled her hands on her weapons as he stalked up the center aisle in arrogant, long-legged strides, his entire demeanor bristling with menace. Yet for all his arrogance and rudeness, he was handsome. She might even have been tempted to call him beautiful, if not for the savage scowl that knit his brow and twisted his full lips into a furious snarl.

Even in rage, his face was arresting. Brutal and fierce, full of hard angles and unforgiving lines, his was the kind of face that would've told anyone looking at him that he was something more than human.

Something long-lived, darkly formidable.

Something very dangerous—all the more so because of his enticing, rugged appeal.

Judging from the many agog faces of her fellow Blades, Valina included, Nahiri had to guess this was one incredibly powerful Incubus.

Hushed whispers drifted toward her from the other Nephilim.

*"Isn't that the Master of Gravori House?"*

*"Heaven save us, if it is."*

*"You know what they call him, don't you?"*

*"Devil Gravori."*

He was nearly to the front of the Chamber now. As captain, it was up to Nahiri to meet this oncoming threat and stop it. If need be, she would call every Blade in the room to attack.

She stepped directly into his path. "Come no farther."

To her relief, her warning sounded steady, unrushed. She felt the weight of more than one pair of Blade eyes on her as she alone moved in to confront the menace that had taken over the room.

The Incubus paused, but those ageless, golden eyes were fixed on her in question.

In piqued challenge.

Nahiri didn't like the wicked gleam she saw in his gaze. It did strange things to her breathing. Made her already racing heartbeat lunge into a harder tempo.

That unsettling citrine stare made her feel examined from the inside out. She felt exposed, vulnerable. As if her every fear and doubt and sinful thought were being laid out for his perusal.

Worse, it took all her focus to keep from losing herself in his eyes, and the wicked promise that seemed to burn in their depths.

She didn't want to imagine what his kind could do to a woman, but it seemed that as soon as she thought it, pictures were already forming vividly— profanely—in her mind. She and this man, this demon, twined around each other under the heat of a summer sky.

She could practically smell the sun warming his naked, tawny skin. She could almost feel the erotic warmth of him under her fingertips, in her grasp, on her tongue…against every fevered inch of her body.

And then it was his fingers roaming over her

bare skin. His lips tasting every inch of her.

His mouth devouring her with a carnal hunger that threatened to consume her…

*Enough.*

Nahiri cleared her throat and struggled to rein in her wandering mind.

*Was he doing that to her deliberately?*

*Did an Incubus Master like him even have to try?*

He moved to step around her. Nahiri moved too. Chin lifting to meet his arrogant gaze, she closed her fingers around the hilts of her weapons.

"Unannounced visitors are not permitted in the temple."

She could have the twin, ten-inch daggers in her grip and poised for combat in a mere instant.

Although she had never used the special blades to inflict harm on anyone, she wouldn't hesitate to use them now.

She wouldn't hesitate to *kill*, if it meant protecting the Three. They were her family—as close to family as she'd ever known, that is.

Those golden eyes seared her. "I'm not a visitor," he growled, his voice dark and deep and powerful. She felt the vibration of it all the way into her bones. "And since I'm already standing here, consider my presence all the announcement anyone needs."

A gasp went up from many of the other Blades.

No one had ever dared such a flagrant show of disrespect for the temple. Nor, more importantly, for the Three.

Nahiri bristled. She drew one of her long daggers. "You must leave. Now."

He glanced at the razor-sharp length of honed obsidian in her hand. One black brow quirked, nearly imperceptibly. Then his face hardened, and the dangerous twist of his mouth turned even more terrifying.

He took another step, not so much toward the stairs now, but toward her. Into her personal space, until there was hardly a hand's width between them.

"You think you can tangle with me, little Blade? I won't go down as easily as my brother, I promise you that," he snarled.

She didn't know what he was talking about.

She didn't know anything in that moment, except the mesmerizing spell of his penetrating gaze and the answering rush of arousal that ran up and down her limbs, making her skin feel too tight, utterly too hot, to bear.

All of the carnal images and wildly erotic sensations she'd felt a moment ago under his stare intensified now. She saw things—*felt things*—that her virgin mind struggled to comprehend, even though her untried body seemed eager for the education.

Her heart raced. Her breath accelerated into soft, shallow pants as a keen ache began to bloom deep inside her. She moaned at the feeling, powerless to bite back her reaction to this intense need. She couldn't break free of his hold on her. All the worse, she couldn't even summon the will to want to break free.

It was unbearable, both the yearning of her body and the humiliation of how effortlessly the Incubus would be able to make her his Thrall, if he wanted.

Her fingers began to go lax around her blade, almost to the point of dropping it.

*No.* She wouldn't go down so easily, either.

Gathering what inner strength she could, Nahiri mentally pushed back at him with all her will.

*No!*

The ache eased up at once. She was still breathless, her nerve endings still smoldering, but at least she had some control of herself again.

As for the demon—Devil Gravori—he cocked his head at her, studying her with more interest than she cared to acknowledge. The look was there and gone in an instant, then he swung his head away from her and addressed the Three directly.

He stalked toward the stairs before Nahiri could stop him.

No one stopped him.

No one seemed inclined to move against him, not even Valina.

Every female face in the room was transfixed on him, not in terror or horror now, but in some small measure of the same boneless compliance that he had inflicted on her.

He had enthralled every Blade in the room.

And now his fury was fixed entirely on the trio of priestesses at the top of the stairs.

"I've come here to demand an explanation from the three of you," he said, his voice booming in the heavy silence of the room. "I've come to demand justice for the offense that's been dealt to my family and my House."

The silence of the Three was staggering. Nahiri

waited to hear one of them, any of them, react to the accusation in some way.

Had he enthralled the powerful Nephilim priestesses as handily as he owned the rest of the High Chamber?

Finally, a voice filtered down from behind the tall screen.

"This is an overstep even for you, Devlin Gravori."

*Devlin*, Nahiri silently acknowledged, *not Devil*. Although she was getting a very good taste for how he might have earned the nickname.

"You've been Master of your House for many centuries," another of the Three said. "Long enough to know that this temple is not a place for violence or accusations. This is a place of peace and mercy. Of wisdom and counsel. And we Three are merely the balance—"

"Fuck the three of you," he growled, more savage than ever. "And fuck your precious balance. My brother was killed last night, along with his human Thrall. I'm not leaving until I have an answer as to why."

He stalked for the stairs leading up to the Three, and started taking them two at a time.

Panic sent Nahiri into motion. She sped up beside him to head him off midway. Her obsidian blade was gripped lightly, but lethally, in her right hand; the second was not even a moment out of reach of her other hand.

"Stop," she commanded the powerful Incubus Master. "You have no right—"

His teeth flashed white behind the furious curl

of his lips. "Don't I, little Blade?"

He slipped his hand into the inside of his suit jacket. Nahiri thought for certain he was about to retrieve a weapon of his own.

And in a way, that's exactly what he did.

"I found this under my brother's body today." He held out his hand, a length of gleaming black volcanic glass lying across his palm. His tone seethed with barely restrained rage. "Whoever killed him left it behind."

It was a broken length of blade.

An obsidian blade.

The kind of weapon only a Nephilim warrior like Nahiri would carry.

# CHAPTER THREE

Dev watched the Temple Blade's expression turn to shock as she looked at the broken length of obsidian in his hand. Smoky dark eyes widened in confusion. In total disbelief.

Was she stunned by the killing, or by the idea that he held evidence of it?

Dev couldn't be sure.

"No," she murmured. A shake of her head sent the rope of her silky black braid swinging like a pendulum behind her lithe body. "No, that's impossible. No one carries a weapon like this. Only a—"

"Only a Nephilim Blade," Dev agreed. "And no Blade would raise her weapon against anyone without the approval of this High Chamber." He swiveled a hard look in the direction of the Three. "Or on its direct command."

He heard her sharp inhalation, felt her tension ratchet up tighter at his inflammatory charge. "You cannot speak to them that way. It's not done. It's not right—"

"It's not right that my brother is dead, damn it." His sharp words echoed in the silence of the temple. He glared down at her. "It's not right that the coward sliced open Marius's throat and left him to bleed out while his lover was stabbed through the heart."

The Nephilim warrior stared at him then, mute, hardly breathing under the blast of his rage.

And despite the boiling fury and grief he felt over his brother's murder by one of her kind, he couldn't deny that this Blade intrigued him.

She was beautiful. Sable-dark hair, fathomless brown eyes that seemed both innocent and ageless in the creamy, soft oval of her delicate face.

But beauty alone meant nothing to Dev. He'd had the pleasure of a lifetime of beautiful women. Several lifetimes.

This Nephilim pricked his interest for her courage, even more than her heavenly face and tempting body, which he noted with far too much interest was hardly disguised by the loose-fitting clothes of the temple.

She had been the only Blade in the temple who'd made a move to stop him. Impressive, though not completely surprising, given that she stood at the right of the stairs as the highest guard.

Looking into her sober, determined face now, Dev would bet that she'd have been the first to step up no matter her rank among the other Blades.

This female was brave, stubbornly so.

She was also strong-willed, the only Nephilim warrior in the temple to push back against his allure.

He'd turned it on hardest for her, and yet she'd managed to hold on to her will. Barely.

That stubbornness made the Incubus in him

rankle with a wicked urge. How far would he have to go to seduce her?

How long would it take for him to make the pretty Blade his Thrall?

Dev shoved the thought aside with a growl. His unholy nature—and the carnal needs that came with it—would have to wait for another time.

Another woman.

Refocusing on his purpose for being in the temple, Dev curled his fingers around the cold obsidian in his palm. He had come for answers. For an explanation of why Marius had been singled out for such savage attack, and which of the Nephilim warriors had dealt it.

Dev had come for an admission of guilt from the Three. For an apology.

For vengeance, if he didn't find any satisfaction in this chamber.

He swung around to address the Three on a snarl. "I demand the truth. Did you send a Blade to kill my brother?"

Quiet filled the vaulted cavern of the High Chamber, and for a moment Dev doubted he would get any reply. Then, at last, a whisper of movement from behind the screen at the top of the stairs.

A low murmur of voices from the Three, before one spoke for them all. "No such order was given. Nor have we ever called for an Incubus's execution."

Dev scowled, doubt tasting like bile on his tongue. It was true; he couldn't think of a single instance when an Incubus had been sought out and killed on the orders of the priestesses during their three-hundred-year tenure. Banishment to the Oubliette was more their style. And yet he sniffed a lie in their response.

He held the proof of the lie in his hand. The sharp length of honed obsidian felt like ice in his grip.

"You're telling me the Blade who took this weapon to my brother's neck did so of her own volition? Or, more incredibly, against the edict of this Chamber?"

It would be unheard of. Neither likely nor even possible, given the Nephilim warriors' devotion to the Three.

A slow exhalation sounded from the priestesses hiding behind their flimsy shield. There was a wealth of disapproval in the heavy sigh. Scorn in the brief silence that followed.

"This intrusion is unwelcome, Master Gravori. Though no more than your accusations."

Dev grunted, unfazed that they'd taken offense. "Tell me why my brother was killed."

"If you feel a wrong has been unjustly dealt your House, we suggest you take it up with the Sovereign—"

"The Sovereign," Dev scoffed. Anger flooded him at their attempt to dismiss him. "You know damned well my request will never be granted. How many years has it been since anyone's even seen him?"

"You have our answer." Short words, sharp with irritation. "We are finished here."

"Like hell we are." Dev seethed with outrage.

He couldn't hold back the roar that erupted from his throat. He pulled his arm back, then let the broken obsidian dagger fly at the screen at the top of the stairs. It shattered against the wall of pierced, painted sandalwood that stood between him and the Three.

They scrambled behind the screen, a chaos of panic.

Dev relished their fear. Although he'd never laid eyes on them, he pictured three faces blanched with alarm, sandaled feet scuffing over the polished marble as the priestesses leapt for cover.

"Blades!" one of them shrieked. "Nahiri, seize him!"

Slender, strong hands clamped down around Dev's arm in that instant. A razor-sharp edge of cold obsidian rested in warning under his chin.

He met the dark eyes that glinted with unswerving determination in the lovely face of the temple's highest guard. If he so much as flinched with harmful intent toward the Three, this exotic beauty—Nahiri—would cut him open right where he stood.

He didn't want to admire that about her, but damn if he didn't find her even more attractive when her doe-brown eyes were narrowed, her entire body vibrating with readiness to fight.

She was levelheaded, stealthy.

Lethal, Dev had no doubt.

She didn't have to worry. As furious as he was, Dev wasn't going to assault the Three.

It was one thing to storm into the High Chamber and demand answers. Quite another to strike against the Nephilim's most sacred beings.

The Incubi and the Nephilim realms had already come through one savage war centuries ago; he wouldn't be the one to start a new clash between their races here and now.

But he wasn't leaving without some kind of satisfaction.

"This is far from over," he warned them. "I will find out who killed my brother, and why. I won't rest until I have those answers. And I promise you, the guilty will not be able to hide for long...no matter who they are."

Dev glanced into Nahiri's determined, doe-eyed gaze. She was struggling to keep her dagger on him, fighting a desperate inner battle against the blast of sexual compulsion he trained on her now with ruthless intent. He gave her more than he had the first time. Her full, pink lips parted on a moan as he flooded her mind and senses with arousal. With raking need.

She was strong, but he was stronger.

And he had no mercy in him.

Only fury.

Only grief and a need to make someone pay.

Until the Three were ready to admit their part in Marius's murder, Dev wanted them to feel some measure of loss too.

Dev wrapped his hand around Nahiri's wrist, guiding the weapon away from his throat with only the slightest effort. As he held her in his grasp, a dark thought took root. A wicked thought that caught fire in his blood, faster than he could rein it in.

"Since this temple values its damnable balance so much," he growled, "it only seems fitting that I take something precious from you."

One of the Three sputtered in outrage. "You would not dare—"

But he already had.

With Nahiri held tight in his grasp and deep in his thrall, Dev dematerialized, taking the Nephilim priestesses' most valued Blade along with him.

# CHAPTER FOUR

Nahiri awoke in the middle of a large bed in a strange room.

She shot upright the instant consciousness dawned, her hands reaching automatically for her weapons.

They were gone.

The leather sheaths that crossed her torso were empty.

*No. That meant her nightmare hadn't been just a dream. It was reality.*

*The Incubus in the temple...Devlin Gravori.*

*He really had taken her.*

Nahiri's eyelids snapped open in panic. Sunlight poured in from an open window across the room, blasting her vision.

Momentarily blinded, she squinted through her lashes, struggling to take quick stock of her new surroundings.

Creamy stucco walls. Dark hardwood floors and masculine-looking furnishings. Thick timber beams high above her head.

And beneath her, a massive bed. The mattress was as cushiony as a cloud, the cotton sheets and silken coverlet calling to mind all manner of sins.

All around her was the scent of intriguingly exotic spices and something even more enticing.

*Him.*

She sensed his presence even before she swung her head in his direction and found him seated in an upholstered chair beside the bed. No, not seated in it, exactly. Dominating it. The same way he seemed to dominate every space he occupied.

His big body lounged negligently where he sat, his powerful thighs spread, one arm draped over the side of the chair, the other propping his head up, fist curled loosely under the square line of his jaw.

He'd shed his suit jacket at some point, and now wore just his gray tailored pants and white business shirt. The collar was opened even farther than she recalled, just one more button loosened, but exposing enough of his tawny skin to make her mouth water with a sudden, unholy urge to taste him.

She wanted to dismiss the impulse as one he planted in her mind, but she could tell from the casual way he regarded her that any curiosity she felt in that moment was hers alone.

Nahiri scrambled off the bed. She backed into the farthest corner of the room, eyeing him warily. "Where am I? Where have you taken me?"

"You're at Gravori House." He cast a nonchalant look around the room. "More specifically, you're in my bedroom."

Even though she could have guessed as much, her heart still climbed into her throat. Since she'd gone to the temple to train at eighteen years old, she hadn't left the sanctuary grounds even once. Let alone spent so much as a minute in a man's bedroom.

She might be a virgin, but she had never been a wilting little girl. She was a grown woman. A skilled warrior. She refused to let him intimidate her.

"It was a bad idea to abduct me from the temple," she informed him. "The Three will see you punished for this, Incubus, regardless of what you mean to do to me. And with or without my weapons, I am still a Blade. I will fight you every step of the way."

"The same way you did in the High Chamber?"

Her cheeks flamed with heat at the reminder. With humiliation. Her weakness had shamed her in front of the other Blades, in front of the three priestesses who'd entrusted her with their lives. With their faith that she was the best, the strongest, of her peers.

And this demon had disproved all of that in a moment.

He would do it again if he wanted to. He could do anything he wanted to her. Nahiri could see it in the hard glint of his golden eyes.

No, for all her skill—for all her dedication to the teachings and training of the temple—Devlin Gravori could destroy her at his whim.

"I'm not interested in fighting you," he murmured, as if he could read the troubled direction of her thoughts.

She swallowed, watching the way he stared at her from across the room. He didn't move, and yet her body trembled as though his hands were already on her, as hot and roaming as his gaze. All the wicked, deviant things she'd ever heard about Incubi appetites poured over her in a rush of dread and terrible anticipation.

"In case you're worried about it, I'm not interested in raping you either," he drawled, the corner of his mouth curling around the sensual growl of his deep, rumbling voice. "Forcing a woman isn't the Incubus way. Never been my way, at any rate."

Nahiri hiked up her chin. "No, you'll just bend my will until I submit. Or make me your Thrall so you can siphon my life's energy for your own. Maybe you'll manipulate my mind until I beg you to drain me completely. I suppose that would be more your way."

He grunted, dark amusement in his tone. "I have plenty of women more than happy to slake my needs—*all* of my needs."

As reassurances went, his did little to relieve her. He steepled his hands beneath his chin, his citrine gaze locked on her. Nahiri could hardly breathe. His dark energy was gathered about him, pulsating and vivid, but not the way she'd felt it in the temple.

He was holding his demonic allure in check now, despite the heat she felt licking along her limbs and putting a flame to her blood. He intrigued her as much as he unsettled her.

Heaven save her, but he tempted her.

Even as he terrified her, infuriated her...he stirred a dangerous longing in her.

*And he knew.*

The way he studied her, he knew she was struggling against an attraction she wanted desperately to deny.

One raven brow quirked nearly imperceptibly. "If I wanted to take you as my lover, Nahiri, or feed from you as my Thrall, I wouldn't need force or Incubus magic to do it."

The combination of her name on his lips and the terrible truth he spoke made her heart stumble in her chest. It beat shallowly, accelerating in time with her breathing.

And she tried not to notice how his gaze tracked every inch of her body, settling on her breasts as they rose and fell with each rapid squeeze of her lungs.

He got out of the chair and stood in place for a long moment. When he finally moved, his steps were measured, unrushed. So confident, as if doubt was something he never had to trifle with when it came to women.

Of course, he'd told her as much, so his arrogance shouldn't surprise her now.

Nahiri stood, frozen, as he approached, his thick-muscled thighs carrying him in a slow prowl across the room. He paused an arm's length away from her.

"Why did you bring me here?" she asked, grateful that the tremors of her body hadn't found their way into her voice. She could not forget for an instant that she was dealing with a demon. "What do you want from me?"

His sensual mouth twisted in contemplation. "I

haven't decided yet. But let me be clear about one thing, little Blade. You may be pledged to the Three and their precious temple, but in this House, I am Master. So long as I have you under this roof, you will obey me. As of now, your well-being, your life—*everything*—belongs to me."

She bristled, outrage shooting through her like fire. She welcomed the anger. It helped eclipse the desire that was still simmering inside her, unwanted and never to be admitted—especially to this overbearing heathen of a man.

Devlin Gravori was mad if he expected her to think of him as anything but her captor.

Her enemy.

And he might as well realize that now.

Nahiri peeled her lips back from her teeth in a furious smile. She squared off against him, ready to do battle even without the benefit of her weapons. "I would rather die before I give anything to you. Willingly or by force. I would see you dead before that day."

He scowled as she hissed the words into his face. When he raised his hand, she thought for certain he would strike her.

Instead, his broad, warm palm came around the back of her neck. He held her in a firm grip, and brought his face terrifyingly close to hers.

When he spoke his voice was raw, as rough as gravel in his throat. "Be careful with your threats, Nahiri. Those are dangerous words. Particularly when my kin are already grieving the loss of one brother to your kind today."

She stared up into his fierce golden eyes,

transfixed by the power she saw there. By the pain and fury that hardened his handsome features and tightened the lush line of his mouth.

"On the other side of this bedroom door, I have a dozen Incubi brothers and cousins who might be tempted to take your threats against me to heart. They might be tempted toward other things too. But not so long as you're under my watch. No one takes what belongs to me."

As he spoke, his gaze drifted to her mouth. It lingered there, and suddenly Nahiri could hardly swallow for the lack of moisture in her throat. Her lips tingled under his gaze, aching for contact. Her temples pounded with her heartbeat, a rising, steady thrum that seemed to echo in the small space between her body and his.

Everything female in her was fixed on this man—this dark, deadly demon—and the unholy need he aroused in her.

"You will obey me," he muttered, the command like velvet on her senses when it should grate like sharp stones. "As of right now, Nahiri the Blade, you belong to me."

~ ~ ~

He wanted to kiss her.

Holy fuck, he wanted to do a hell of a lot more than that with Nahiri, and he didn't trust himself to be alone with her for one more second the way his need was churning inside him.

As an Incubus, he thrived on pleasure. Sex was at the core of who he was; it sustained him the same way food nourished a human. But it wasn't physiological necessity he felt around the gorgeous Nephilim in his custody.

It was lust, pure and simple.

It was craving, deep and raw and all-consuming.

He may have prided himself on never taking something from a woman that wasn't freely given, but his cock had other ideas where Nahiri was concerned.

Very tempting, very carnal ideas.

Which is why Dev found himself on the other side of his closed bedroom door, standing in the hallway with a massive hard-on and an attitude just short of hellacious.

Ramiel came walking toward him in that moment, up from the other end of the hall. He stopped dead in his tracks as soon as he saw Dev's ferocious scowl.

The Watchman smirked. "Now tell me it wasn't a mistake to bring the woman here."

Dev snarled a wordless reply. Ram had been incredulous when Dev had teleported out of the temple with an enthralled, unconscious Blade in tow.

He'd tried to convince Dev to rethink the impulse that made him grab Nahiri as some kind of collateral for the justice Dev sought for Marius's slaying. But Dev's mind had been made up. He couldn't let the Three lie to his face on top of the murder he was sure they had a hand in.

They had to feel some pain today too.

They deserved to weather some degree of loss.

As for Nahiri...her only offense was having the

bad luck to be standing in the crossfire of his wrath.

Not that he had any sympathy for the Blade.

No, at the moment, sympathy was pretty damned far down the list of things he was feeling for her.

He stepped away from the closed door to meet his Watchman at the other end of the hallway. The two Incubi headed downstairs to the main floor of Gravori House.

"Shall I post one of my men to guard your prisoner?"

Dev gave Ram a dark look. "That won't be necessary. She's not going to try to escape."

"How can you be sure?" Ram glanced at him sidelong, brows raised in question. "What'd you do, threaten to dangle her pretty Nephilim arse like candy in front of every Incubus in the citadel? I can only imagine the feeding frenzy that would cause."

The thought put a stab of violence in Dev's already dangerous mood. He glared at the captain of his guard. "No one will touch her, understood? No one. But she doesn't need to know that. All she needs to know is so long as she's in my keeping, she is at my mercy alone."

Ram gave him a nod, but didn't seem able to keep from snorting a low chuckle. "At the mercy of Devil Gravori. Does she realize that's even more dangerous than facing a pack of sex-hungry Incubi?"

Dev grunted, leading the way through the living area of the sprawling Mediterranean-style villa. Most of the House was having lunch in the sun-filled courtyard outside, his brothers and cousins seated soberly around large tables set up on the tiled patio while the Gravori children—a handful of Incubi boys and a couple of Nephilim girls, offspring of the mated members of the family— played a raucous game of chase through the hedge maze in the gardens.

Dev watched a towheaded boy in particular. The five-year-old leapt up onto a large rock with a jubilant shout, his face lit up with triumph as he declared himself the winner. A few of the other boys jumped up to challenge, playfully toppling him, and off they went together in a cacophony of shouting and mock battle.

"I take it Kai and the other children haven't been told about Marius yet."

Ram shook his head. "Arionn thought it best for you to tell the boy about his father's death first. Then he'll gather the other children and explain the situation to them all together."

Dev glanced at his mated brother, the calm and steady one. There were times he felt Ari would have been better suited as Master of Gravori House. He certainly had the better temperament, and the compassion required to rule. Although Ari had tried for the seat, it was Devlin who had won it instead.

As for the rest of his brothers—Bannor, Naell and Zaban—none had wanted the responsibility to lead. Least of all Zaban.

And if there was one Incubus in the villa whom Nahiri needed to fear as much as Dev, it was the libertine black sheep of their demon clan.

"I'm surprised to see Zaban's sticking around today," Dev murmured. "Not like him to linger when things get too dramatic around here."

Ram shrugged. "Apparently even he is grieving Marius. Ari told me Zaban will stay until after the rites."

"How noble of him." Dev grunted, his gaze clashing with that of his dark-haired younger brother, who saluted him grimly over a glass of blood-red wine. He looked away from Zaban without acknowledging him.

In the garden, the children were still playing, laughing brightly. Dev glanced with regret at Marius's only progeny. The Harem-born little boy's face was alight with glee, innocently unaware of the crushing news that awaited him. "Bring Kai to me after his game is over. I'll be in my study, making arrangements for tomorrow night."

# CHAPTER FIVE

Nahiri didn't see her demon captor again the rest of that day or night.

She'd avoided the tempting comfort of the bed—*his bed*—and had instead spent the night curled up on the hardwood floor, trying her best to keep from sleeping in case he decided to return to his bedroom and make good on any one of his disturbing threats.

As much as she knew she should fear all of the Incubi in this unfamiliar, enemy terrain, it was Devlin Gravori who frightened her the most.

Not because she dreaded what he might do to her.

Because deep down, to her horror, she dreaded that what he'd said was true: *If he wanted to make her his lover, he wouldn't have to resort to brute force or Incubus tricks to persuade her.*

The words had haunted her all night.

They were still heavy in her mind that next morning, when the bedroom door opened without a knock of warning and in walked the arrogant, disturbingly attractive demon.

If possible, his black scowl seemed even more dangerous now.

Nahiri got to her feet, throwing her long braid behind her as she eyed him warily. His handsome face was more rigid today, his square jaw clamped tight, unforgiving. Deep lines scored the sides of his sensual mouth. Dark shadows rode beneath the startling canary hue of his eyes.

"You're up early. Good," he muttered, looking her up and down as he entered the room. He carried clothing folded neatly over his arm, something feminine by the look of it, the tropical blue fabric adorned with a smattering of tiny, delicate flowers. "I brought you something to wear."

Nahiri smoothed her rumpled, undyed linen tunic and pants. "I have my own clothing."

He didn't bother to acknowledge that, just stalked farther into the room and thrust the sundress at her. "There's a shower and anything else you might need in the en suite. When you're dressed, meet me downstairs."

Nahiri stared at him. Meet him downstairs— why? Had he decided to throw her on the mercy of his Incubi brothers and cousins after all?

Was he telling her to shower and dress to face her executioners…or worse?

She had to know. "What's waiting for me downstairs?"

"I will be," he said. "Fifteen minutes, Nahiri, no more. Or I'll come back and personally see that you do as I tell you."

He gave her no chance to argue, no chance to demand more information.

Pivoting away from her, he was gone from the

room in the next moment, shutting her in once more. Nahiri looked at the dress that was so different from anything she'd put on in the past ten years. It was nothing she'd wear now either, and she wanted to despise the dress as much as the man who brought it to her.

With thin straps at the shoulders and a skirt that flowed in a loose drape probably to her ankles, it was both sensual and modest. The fabric was soft and cool to the touch, probably silk.

Nahiri held it up to her body, surprised to see it was just the right size.

She didn't want to put it on.

Nor did she want to leave the room and face whatever humiliation or torture he had arranged for her downstairs.

But she refused to consider the alternative—having him return to make sure she obeyed his commands.

His arrogance made her normally calm demeanor seethe.

She was not his plaything. She was a Blade. The right guard of the temple's High Chamber.

If Devlin Gravori wanted to lead her into some kind of judgment today, or some Incubi means of degradation, she would walk into his wrath with her head held high.

She showered and dressed in less than ten minutes.

It felt strange to leave the bedroom and make the trek down the long hallway by herself. In the villa below, the smell of food drifted—smoked meats and fresh-baked breads, the citrus tang of

39

oranges, the nutty aroma of brewing coffee. Nahiri breathed it in, more accustomed to the temple's pervading scents of hot sand and incense.

Instead of waking to silent meditation, this place was busy with activity. A large group of people were gathered somewhere downstairs. Groups of men and women conversing, plates and silverware clinking, chair legs scraping over smooth tiles. Here and there, the bright chirps of children's voices.

Nahiri inched her way down the stairs, peering into the heart of a lavish Mediterranean mansion.

As she descended, the group gathered in the open-air courtyard stopped talking, everyone turning to look at her. A few of the men—large, imposing Incubi—stood to glower in her direction.

At the breakfast table, a pretty red-haired woman set down her utensils and motioned for two young boys to come to her side. She immediately pulled them close in a suspicious, protective stance.

*Protecting them from me*, Nahiri realized, astonished to consider it.

She didn't know what to do.

She didn't know where to look or where to go.

She felt even more uncertain wearing the long-skirted floral dress with her temple sandals, instead of her Blade's garb. The minuscule straps holding up the bodice felt no better than the thinnest threads as she stood before these people. Her bare arms raced with heat, then chills, making her feel exposed, self-conscious.

She crossed her arms over her breasts, trying not to feel so awkward and afraid. So out of place and unwanted.

"You finished sooner than I expected."

Even though it sounded like an accusation, Gravori's deep voice was a comfort under the weight of so many unwelcoming stares. He came to stand in front of her, taking an unrushed measure of her appearance. His mouth tensed slightly, nostrils flaring nearly imperceptibly.

When he met her eyes again, she saw a dark satisfaction in his. An unmistakable hunger. And whether or not he wanted to enthrall her, she could feel the caress of his preternatural allure. It reached out to her like a physical stroke.

He moved closer, blocking her from the disapproval of these other people.

His family, all of whom seemed to regard her as the intruder when it was she who'd been forced here against her will.

"Come with me," Gravori said.

He started walking. This time, Nahiri was glad to obey him.

She followed him through the courtyard, toward a stone path cut through a lush garden. When they were out of view of the gathering, Gravori paused and turned toward her, frowning. "Undo your braid."

"Why?" Instinctively, she reached for the long tail that swung behind her with each step.

"Because I asked you to," he said in low, sensual tones that conveyed something more than simple arrogance. "And because it reminds everyone here of what you are."

"The enemy," she murmured. "Is that why you

made me put on this dress too?"

He cocked his head as he made another slow appraisal of her from head to toe. "No. I made you put it on because I wanted to see you in it. Now, undo your braid."

Maybe because her heart rate had just gone a bit hectic, Nahiri found herself slipping off the thin leather thong at the end of her braid. She speared her fingers into the woven strands and worked them loose all the way up to her nape.

As her long black hair sifted around her shoulders and down her spine, Gravori's chest rumbled with a quiet growl. The air thickened as though a wave of heat had just rolled into the garden to twine around the both of them.

"This way," he snarled, and set off once more.

On the other end of the manicured bushes, flower beds and maze of tall greenery, a paved path led across the lawn to where a black helicopter sat on a concrete pad behind the estate. Emblazoned on the cockpit door was the symbol of a scorpion, painted in gold.

The Gravori sigil.

Each of the ten Incubi Houses had their own symbol, their own totem that represented the family through the eons. Every Nephilim knew the sigils. For those Nephilim born of the Harem, like Nahiri, their fathers were Incubi, so the sigils were part of them too.

Nahiri looked at Devlin Gravori, striding alongside her with grim purpose.

Like his House totem, he was volatile and dangerous.

He was fierce, unforgiving, and yet his hand came down gently on the small of her back as they reached the helicopter. A pilot sat at the controls. An Incubus as well, Nahiri guessed, feeling her skin prickle with mild awareness of the demon.

Although the flat look he gave her through the window might have been enough to tell her he was also a member of Gravori House.

"My brother, Naell," Devlin said as he opened the cockpit door to Nahiri.

The sandy-haired demon grunted, his expression unmoving.

"Where are we going?" she asked.

Gravori didn't answer. He gestured to the open door and the cabin within. "After you."

Warily, she climbed up into the cabin and slid into one of four bucket seats, the two pairs facing each other inside the small compartment. Gravori got in behind her and took the seat right next to her. After strapping her into the restraints, then fastening his own, he gave a nod to the pilot to take off.

The engines whined, the propeller began to chop, and the helicopter lifted up from the ground.

Nahiri had never felt anything so extraordinary. She'd never seen the Earth from above, had never realized how awe-inspiring hills and rock and trees could seem from so high off the ground. And up ahead, the ocean.

It glittered, impossibly blue, sunlight twinkling like stars across the rippling surface.

Nahiri pressed her face as close to the window as she could get.

"You've never flown before?" Gravori's low voice sounded right up against her ear.

She gave a small shake of her head, unable to summon words with him so close to her. She'd been so engrossed in the scenery, she hadn't realized he'd unbuckled his seat belt and sidled up behind her.

Now she was powerfully aware of him. His heat permeated the thin silk of her dress. His body's warmth skated over her bare arms, making an all-new, liquid warmth bloom deep inside her.

She tried to ignore the intensity of their close quarters, and the fact that the outside of his thigh was pressed up against hers as he leaned in beside her. His long, muscled arms caged her in on either side of the small compartment, one hand on the upper back of her seat, the other braced on the opposite side of the cabin.

Nahiri wanted to ignore the way her pulse was hammering in her breast and in her temples…the way it was throbbing in the sensitive apex of her thighs.

"You know, the Incubi have always envied your angel ancestors for their wings," he murmured, his mouth beside her ear.

"The Nephilim too," Nahiri said. She gazed in wonder as they soared over a verdant, hilly landscape. Neatly tended rows of vines combed the Earth as far as she could see. And embracing the edge of the rolling green inclines and fertile brown tracks of soil was the breathtaking crystal blue water of the ocean. "Being earthbound, I never understood why I should envy the angels. Until now."

She made the mistake of turning slightly to look at him.

His penetrating stare seemed to reach right into her eyes, into her soul.

"There are other ways to fly, Nahiri. You only have to be willing to let go."

His voice was velvet against her nerve endings, a temptation as overwhelming as his immense body, crowding her too intimately in the tiny compartment. His gaze dropped to her mouth and lingered there, making all the moisture evaporate from her lips.

She swallowed, wanting desperately to think he was flexing his Incubus powers of seduction on her.

Anything to keep from admitting to herself how much she hoped he would kiss her.

This man—this demon Incubus—made her yearn for dark, dangerous things.

And she wasn't alone in that yearning. She could read it plainly enough in his unflinching face. She could see it in his too-serious expression that made her feel both wildly uncomfortable and recklessly bold.

He lifted his eyes to hers, then his fingers brushed tenderly along the side of her cheek, coaxing her face toward his.

Nahiri knew she should draw away from his touch like she would an open flame. Instead, she couldn't even draw breath.

Heaven save her, but there was nothing she wanted more in that moment than to feel his lips against hers.

He leaned in closer, then closer still.

A dark rumble vibrated through him, though whether it was a chuckle or a growl, she couldn't be certain. His hand fell away abruptly, leaving an empty chill on her cheek.

"We're here," he said, a gruff announcement.

He sat back in his seat, all the tenderness of the moment gone in an instant.

Nahiri mentally snapped herself out of her daze to look out the window again. Below them, the green vineyards and rich brown soil stretched toward a compound of cream-colored buildings capped with red tile roofs.

There was nothing else around for miles and miles.

Nahiri shot a troubled look at him. "What is this, my new prison?"

His mouth quirked, but his gaze was gravely serious. "This is the Gravori family business. I have matters to attend today and I wasn't about to leave a Blade in my home without me there."

She sat back against the cushioned seat, watching as the helicopter gently descended to the ground outside the complex of buildings.

After they landed, Nahiri reached up to unfasten the restraints. Before she could manage it, Gravori's hand came down atop hers. "The employees here are human. They don't know what I am, and I mean to keep it that way."

He leaned toward her, no softness in his citrine eyes, or in the dark velvet voice that grazed her ear. "Whatever I say in there, I advise that you play along."

# CHAPTER SIX

Heads turned as Dev walked into the Gravori Vineyards corporate office with Nahiri.

It wasn't unusual for the female employees—and a few of the men—to pause whatever they were doing and look up in eager anticipation when he or any other Incubus entered a room.

The sensual allure of a sex demon was a powerful thing. It was a reaction Dev and his kind had learned to take in stride. So much so, he hardly noticed anymore.

But today it was different.

Today, the object of everyone's interest was the dark-haired, exotic beauty at Dev's side.

He glanced at Nahiri and saw what the humans did in that moment:  a tall, elegant goddess with absorbing, intelligent brown eyes and a tempting, sensual mouth, set in the delicate face of an angel.

Maybe he should have thought better of making her wear the spaghetti-strap sundress with its plunging neckline. He'd sent Ram to the mainland last night to buy various supplies, and told the Watchman to pick up a few things for Nahiri to wear. Of the handful of garments Ram returned with, the tropical blue dress had immediately caught

Dev's eye. He knew the body-skimming, sexy dress would look spectacular against Nahiri's smooth skin and pleasing curves, and he'd been right.

Damn, had he ever been right.

The way the half-dozen human men in the room were gaping at her, Dev would have rather had her covered from head to toe in the shapeless, undyed linen from the temple.

One of the older women stepped around the reception desk to greet them. "Good morning, Mr. Gravori. And, ah, your…guest?"

"Good morning, Louisa," he said, giving his capable general manager a nod. He sent a flat look and a tighter nod of greeting to the rest of the room—the men in particular. "This is Nahiri."

Although he didn't have to say it, every male pair of eyes in the room blinked with understanding.

This unearthly beauty was Nahiri, and she belonged to Dev.

At least as far as any of them were concerned.

He glanced back to Louisa. "Is everything ready for me?"

"Yes, Mr. Gravori. This way, please."

He paused to let Nahiri step in front of him, gesturing her into motion with his palm at the base of her spine. He felt her sudden intake of breath at the moment of contact. The jolt of awareness—her little tremor of startled pleasure—vibrated against his palm, a sensation that stayed with him even after he'd drawn his hand away and fell in behind her.

With pleasure, he followed her as Louisa took

them through the old stucco-and-tile building that had been the headquarters of the Gravori family business for hundreds of years. It was impossible to walk behind Nahiri and not imagine what her long, lean legs would feel like wrapped around his waist. And seeing the tight curve of her backside made him instantly hard and hungry with the urge to mount her, to bend her over the nearest surface and ride her sweet ass until she was screaming his name for all to hear.

Especially the men in the other room, who'd looked at her as if they were having similar thoughts.

Dev felt a scowl crease his brow.

He had no right to feel any such things—least of all the jagged edge of possessiveness that cut into him while he strode behind Nahiri toward their destination.

She didn't belong to him, despite the threat he'd delivered yesterday in his bedroom.

She belonged to the temple, to the Three.

She belonged to a race of beings he didn't trust and should despise for what had been done to his brother and the human Marius had taken up with.

And yet, Dev craved this Nephilim Blade.

He wanted Nahiri with an intensity that shook him.

Damn it, he should have kissed her in the helicopter and gotten it out of his system. Now, the question—the temptation—was going to hang over him all bloody day.

And it wasn't going to be easy to pretend he'd brought Nahiri with him purely for the security of his House and family when he was stalking after her now, sporting a raging hard-on.

"Here we are, Mr. Gravori," Louisa announced, pausing at an open doorway. "A bottle from each of our finest vintages, just as you requested."

"Thank you," Dev murmured. He motioned for Nahiri to step inside the tasting room with him. Across the sunlit plank wood floor and antique Persian rug was a blood-red leather sofa and a large mahogany cocktail table where ten bottles of red wine stood uncorked and waiting to be sampled. "That will be all, Louisa. I'll let you know when I'm finished in here."

"Of course, sir." She smiled and obediently disappeared.

Nahiri glanced at all the wine before looking back at him in question. "This was the important business you had to attend today?"

"Wine has been my family's business for centuries. It's my passion." He cleared his throat. "One of them, at any rate. And yes, Nahiri. This is important."

He closed the door behind them as she wandered farther into the room.

Instead of sitting down, Nahiri drifted over to the large wall of windows that overlooked the sun-washed vineyards outside. "All of the vines we flew over are yours?"

"Every last one of them." Dev joined her at the glass. "The entire island belongs to the House of Gravori. The winery and vineyards date back to Roman times."

"It's lovely," she murmured. "And...not what I

expected."

Dev stared at her. "I agree."

Her gaze flew to his, her fine brows raised. Whatever she might have thought or said was lost when movement outside drew her attention back to the windows. "There goes your brother. Naell, was it?"

Dev grunted, following her line of vision. Naell strode toward one of the rows of vines. He wasn't alone. The Incubus was hardly ever without female company, and Dev didn't have to guess what his sibling was up to now.

"Isn't that one of the women we saw when we came in?" Nahiri asked. The words had barely left her lips before she glanced away abruptly. "He's taking off her clothing in broad daylight."

"Yes," Dev replied. "Incubi don't have modesty issues. Apparently, neither does Naell's choice of Thrall today."

Dev watched only long enough to see Naell sling the half-naked, giggling young woman over his beefy shoulder and tromp off into the vines with her. When he looked at Nahiri, her cheeks were flamed pink.

"Do you use the women here like that too?"

"Never," he said. But he had to admit a pang of envy for his brother, who took his pleasure anywhere, and with anyone, he pleased. If Dev were more like Naell, or most of his other brothers, Nahiri's cheeks wouldn't be the only part of her that was flushed with heat. "I prefer to keep my business and personal lives separate," he told her. "Fewer complications that way."

"Your brother doesn't seem to care about any of that."

Dev shrugged. "Naell does what he wants. Marius did too."

"Your brother who died," Nahiri murmured.

"My brother who was murdered," he corrected.

With a gesture of his arm, Dev guided Nahiri to take a seat on the sofa while he poured them each a sampling from one of the bottles of wine. He sat down beside her and handed her a glass.

She sipped at his direction, and Dev waited for her reaction. Although she didn't seem to dislike the wine, her unaffected expression didn't applaud it either. Dev offered her a cracker to prepare her palate for a different selection. She munched it demurely, then took the new glass he offered her.

"Marius couldn't resist human women, even more so than Naell," Dev continued. "Marius used to say he enjoyed the freedom, the fact that he never risked a mating bond with a human."

"Unlike a Nephilim," Nahiri added.

Although the Incubi and Nephilim were opposing races, they were also dependent on each other for continuing their lines. In an odd demonstration of cosmic balance, offspring were born only to an Incubus/Nephilim joining. Without the Nephilim, the Incubi Houses would all eventually perish. Without the Incubi, the Nephilim would cease to exist.

The Harem helped ensure that balance was met with sanctified regularity. It also helped avoid the added complication of the mating bond, which formed if a pair made love together a total of eight times.

The bond was eternal, unbreakable. And there were few Incubi willing to entrust their sustenance and all of their future progeny to a single Nephilim.

Over the eons, only a few Gravoris had taken Nephilim as their bonded mates.

For the rest, Dev included, in order to keep the Gravori line intact, a visit to the Harem was required.

Dev had successfully avoided his call of duty for a couple of centuries.

He thought of Marius, and the Harem-born son he left behind. "I keep trying to make sense of the slayings, but there is no sense in it."

Nahiri stared at him in silence for a long moment. "A killing like that would only happen if a law was broken. A very high law. And no Blade would carry it out unless commanded to."

"Marius broke no laws. And what about the woman he was with that night? Why kill her along with him?"

Nahiri frowned. "The Three do not approve of sexual relations between Incubi and humans. In the old times, it was forbidden—"

Dev scoffed. "An old law that went extinct with the last Succubus a very long time ago."

"Those offspring between humans and Incubi were an abomination," Nahiri said, no doubt quoting from the teachings of the Three.

"They were sisters to my kind," he said. They were female sex demons and very powerful beings, some of whom had incited an ancient war between the demon realm and the Nephilim. "Nature seems to have taken care of that problem for everyone. There hasn't been a successful Incubus/human breeding for as long as I can remember. As for Marius, he did nothing to deserve that kind of death. He was a good man. A good father to the son who hardly had the chance to know him."

"A son?" Nahiri asked, her voice soft, compassionate. She'd taken one sip of the second wine now, licking her lips as she swallowed. She took another sip, nodding her approval.

Dev lifted a brow, pleased. He reached for another bottle and gave her a fresh glass while he tasted the one Nahiri had enjoyed. He liked it too. If only for the way it pleased her.

And as much as he didn't want to admit it, he was finding Nahiri easy company. Too comfortable, considering that just the day before she'd been standing off against him, wielding her daggers on behalf of the Three.

He didn't want to think of her as a woman first and an enemy Blade second, but seated beside her on the leather sofa, sharing wine and conversation, Dev had to acknowledge the danger here.

He couldn't hold on to his fury about his brother's death when he was with Nahiri. He couldn't blame her for it, simply because of her connection to the ones who killed him.

Worse than that, he couldn't deny that he liked Nahiri, in spite of everything that stood between them.

And that on its own was the more troubling danger.

Dev cleared his throat, wrangling his thoughts

back to his brother. "The boy's name is Kai. Marius sired him in the Harem five years ago."

"I was born in the Harem too," Nahiri murmured, setting down her glass. She had abandoned the new vintage for the one she'd liked better. "My mother is still there. She's happy living in the sanctuary."

Dev couldn't pretend he wasn't interested in Nahiri's background, the things that made her who she was. "And your father," he said, reaching to pour them each a fresh serving of the second bottle. "Do you know him?"

She shook her head. "I never met him. I heard he died not long after I was born. He was from the House of Akana, one of the last of his line, from what I understand."

Dev acknowledged the now-extinct House with a grave nod. "Akana was a strong House. They were known for their skilled warriors."

He could see Akana in her now, the dark eyes and exotic beauty. Not to mention Nahiri's accomplished position as the highest ranking Blade in the temple.

"Akana was an honorable House," he added, in case she wasn't aware of the good in her Incubus father's people. "It's too bad theirs was the first Incubus line to die out. I'd have rather seen Marakel go that way first."

Nahiri all but choked on her wine. "You're speaking of the Sovereign. You shouldn't say such things about the one seated on the Obsidian Throne."

Dev shrugged. "I never wanted their House to

have the Throne, and I'm not afraid to say that to anyone. Imothus Marakel is no ruler. If it had been up to me alone, I would've put any one of the other Houses on that seat. You're too young to know this, but it was supposed to be the House of Romerac in power now, not Marakel. Canaan Romerac would've been the best choice by far, if he hadn't abandoned his House with no explanation centuries ago."

Dev took a drink of wine, scoffing as he set his glass down. "Hell, I'd gladly take the lethal spies of Xanthe over Marakel now. Or even Vipera's barbarians with their twisted passions. Marakel is weak, and there are others in power around him who know this. The question is, who has the Sovereign's ear, and what will his weakness cost us all in the end?"

Nahiri regarded him warily over the rim of her wine glass. "The Sovereign has power, but it's not without limits. The Three will ensure the balance."

"Will they?"

"They always have," she replied, resolute. But despite her devotion, Dev saw the smallest flicker of uncertainty in her eyes. She shook her head as if to scatter her doubt. "Anyway, I'm glad to be removed from all of the politics. I'm even more glad to be removed from the obligation of being chosen for the Harem."

Dev nodded, aware of the exclusion of Blades being sent to breed in the sanctuary. Still, he was curious to know more about Nahiri. "Most Nephilim consider it a great honor to serve in the pleasure palace."

"Most," she agreed, "but not me. It would've driven me mad. Lazing around on silk cushions all day with nothing to do but primp and weave flowers into my hair? Batting my eyelashes at every Incubus who swaggers in, and praying for the chance he might debauch me so I can give him a child I might never see again? No, thank you."

Harem life wasn't the oppressive indenture she described, but Dev was too intrigued to contradict her. Instead, he listened with rapt interest to the way she spoke so freely with him now.

Her candor was partly due to the wine, no doubt. But she was relaxing moment by moment. Her guard had come down, and it was clear she was feeling as comfortable with him as he was with her.

Dev stared at her, mesmerized by her sweet mouth, and by the way she looked at him with those soulful, fathomless brown eyes. He couldn't keep himself from reaching out to tenderly stroke the back of his knuckles along her soft cheek. She drew in a shallow breath at the uninvited contact, but she didn't pull away.

Dev's voice came out thick and rough with desire. "I'm glad to know the Harem will never have you, little Blade."

A woman like Nahiri would have been in high demand. And the thought of other Incubi touching her, lusting for her, annoyed him deeply. Aggressively so.

*For fuck's sake, what was he doing?*

More to the point, what the hell was he *thinking,* letting himself feel any kind of jealousy or possessiveness toward this woman?

Need swamped him, swift and fierce. Heat raced through him, settling uncomfortably, and quite obviously, between his legs.

He shifted on the sofa, for all the good it did.

He poured himself more wine and downed it in one savage gulp.

If he was smart, he'd put an end to this right now. There was still a chance to clamp the brakes down on what he was feeling for Nahiri. Time enough for him to rein in his temptation and deliver his pretty prisoner back to the villa.

Better yet, back to the temple where she belonged.

He felt her gaze on him. It was as warm and tender as any caress. "I'm sorry, Dev," she murmured gently. "About what happened to your brother and the woman he was with…I'm sorry for your loss."

He swung a hard look at her, wanting to refuse her sympathy with a harsh remark or a cutting accusation for the trio of priestesses she served.

But he couldn't do it.

The sound of his name on Nahiri's lips had done something to him. All the worse after the time they'd spent here together, getting to know each other as a man and a woman, instead of the vengeful Incubus Master and the devout Nephilim Blade.

Dev wanted to feel animosity toward her.

He wanted to cling to the rage that had sent him to the temple in the first place. The same rage that had made him seek to inflict some measure of his grief and pain on the Three by taking something that belonged to them.

Maybe there had been a part of him that thought he'd find some sense of justice in sullying their finest weapon, their brightest Blade.

But not now.

He couldn't get a firm grasp on any of those malicious intentions when Nahiri was looking at him so openly.

So trustingly.

His gaze fell to her parted lips. His heart pounded with the urge to crush her mouth beneath his.

"I want you, Nahiri." The admission was as dark and unapologetic as he felt. "I've wanted you from the moment I saw you in the temple." He hissed out a curse. "I want you so damned bad right now, it's all I can do to keep from letting the demon side of me loose to enthrall you if that's what it will take to have you naked beneath me."

Her eyes widened, but she didn't flinch. She didn't move away from him or his carnal warning. "I thought you had plenty of other women at your disposal," she said. "Willing women you don't have to persuade with Incubus magic?"

He smiled, taking far too much pleasure in the fact that his boast struck a nerve in her. "What are you really asking me, Nahiri?"

She plucked at a tendril of her long, unbound hair. "Do you have a mate, Dev?"

"No."

She glanced up at him in question. "A lover?"

"No lover who means anything to me," he said. And not a single name or face even came to mind when he was looking at Nahiri.

She was tipsy from the wine. He could see it in her dark eyes, and in the relaxed, curious tilt of her head as she studied him from under the thick black fringe of her lashes. "I suppose you prefer a stable of Thralls, eager to satisfy all your needs instead?"

He smirked. "Are you volunteering for the job?"

"Never." It was a quick reply. Too quick to be a true denial. She was looking at his mouth now, her pink tongue darting out to moisten her lips.

It was all the confirmation Dev needed.

He leaned in and caught her nape in his palm, dragging her close.

Then he took her mouth in a hungry kiss.

# CHAPTER SEVEN

Nahiri had longed for his kiss from the first instant she'd seen Devlin Gravori.

Her initial craving had been all his doing—the blast of seductive energy that had rolled into the temple along with him, making every Nephilim in his path feel the urge to strip off her clothes and beg for him.

Later, after he'd brought her to his island citadel and declared her his hostage, she'd craved his kiss all on her own. Shamefully, undeniably. Powerfully.

During her time with him today, she'd begun to desire Dev in a whole new way.

With a need that staggered her.

And now, as his mouth crushed down on hers in a deep, masterful kiss, she realized that she was about to cross a threshold from which she might never return.

She wanted more of him than just his kiss.

She wanted all of him.

There was no resisting the hot demand of his lips. No denying the dizzying sweep of his tongue as he tested the seam of her mouth, then plunged inside. His kiss was scorching, ferocious, as devilishly seductive as the man himself.

Nahiri had no defenses now, and no wish at all to make this dangerous moment stop.

Overcome with sensation, melting with erotic pleasure, she speared her fingers into Dev's silky black hair, holding him close, surrendering her mouth—her entire being—to his command.

He pressed her back onto the blood-red leather cushions, then moved atop her as his kiss delved deeper, hotter. More hungry by the moment.

Nahiri moaned, her spine arching up to meet his hard body. She couldn't get enough of him. Couldn't get enough of the delicious friction of their hips, where the thick ridge of his sex ground profanely against her mound.

Some thin shred of sanity warned her that as good as he felt, he was still her captor. It could be a costly mistake to trust him.

"What are you doing to me?" she managed to whisper. "Dev, we shouldn't..."

He lifted his head, only far enough to meet her pleasure-drenched gaze. He stroked her cheek, strong fingers caressing her with infinite tenderness. "No, we shouldn't, Nahiri. I damned well shouldn't want you like this...but I do."

She closed her eyes, sighing at the pleasure of his touch. "It's wrong."

"It's real." He lifted her chin, imploring her to look at him. He shook his head, exhaling a curse. "What's happening here is real, whether either of us wants to admit it or not. And if you want me to stop, by everything holy, you'd better say so now."

The words wouldn't come.

She searched her soul for the will to reject what

she was feeling, to convince herself that it was only demon magic that had her so enthralled with him, but Dev was right.

This was real.

And she was lost to him.

She drew him back down to her. His answering growl vibrated against her, a sound so raw and masculine it made everything female in her coil in eager response.

Dev kissed her again. Moaning deep in his throat, he plunged his tongue into her mouth and ravished her lips. His hand began to roam over her breasts. He slid his fingers into the low vee of her dress's bodice, fondling her nipples, which beaded tight and aching under his touch.

He tore away from her mouth on a snarl. Moving lower, his dark head dipped down to kiss her breasts. As he suckled, Nahiri went boneless, pleasure flooding her.

Just when she didn't think she could take any more, Dev came back up for another kiss. His hand lifted her long skirt, his warm palm skating up her bare thigh. Nahiri gasped, trembling at the feel of his touch skimming toward her sex.

He found her in that next moment, his fingers wading between her folds. He groaned against her mouth, his voice nothing more than a rasp.

"Ah, fuck, Nahiri. Your pussy is so soft and wet and hot. All for me…"

His raw words had the same effect on her as his questing fingers. Her vision started to blur as he stroked her, sensation racing through her like electrical charges. Each caress and tweak made her pleasure ratchet tighter. Her desire coiled taut, on the verge of a delicious explosion.

Dev kissed her deeper now, his fingers toying with the tiny nub of her sex, making her wild with the need for more.

"I want to be inside you," he murmured thickly. "I need to be."

His finger slipped through her wetness and into the tight entrance of her body. He penetrated her slowly, but deeply. Nahiri's body went molten. Although she was a virgin, there was no pain for her kind, only pleasure. And the measured thrusting of his finger inside her only made her long to know the fullness of a true joining with him.

She moved in time with his strokes, unable to hold back her whimper of mounting arousal. "Please, Dev…"

His rhythm slowed, then he eased out of her. She cried out in protest, lifting her head to find him bringing his fingers to his mouth. Her moisture glistened on him. He licked it away, his gaze locked on hers in sensual promise.

"Mmm…sweet as Heaven," he murmured, looking dark and demonic and so very wicked. He peeled off her dress, baring her to his brilliant citrine eyes. When she was naked, spread out before him, he smiled. "And sexy as sin, little angel."

He was still clothed, the front of his black suit pants tented at the front. Nahiri couldn't look away from him. She quivered in anticipation, wanting to feast her eyes and fill her senses with him too.

Dev arched a brow, grinning as if he could read

the wanton direction of her thoughts. He took hold of her ankles and pivoted her on the sofa. Sitting at the edge of the soft leather, she could hardly summon breath as he reached down and spread her legs wide before him.

"So sweet and sexy," he growled, his hot gaze taking her in. "I want to eat you up."

He sank down between her thighs. His dark head descended on her core. The instant his mouth touched her, Nahiri arced up on a jagged cry.

He caught her hips, holding her steady beneath him as his tongue licked her cleft in maddeningly erotic strokes, from the swollen, throbbing pearl at its crest to the tight rosebud nestled between her cheeks.

Pleasure poured into every cell in her body. Her senses lifted, rising higher, then higher still.

Dev kept on suckling her, and soon that rising pleasure began to concentrate and build.

It exploded, bright white, brilliant.

She gasped a sharp scream of ecstasy as Dev's mouth sent her soaring, weightless, utterly free.

As she slowly drifted back down into her skin, she found him looking up at her. His mouth still moved over her sensitive sex, but tenderly now. Gentling her descent back to Earth.

"You were right," she murmured, panting. Her body was still electrified, shuddering with aftershocks. "What you told me in the helicopter earlier. There *are* other ways to fly."

Dev's grin was devilish, one dark brow notched over his gleaming eyes. "Angel, we're only getting started."

~ ~ ~

Her sweet taste lingered on his tongue as he rose from between her creamy thighs. He had no patience for his clothing now, stripping it off with rough, careless hands while Nahiri watched him.

He stood before her naked, his cock stiff and upright, the heavily veined shaft on fire, its swollen, blood-engorged head weeping with the need to be buried inside her.

She reached for him and he obliged, moving forward until her slender fingers wrapped his girth in a warm, tentative grip. Curiosity shone in her dark eyes, amazement in the soft gasp that slipped from her parted lips.

Dev steeled himself for her exploring strokes. His legs spread slightly, hands fisted at his sides, he had to focus just to stand there and breathe as Nahiri traced her fingertips along his length, then through the clear bead of moisture that oozed from his tip and ran down the underside of his cock.

When she leaned forward to press her mouth to him, his blood spiked as though he'd just been hit with a bolt of lightning. The demon in him snapped awake with hunger, urging him to feed.

He'd been careful with Nahiri so far, not wanting to scare her off with the siphoning energy of his Incubus nature.

But it was no small feat to keep the demon in check while she caressed him, kissed him…making him ravenous for her in every possible sense of the word.

On a snarl, Dev drew her away from him and eased her back down onto the sofa. He followed her there, covering her gorgeous body with the tense, muscled bulk of his.

"I can't wait any longer," he muttered, then took her mouth in a savage kiss as he guided his cock to the slick cleft of her pussy. Her heat engulfed him, and he slid home with one sure thrust. "Ah, fuck. This right here...this is Heaven."

She moaned as his hips found the perfect tempo. He guided her long legs around him, an unspoken instruction for her to hold on tight while he gave his passion free rein.

He pumped into her in a frenzy, never having known such a ferocious need for any other woman. This woman—this Nephilim he'd known less than a day, the Blade he should despise on behalf of all her kind—instead had turned him inside out.

Less than a day with Nahiri and he wanted to possess her.

How much longer before she owned him completely?

Dev roared with the realization of how fast he was falling for her. His hunger swelled, need overcoming him. He rocked against her, merciless as he watched another orgasm rise up to take her.

"Come for me," he rasped. "Do it now, angel."

She screamed as the pleasure swamped her. Dev soaked it up, unable to keep from drawing her sexual energy into him as his own climax rolled over him like a tsunami.

The sweet honey taste of her juices was like nectar in the back of his throat. The even sweeter force of her orgasm fed the demon side of him, all of it proving too much to bear.

Dev plunged deep, his entire being gripped by the power of his own release.

He never spilled his seed inside a lover. Not any of the humans he'd seduced over the years, and most definitely never with a Nephilim.

Not once, not in centuries of living.

And yet, he couldn't stop the flood of heat that rushed through him now—a wracking wave that exploded out of him as he buried himself to the root in the tight velvet glove of Nahiri's womb.

He swore viciously, shouting with the intensity of his orgasm.

And even after he was spent, Dev couldn't summon the will to withdraw. He couldn't keep his hips from pumping into her, nor his cock from rousing right back to life, ready to do it all over again.

Had he told Nahiri this wasn't wrong?

Christ. What a bastard he was.

Because real or not, right or wrong, he knew this thing between them could not continue. He couldn't allow it.

He had to send her back to her home. Back to the temple, where she belonged.

And soon.

Before he took anything more from her.

# CHAPTER EIGHT

He seemed different after they had freshened up in the tasting room's private bath, and were dressed once more.

Nahiri couldn't decide what had changed in Dev, or precisely when, but their conversation in the time after they'd made love had taken a markedly less familiar turn. Gone were the questions about her past and her life at the temple. And his replies when she attempted to engage him were perfunctory at best.

There were no more intimate glances or tender, seductive caresses. Dev still looked at her with hunger, but there was a sharper edge to his gaze now.

There was reservation in his golden eyes. Darkly troubled contemplation in the flat line of the sensual mouth that had given her so much pleasure just a short while ago.

She had asked him if she'd done something wrong, but he'd denied it with a stern scowl and clipped words that hadn't done much to reassure her.

For the past several minutes, he'd been talking in private outside the tasting room with his brother,

Naell.

The two Gravori men stood in the hallway, conversing in low, serious voices. Every now and then Dev sent a grim look her way as he and Naell spoke. Nahiri couldn't pretend his sudden distance and grave regard didn't put a lump of coldness in her chest.

She felt his abrupt detachment as if a wide crevasse had opened up between them.

It confused her.

Wounded her more deeply than she might have imagined.

Finally, the Incubi brothers finished talking. They both strode into the room where she waited, feeling awkward and out of place on the sofa where she'd given Devlin Gravori her virginity.

She'd given him a piece of her heart today too, if she were being honest with herself.

And she couldn't deny that she felt a bit used now, looking into Dev's impassive face when her body still thrummed from the intensity of their lovemaking.

"Naell will take you back to the citadel, Nahiri."

She glanced at his handsome, sandy-haired brother before looking back into Dev's sober gaze. "What about you?"

He gave a small shake of his head. "I have things to settle here. It could take a while yet. You go on ahead of me."

She cocked her head at him, eyes narrow. "Aren't you concerned about leaving an enemy Blade in your House without you there to ensure your family's safety?"

His mouth flattened in a wry, regretful smile. "You're not the enemy, Nahiri. You never were, and you never will be."

But she wasn't a part of his House either. Not a part of his family.

Nor would she ever be.

A bitter thought—an unfair one too, perhaps. He hadn't made her any promises, after all. She had been the one who let him into her heart. If she'd walked willingly into an Incubus trap today, naively trusting that she wasn't just one of Devil Gravori's stable of willing Thralls, then she had no one to blame but herself.

She didn't want to believe the worst of him, but she also wasn't fool enough to think this wasn't some kind of good-bye.

"Go with Naell," he told her. "I'll be back at the villa in a few hours. We'll talk then."

The gentleness of his voice made it clear to her.

He regretted what happened between them today. He'd told her it wasn't wrong, that it was real, and now he was looking at her as though he wished he could call the words back.

The hurt of his rejection sapped all the moisture from her mouth. She had no voice, which was probably the only thing preventing her from making an even bigger fool of herself in front of not only Dev, but his brother too.

Praying he couldn't see her wounds through her eyes, Nahiri nodded, then followed Naell out of the room. Dev stood in the threshold behind them, watching her go.

Watching, but making no move to stop her.

Nahiri tried to tell herself it was for the best if they kept their distance from each other.

She needed to remember that she wasn't his lover. She wasn't even his guest.

She was his prisoner.

At worst, she was merely a pawn to him. A piece he'd swiped and would keep until he decided he no longer needed her.

Those troubling understandings followed Nahiri for the duration of the flight back to Gravori House. She didn't look at the breathtaking scenery this time. She sat numbly in her seat, staring straight ahead and wondering how she'd allowed herself to feel so strongly for Dev.

It was worse than that, in fact.

She was falling in love with him.

Maybe she already had.

The realization astonished her. It had happened so quickly, and taken root so deeply.

But her entire being had responded to him as if it recognized he belonged to her the moment he walked into the temple. She couldn't blame it all on Incubus allure, as much as she might wish to.

His brother had no such effect on her. She felt his innate power emanating from the cockpit the same way she might notice the thickening of the air before a storm.

With Dev, he *was* the storm.

He swept her up, twisted her inside out. Left her breathless and trembling.

Heaven help her, but he would leave her crushed and broken if it turned out that today meant nothing to him.

And if it turned out that *she* meant nothing…?

"Here we are," Naell announced from behind the helicopter's controls, dragging Nahiri's thoughts back to her surroundings. He touched down lightly in the villa's courtyard and killed the engine.

"I suppose you've been ordered to put me back in my cell now?" she asked.

Naell shook his head. "You're not Dev's prisoner. Not anymore. He said you can make yourself comfortable anywhere in the villa you like. We'll leave for the temple after he returns."

"The temple." She went very still as the news settled over her.

*He was letting her go.*

No, he was pushing her away.

Back to her old life. Back to the place where they would never see each other again.

"You didn't know," Naell ground out. "Son of a bitch. You mean, he didn't tell you?"

She couldn't speak. She fumbled with the complicated set of buckles on her seat belt, then burst out of the helicopter as soon as she was free of the restraints.

She took off running, into the maze of gardens and tall hedges.

Naell didn't follow her.

He had to know she wouldn't want the company. He probably saw the misery in her face and preferred to steer clear of the tears that were sure to start falling any second now.

She didn't wait to find out. Ducking down one twisting passage then another, Nahiri soon found herself deep within the garden maze. In a small elbow of the labyrinth, she came upon a stone bench and plopped down on it, her face sagging into her open palms.

What an idiot she was.

What a gullible fool.

Her heart ached, throat burned. Her vision swam with hot, welling tears.

"Did you get hurt?" The child's voice sounded from just a few feet away.

Nahiri looked up and met the concerned, inquisitive face of a lovely little boy. An Incubus, although he was easily a couple of decades away from maturing into his demonic powers. A mop of pale blond hair drooped into his eyes and fell around his seashell-pink cheeks. He held a large red ball in his arms, his breathing rapid as if he'd been racing through the maze too.

She sniffled and wiped the moisture from beneath her eyes. "I did get hurt, but I'll be all right." She managed a genuine smile for him. "Do you live here?"

He nodded, walking over to sit next to her. His bright blue eyes lifted up to her. "Do you live here now too?"

"Oh. No, I don't," she said. She wasn't sure how to explain her presence at the villa to a child, and anyway, Dev's planned dismissal of her made it unnecessary to try. "I'm only staying for a little while."

"Don't you like it here?"

She stared into the guileless little face and found she couldn't lie. "I think I probably could like it here, very much. But it's not my home. I can't stay."

"Oh," he said. "That's too bad, huh?"

"Yes, it's too bad."

Restless with energy, he hopped back to his feet, shifting the ball to under his other arm. His pale brows knit together now. "What's your name?"

"Nahiri."

"I'm Kai," he said. "Come on, Nahiri. See if you can catch me!"

*Kai.*

*Marius's son.*

She watched him vanish into the greenery, feeling her heart twist with a new kind of pain. The last thing she felt like doing was playing a game of hide and seek in the gardens when her world was about to shatter in a few more hours, after Dev returned.

But she couldn't refuse the little boy.

If for no other reason than to help give the dead man's only child a reason to smile and laugh for a while. Her problems would still be waiting for her after her game with Kai.

"Nahiri, are you coming?"

His shout drew her to her feet. "You'd better run fast, or I'm going to find you!"

She hurried in the direction he'd fled, darting down one of the passages that cut to the left. She could hear his footsteps beating somewhere to her right, a few yards ahead. Smiling, she worked her way over to another hedge row and jogged toward the area she last heard him.

He wasn't there.

She crept forward, listening for any sounds of

movement. He'd gotten so quiet. Hiding from her, but she knew he had to be close.

She ducked around another corner of the maze and paused, searching with her eyes and ears. "Kai?"

The red ball rolled out from a row that cornered into another one up ahead.

Nahiri's stomach sank inexplicably.

Although she had no cause to feel the dread that settled in her belly, she crept toward the errant ball, her heart pounding frantically in her breast.

*Please, don't let him be harmed.*

She reached the end of the row and turned to see what waited there.

A pair of Nephilim Blades.

Not from the temple, but from the ranks who served the Three on the outside, in the realm of man. They wore black instead of undyed linen. Boots meant for stealth instead of the simple leather sandals that Nahiri wore now.

One of the Blades held Kai under her arm, the edge of an Obsidian dagger pressed under the boy's chin. Scornful gray eyes looked Nahiri up and down, taking in her blue sundress and unbound hair with an obvious look of disdain.

"We were told you were abducted by the demon Master of Gravori House," the other Blade sneered. "The Three gave us orders to bring you back, and to let no one stand in our way."

Nahiri stared at them, appalled. "Take that weapon off him. He's a child."

"He's an Incubus," muttered the one who held him. "They're all the same to me."

Nahiri reached for her own weapons, prepared to kill in order to protect him. But her weapons were gone.

"Release him," she said, looking at Kai's innocent face. He wasn't scared. He was a brave boy. He would have made his father proud, Nahiri had no doubt. "Release him. You've come to collect me and bring me back to the Three, so let's go."

~ ~ ~

"The Pinot noir you selected is being crated for shipment to the villa within the hour, Mr. Gravori."

Dev looked up from the paperwork laid out in front of him on his desk. "Thank you, Louisa."

He hadn't been the one to select the wine for Marius's celebration of life tonight. Nahiri had chosen it. And now every time Dev drank that particular vintage, every minute he spent at the vineyard from now until forever, he would think of her.

Damn it.

With Louisa heading back down the hall, he got up to pace in front of his office windows, anxious. Frustrated. Brooding.

Wondering how the hell he was going to make it work between himself and a certain Nephilim Blade who'd managed to get under his skin.

Nahiri had gotten in further than that; she'd found her way into his heart.

She hadn't been gone ten minutes before he realized what an ass he was. He'd hurt her by sending her off without him, especially when his aloof send-off came on the heels of the incredible sex they'd shared.

He'd been an idiot to think he could remove her from his life, even if he was sure it was the best thing for Nahiri to be away from him.

Now, going on a hour since she'd left with Naell, Dev's world was stale and empty, less interesting.

Passionless.

And that alone was a big problem for an Incubus who thrived on passion the way a human required three square meals in order to sustain himself.

He couldn't send Nahiri back to the temple. He knew that now.

He wanted her in his life, in his House, in his family.

As his mate.

The realization staggered him.

He'd avoided the shackle of a bond for many long centuries, yet now, after a handful of hours, he was contemplating how he might convince Nahiri to stay. To belong to him.

Forever, if she'd have him.

And he wanted forever to start as soon as possible.

He was already stalking out of his office and down the hall when his mobile rang. Naell's number came up on the display. Dev answered the call without a greeting. "I'm heading back to the villa now. Tell Nahiri I want to talk to her as soon as I arrive—"

"Dev." His brother's deep voice was grim, hesitant.

"What's wrong?"

"It's Nahiri...she's missing."

Dev's heart lurched to a halt in his chest. "Missing. You mean, you can't find her?"

"She's gone, Dev. Kai just came in from the gardens to tell me. He said two angels with black knives took her back to the temple."

Dev's feet stopped moving. Every cell in his body froze, cold with dread. "Tell Ram to arrange for the jet and a pilot. Tell him to get it fueled and ready for me right now."

The helicopter would be ready faster, but it couldn't make the long flight to where Dev needed to go. And although an Incubus could teleport, it would be too taxing to travel that distance and still be ready for battle on the other end.

And if it was a battle that awaited him with the Three or any of their Blades, he would go through every last one of them in order to get to Nahiri.

"You're going after her," Naell said, no surprise in his tone at all. "You care for this Blade, brother?"

"Yeah," Dev said. "I don't want to live without her."

"Then I'll take you there myself," Naell said. "Ram and I will be waiting for you."

"I'm on the way now."

Dev pocketed his phone, then vanished in a tempest of swirling demon magic.

# CHAPTER NINE

The pair of dark-garbed Blades brought Nahiri into the temple's High Chamber as though she were the condemned being taken before her executioners.

As Nahiri was escorted up the center aisle of the vast hall, toward the stairs leading up to the sandalwood screen and the trio of Nephilim priestesses behind it, she realized just how apt the feeling truly was.

The eyes of her fellow Blades of the temple took in her outsider's attire with open but silent disapproval as she was led forward at knifepoint by her guards. She felt conspicuous in the bright turquoise sundress and her unbound hair. Worse than naked without the comforting presence of her linen clothes and leather weapon sheaths.

Up ahead of her, Valina stared at her approach. The blond Nephilim stood in the position right of the High Chamber stairs today. Another Blade had been promoted into Valina's former post.

One day gone from the fold, and Nahiri had already been replaced.

Forsaken, based on the looks of everyone who watched her now.

"Bring her forward," one of the Three commanded from atop their lofty perch.

The two Blades shoved Nahiri into motion, the gray-eyed one using more force than necessary. Nahiri swung a glower on the Nephilim, still seething for the way the Blade had also been so harsh with Kai back at the villa. "You disgrace your station, if threatening children and unarmed opponents gives you such pleasure."

The Blade smirked thinly. "Don't talk to me about disgracing my station...whore."

Nahiri hissed at the whispered insult. Furious, she struggled against their hold on her.

"Enough." The censure spoken from atop the stairs was curt, severe.

In the answering silence, Nahiri glanced at the other temple Blades for signs of support. Not one of the solemn gazes would meet her eyes. It was as if they all knew where she'd been, what she'd done...and with whom.

It was as if they all shared the gray-eyed Blade's assessment of her.

Did the Three as well?

She squared her shoulders and lifted her face toward the obscuring screen above. "Your Graces," she said, refusing to show any fear or shame. "What is the meaning of my return, if not to take my place again here in the temple? Why bring me back?"

"You are a Blade, Nahiri." Simple statement, no affection or forgiveness in the tone or the words. "A shame you forgot that fact so quickly under the thrall of the demon from Gravori House."

"I wasn't under his thrall," she replied.

"Anything I've done was of my own volition. And never once did I forget that I am a Blade. Devlin Gravori was able to look past what I  Can any of you say the same now? Can anyone here see me beyond what my station was here in this temple, or the shame you think I've brought to it?"

"You've proven yourself weak, Nahiri," said another of the Three. "But you're also young, and for that reason, we've decided to be lenient. We will make a place for you in the Harem—"

"What?" She recoiled at the idea, vigorously shaking her head. The gray-eyed Blade tightened her grip on Nahiri, forcing her arm to a painful angle behind her back. "No. You can't do that. I won't go."

"You will, Nahiri. Even if we have to place you under lock and key."

She couldn't believe this. She refused to accept that she might be sent somewhere for other Incubi to touch her, lie with her. There was only one man's touch she wanted now, and if he didn't want her, she could never give herself to anyone else. Panic and outrage seeped into her veins. "You would banish me to the Harem simply because I made love with Devlin Gravori?"

"No, Nahiri. Because you're carrying his child."

Distantly, she heard the wave of gasps travel the High Chamber. Even Valina appeared stunned by the revelation.

No one was more shocked than Nahiri.

Could it possibly be true? The idea astonished her. She knew an instant flood of emotion in that moment. Elation. Wonderment. Sadness for the thought that Dev hadn't really wanted her, that he'd been intending to send her back to the temple himself.

And she felt confusion too.

"How can you possibly know something like that?" she asked the Three. "If it's true, it can't have happened more than a few hours ago."

There was only silence for a while, then one of the priestesses replied, "We always know the instant there's a demon seed planted in a woman's womb."

"It's all part of the balance," another added.

"Our divine duty," said the third.

As they spoke, a new kind of dread began to take shape inside Nahiri. Something was very wrong about what they were saying. "What do you mean, it's your divine duty? What have you been doing?"

"You will go to the Harem," one of them said. "You will have your child there, then we'll decide what to do with you."

"No." Nahiri snarled with anger. "I refuse to accept this. You can't force me into the Harem, and I won't let you have any say about my baby."

"We can send you to the Oubliette instead."

The threat slammed into her like a physical blow. Their arrogance sickened her now. "Dev was right about you. You're far from holy. All your talk of balance is a farce."

Behind her, the gray-eyed Blade wrenched Nahiri's arm almost to the brink of breaking. She cried out with the pain, then went very still as the cold edge of an obsidian dagger came to rest meaningfully under her chin.

Nahiri didn't struggle. She wouldn't fight now, if only for the sake of her unborn child.

"Take her away," one of the Three commanded. "Lock her in the cloisters to await transport to the Harem."

"With pleasure," the gray-eyed Blade hissed near Nahiri's ear.

"Not you, Terah," the priestess added. "You stay. Valina will go in your place."

Nahiri watched her old rival step forward to carry out the order. The blond met her gaze only for an instant, pity and some other, unreadable expression in her solemn stare.

"This way," Valina murmured.

The other dark Blade shoved Nahiri into motion, taking her out of the High Chamber under the scornful glances of her former friends and peers.

~ ~ ~

The hours it took to make the flight to the desert were pure agony for Dev.

Too mad with concern for the woman who meant the world to him, he had no patience for the drive that would take him into the mountain valley where the temple was hidden. Instead, as soon as the private jet touched down and came to a halt on the crude tarmac, he leapt out of his seat and tore open the exit door.

He glanced back at the Incubi who'd accompanied him on this quest. "If I'm not back in an hour, leave."

"Like hell we will," Naell said.

The rest of his brothers—Arionn, Bannor, even Zaban—all nodded their agreement.

Ram stepped forward with half a dozen Watchmen behind him. "If you're not back in an hour, we're coming in after you and we'll tear the bloody temple down."

He appreciated the support. However, if he ran into trouble he couldn't resolve with brute force or demon magic, then the last thing he wanted was his kin to come under fire.

And if he managed to get into the temple and find Nahiri, only to have her reject him?

He didn't want to consider that possibility.

Because he didn't trust himself to let her have that choice.

He loved her, and come hell or high water, he was bringing her home.

Dev nodded grimly at the other men, then dematerialized.

Moments later, he was standing the temple's High Chamber.

The room was quiet, empty but for the pair of Blades posted at the base of the broad stairs.

Nahiri wasn't one of them.

The blond Nephilim who'd been there the day he first intruded on the Three was. She'd been promoted apparently, during Nahiri's brief absence. The new captain of the temple guards went a bit pale as soon as her eyes lit on him.

Then she charged forward on a throaty war cry, drawing her obsidian daggers at the same time. Her second, a brunette, followed right behind her.

Dev blasted the pair with his power.

They slowed, expressions muting from flashing fury to melting arousal. The lower guard dropped her blades in a clatter and started fondling her small breasts over the linen tunic she wore.

The blond was struggling to withstand his allure too, but she had little fight in her when Dev charged forward and wrestled her knives out of her hands. He locked her head under his arm.

"Where is Nahiri?" he growled against the Nephilim's ear. "What have they done with her?"

The Blade panted, her pretty face slack with forced desire. "You don't want her. You can have me."

"Tell me," he seethed.

"The Harem," she murmured.

Dev's chest went suddenly cold, hollow with dread. "When? Damn it, how long has she been gone?"

"Not yet," the blond slurred thickly. Drunk with lust, she reached up to pet his cheek, but he flinched away from her touch on a growl. "She's not gone there yet, but soon…because of the baby."

The Nephilim wasn't making sense now. Was it possible he'd addled her mind when he enthralled her and the other temple Blade?

"What baby?" he demanded. "What the hell are you talking about?"

The blond smiled up at him, the kind of smile that would turn any other man into putty in her hands. Any man but him. There was only one woman capable of doing that to Dev now.

"Didn't you know?" she asked. "The Three know. They're not very pleased with Nahiri right now." The Nephilim looked at him, her gaze drunken from his power, unfocused. She lowered her voice to a conspiratorial, husky whisper. "She's having the devil's baby. Devil Gravori's."

Dev went numb.

It couldn't be true...*could it?*

They'd made love only today. Just hours ago.

And he'd been so out of control, reckless enough to spill his seed in Nahiri. There was a part of him that couldn't regret that, even though she wasn't his. He couldn't regret any of the time they'd had together, except for the fact that it had been far too brief.

Did he dare believe what this lust-drunk Nephilim was telling him? Could Nahiri actually be carrying his child after just one time together? And if she were, how was it that the Three were already aware of it?

He didn't have time to try and figure out how any of that was possible right now.

All that mattered was Nahiri. He wasn't leaving without her.

"Take me to her. Quickly," he commanded the blond Blade.

She brought him out the back of the temple, to the cloisters where the Blades apparently lived. In the back of the long barracks was a locked door.

A windowless cell, he realized as they approached.

His senses came alive with outrage—and the certainty that Nahiri was trapped inside the dismal place. "Open it."

The blond took out a key and twisted it in the heavy iron lock. It fell open, and it was all Dev could do not to shove the other Nephilim aside as he lunged to open the door.

"Nahiri."

She sat on the dirt floor in the darkness, her arms wrapped around her knees. Her head had been drooped down toward her breast, but it came up the instant she heard his voice.

Hope flashed across her face, then her expression settled into a wary uncertainty.

"My love," he said, two strides carrying him to her.

She cried out, a muffled, wordless sound of relief as he pulled her into his arms and held her close. She felt so good in his arms. Warm and strong, and, blessedly, all his.

"Dev," she whispered against his chest. "I didn't think you'd come. Naell told me you were going to send me back to the temple, so I didn't think I mattered—"

He silenced her with a fierce, desperate kiss. He drew back, framing her beautiful face in a tender grasp. "You're all that matters. You are everything to me, Nahiri."

Her choked cry was full of joy and relief. Her dark eyes were filled with so much affection—so much love—he could hardly breathe for the sight of it.

"Dev, there's something you need to know…"

"Do you love me?"

"Yes," she answered, no hesitation at all. "I love

you, Devlin Gravori."

"Then that's all I need to know right now."

He kissed her again, then swung his attention back to the blond Nephilim slumped against the doorjamb. Her gaze was still heavy-lidded, the female still fully under his thrall.

"Go now. Tell the Three that I came to claim what they owed me," he growled. "If they come after this woman or anyone else in my family, they will answer to me. And there will be no mercy for them."

As she nodded and pivoted around to leave them, Dev wrapped Nahiri in his arms. He pressed his mouth to hers, summoning the demon magic that would teleport them to freedom. The energy swirled around them. "Are you ready to fly with me again, little angel?"

"Yes." Nahiri's smile lit him up like nothing else could. "Take me out of here, Dev. Take me home."

# CHAPTER TEN

Nahiri lay naked in Dev's decadent bed, enjoying the feel of him stretched out alongside her as they both floated back down to Earth after a soaring orgasm. They'd been home for two days, everything that happened at the temple seeming like nothing more than a bad dream.

Home.

Nahiri was slowly getting used to the idea that this villa and island citadel was her home. She was a member of this Incubi House now. This was now her big, raucous family. Her brightly colored, passionate, incredible new life.

And Dev, her demon lover.

Her mate.

The father of the tiny miracle growing inside her.

She'd never imagined having all of these gifts, least of all Dev and the baby they would have nine months from now.

Now she couldn't dream she'd ever need anything more.

It would weigh on her forever that her happiness with Dev had come on the heels of such terrible violence and death. Nahiri had made it her personal mission to make sure Marius's young son never felt alone. She and Dev couldn't replace Kai's father, but between the two of them and the rest of the Gravori clan, the boy would always have the care and attention of family who loved him.

As would her baby.

She sighed softly as Dev caressed the flat plane of her belly. He'd been infinitely tender with her each time since they'd returned from the temple, making love to her slowly, patiently, as though she might break.

Honestly, it was driving her to the brink of madness.

She reached up and took his head in her hands, pulling him down for a deep, sensual kiss.

He grunted in surprise, but it took no convincing at all for him to let her tongue sweep inside his mouth to tangle with his. He chuckled as she maneuvered him underneath her and climbed on top to straddle his nakedness. He moaned thickly, his cock jerking against her wet heat when she positioned her cleft over his length, then sank down to the hilt.

"Ah, shit. Nahiri, don't," he croaked, holding on to her hips as she began a deep, relentless rhythm. "We should be careful—"

"We'll have plenty of time to be careful." She rocked against him, building her tempo. "Right now, I want to fly."

"Fuck yes," he murmured, his citrine eyes locked on her in pure need.

She felt his demon energy wreathing her as she rode him harder, mercilessly. For all the pleasure she took being Devlin Gravori's lover, knowing it was her passion alone that sustained this powerful Incubus Master made their sex even more explosive and consuming.

And when they both eventually came this time, their combined shouts of release shook the thick timbers of the bedroom.

Dev rolled her over and kissed her breathless. His cock nudged her hip, ready for another round already. He grinned. "You might regret giving me permission to do my worst, little Blade."

She laughed, gazing up into his loving eyes. "Your worst is the best."

As they kissed again, a knock sounded on the door. Dev growled, pulling her toward him. "Go away. I'm making love to my mate."

"I'm sorry, Dev." Arionn's voice, edged with apprehension. "There's a woman downstairs. A Nephilim. She's asking to see you and Nahiri."

They scrambled out of bed without words, dressing hastily, neither one of them daring to guess at what might have arrived on their doorstep.

Nahiri hurried down the hall with Dev, then froze at the top of the stairwell. She was astonished to see the familiar face so far away from the High Chamber. "Valina."

"I didn't know where else to go," the Blade murmured.

Nahiri and Dev went down together to meet her. "You left the temple."

She nodded. "I couldn't stay. I couldn't serve the Three anymore. Not after what I learned."

"What happened?" Dev's voice was level, but

Nahiri could sense her mate's dread.

"After you were gone, I went to deliver your message to the Three." Valina glanced from Dev to Nahiri, clearly upset. "They were meeting with Terah—"

"The Blade who came to take me back to the temple," Nahiri explained to Dev. "The one who threatened Kai with her dagger."

Valina nodded. "It was Terah who killed Marius and his lover. And the Three knew. They issued the order."

Dev's answering curse was violent, lethal. Arionn's was equally profane, and the conversation taking place in the foyer of the villa drew the rest of the Gravori brothers and half of the Watchmen as well.

"You're certain the Three did this?" Dev asked, fury in every word. "They ordered my brother's murder?"

"Not your brother's," Valina said. "That was Terah's doing. That was her overstep. The Three executed her for it."

Dev frowned, but it was another brother who spoke now—dark-haired Zaban. "If Marius wasn't the intended target of the assassination, then—"

"The human woman?" Dev asked.

Valina nodded. "She was pregnant…with Marius's baby."

"Impossible," Naell interjected. "There hasn't been a human/Incubus pregnancy for centuries—"

"Because the Three haven't allowed it," Nahiri murmured. It was all making sense to her now. The killings, their odd admissions to her before they condemned her to the Harem. "They always know the instant a demon seed is planted in a woman's womb. That's what they said."

"And it's their divine duty to keep the balance," Valina added grimly. "They've been killing them, Nahiri. They've been making sure no child is ever born to a human and an Incubus."

"How far has this corruption seeped?" Arionn mused darkly.

One of the other Gravori brothers guessed, "Maybe all the way up to the Obsidian Throne."

Nahiri felt a chill sweep over her as she looked at Valina's worried gaze and the sober, dangerous faces of the Gravori men.

With Dev and his Incubi kin, she'd found a slice of happiness—the truest sense of peace and belonging she'd ever known—but it was clear that the strife between their two worlds was far from over.

Dev pulled her close, under the strong shelter of his arm. "If this proves to be fact, if the Sovereign and those around him turn out to be conspirators and killers, then let them be warned— the war that's coming to them from this House and the seven others still remaining will shake the gates of both Heaven and Hell."

~*~

# ABOUT THE AUTHOR

**LARA ADRIAN** is a New York Times and #1 internationally best-selling author, with nearly 4 million books in print worldwide and translations licensed to more than 20 countries. Her books regularly appear in the top spots of all the major bestseller lists including the New York Times, USA Today, Publishers Weekly, Indiebound, Amazon.com, Barnes & Noble, etc. Reviewers have called Lara's books "addictively readable" (Chicago Tribune), "extraordinary" (Fresh Fiction), and "one of the best vampire series on the market" (Romantic Times).

Writing as **TINA ST. JOHN**, her historical romances have won numerous awards including the National Readers Choice; Romantic Times Magazine Reviewer's Choice; Booksellers Best; and many others. She was twice named a Finalist in Romance Writers of America's RITA Awards, for Best Historical Romance (White Lion's Lady) and Best Paranormal Romance (Heart of the Hunter). More recently, the German translation of Heart of the Hunter debuted on Der Spiegel bestseller list

With an ancestry stretching back to the Mayflower and the court of King Henry VIII, the author lives with her husband in New England.

Visit the author's website and sign up for new release announcements at **www.LaraAdrian.com**.

# SOULLESS
## House of Romerac

# Donna Grant

# CHAPTER ONE

The wails and screams of the damned stuck in the Oubliette were mixed with the laughter of their tormentors. All of it was a constant reminder that Canaan would never be free of the supernatural prison to exact his revenge on the ones who had betrayed him.

He didn't know how long he had been in the Oubliette or exactly why he had been deceived by his brothers.

"You're weakening, Canaan. I can see it."

He hid his grimace and let his gaze slide from the row of cells and the prisoners within to the Warden—a female so hideously ugly in her beastly visage that few could gaze upon her.

Canaan looked long enough to see her leathery bat-like wings tucked, her long tail still, and her claws hanging by her sides. It wasn't even her crimson-colored skin that made people gag. It was the snakes sliding over her skin and the smell of sulfur. Not to mention the blinding white light coming from her eyes that made it impossible to look directly at her.

Muriel was right. He was weakening, but then again any Incubus would when they held off sexual pleasure. It wasn't that Muriel didn't have beautiful women for him to choose from. There was something else preventing him from feeding.

"I'm fine," he stated in a firm voice.

Muriel's laugh was deep and almost seductive, if it wasn't for the forked tongue that licked at her lips. "You can't fool me, Incubus. How many times did I bring you to the brink of death only to pull you back with a small measure of sex with human slaves within my walls? Too many to count. And you know it."

Canaan faced her, forcing himself to look into her grotesque face—but not her eyes. "You think I don't remember the torture?"

"I think you're still looking for a way out. There isn't one."

He didn't understand how Muriel always seemed to know the thoughts of those within the Oubliette, but she hadn't been wrong once. It was a fact that he did look for a way out.

His first step had been giving up his soul to her. It had been surprisingly painless. Or perhaps he had suffered for so long that he no longer recognized pain.

By freely giving his soul, he went from being tortured to doling out torture to others. As a sex demon, his goal was pleasure, not pain. Oddly, he didn't think twice about it.

"You'll never leave this place," Muriel said again.

Canaan glanced over her shoulder to the wall lined with shelves. Upon those shelves were clear jars that held the souls she collected. Each soul was a different color, depending on the creature or demon.

He knew exactly what color his soul was — red. There were more than a dozen red jars upon the shelves. If only he knew which was his.

"I know," he said. "I'm here forever."

She limped around her room, her claw feet loud upon the stones. "You were Master of your House. The Romeracs are a powerful Incubus family. You'll be happy to know they remain so with Teman at the helm."

Canaan inwardly seethed, careful to keep any emotion from showing. He still couldn't believe Teman and Levi had turned against him. After their father's death it had just been the three of them.

They had been strong together. What had torn them apart?

"That's good to know." Canaan turned from Muriel and looked at the table of torture instruments for him to choose from. He was set to punish a Alp demon who gave nightmares to humans.

"The sooner you let go of your old life, the sooner you will make a home here," Muriel said from right behind him.

She moved slowly, loudly. And yet she had managed to sneak up close behind him without Canaan even knowing. There was obviously more to Muriel than he realized.

He turned his head so that he could see her out of the corner of his eye. "I wouldn't have given you my soul if I wasn't prepared to make this my home."

"Just what I wanted to hear." She began to walk away before she paused and said, "Oh, and don't forget to visit the humans."

"I don't like to have sex with the same woman more than once."

"Of course," Muriel murmured. "I forgot. But I thought you Incubi were only hindered from sex with the same female when it pertained to the Nephilim."

Canaan chose a long curved blade and vise-like clamps as his weapons before he turned to Muriel. "Incubi don't have sex with the same female—human or Nephilim—more than once as a precaution. If the Nephilim can become immortal after repeated mating with an Incubus, what's to say that a human can't as well?"

"The angel blood coursing through the Nephilim veins," Muriel stated flatly.

From the first moment he had been cast into the Oubliette, Muriel had been hounding him for information about the Incubi. He had refused at first, but it hadn't taken him long to think that Muriel knew more than she let on.

"Why are you so interested in the Incubi?"

She waved a clawed hand. "I'm curious about all the creatures I oversee."

Canaan wasn't a fool. She was more than merely curious about his race, the Nephilim, and the humans. The why of it he had yet to discern. But he would.

He had eternity stretching before him.

With his tools in hand, he walked from the room down the endlessly long corridor to his awaiting target. Inside was a demon who sported thick horns coming out of the side of his skull, flaxen hair, and dark gray skin. As soon as Canaan neared the cell, the iron bars became transparent, allowing him inside.

"It's time," he said to the Alp demon.

The male jerked at the chains latched around his wrists and holding him upright with his arms outstretched against the stone wall. "I know who you are."

Canaan paused. This was a different tactic. Usually his prey begged, crying and pleading, for him to hold off or go easy.

This was his first time torturing an Alp demon, who were known for their deceit and duplicity. And yet there was something in the demon's eyes that gave him pause.

"Who am I?" Canaan asked.

"Canaan Romerac, Master of the House of Romerac, an Incubus with incredible strength and the ability to shake the world."

He could only stare at the demon, unsure if it was a trick or not. "I've never met you, and the Alp demons have no connection to the Incubi. How do you know me?"

"I'll explain everything after we escape."

Canaan should have known. "There is no escape from the Oubliette. Every creature knows this."

"But there is," the demon insisted in a soft tone. He jerked on the chains again and pressed his lips together. "Look, the prison constantly moves, right?"

"Right," Canaan agreed in a bored tone.

"But there are only a handful who know when the walls between this prison and the outside world are so thin you could walk through them. Thereby escaping."

It was too good to be true. Of all the tales he had heard of the infamous supernatural prison, not one prisoner had escaped. Ever.

"You're lying."

The demon shook his head viciously back and forth. "I'm not. You need to believe me, because it won't last long. Just a few minutes."

"Why should I believe you?"

"Because I know who betrayed you."

Canaan leaned a shoulder against the wall next to him and narrowed his gaze on the demon before him. "So do I."

"You only know some of what happened. I know all of it, Canaan."

He slowly straightened, his grip tightening on the instruments he was ready to use to torture the demon. "Tell me."

"After we escape."

Canaan took a step toward the demon and lifted the blade. "You'll tell me now."

"If I tell you now, you won't take me with you."

"If you don't tell me," he said and closed the distance between them, "you'll feel how persuasive I can be."

The demon visibly swallowed, his gaze on the weapon. "The idea to toss you in here wasn't your brothers'. It came from higher up."

"The Council?" he asked in confusion. "Why

would the other Incubi Houses want me out of the picture? The House of Romerac is still strong."

The demon was shaking his head well into the middle of Canaan's words. "Higher, Canaan."

The only thing higher was the Obsidian Throne. To have the Throne was to have the greatest power on Earth. For the Sovereign controlled the gates to Heaven and Hell.

"Yes," the demon said. "Now you understand."

Canaan might understand who had betrayed him, but he couldn't fathom why. "How do you know all of this?"

"I was part of it," the demon admitted after a brief hesitation.

Fury, dark and thick, rose within Canaan. The pommel of the dagger shattered in his hand and the ground rumbled.

"If you kill me now, you'll never learn the rest," the demon hastily added.

It took Canaan all of his considerable control to pull back his rage. As he did, the shaking walls halted.

The demon let out a long sigh. "I was put down here because I know too much. No one realizes that you're no longer being tortured and are now doling it out. The Sovereign would never have sent me here if he thought we might talk."

"Why did he target me?"

"I told you. You're strong, Canaan. With merely a thought you can start an earthquake or erupt a volcano somewhere in the world. The Sovereign's time is coming to an end, and your name was at the top of the list to take his place."

Canaan was as surprised as when he was dragged from his bed in the middle of the night and tossed into the Oubliette. Every House's Master in the Incubi world was powerful.

And every House wanted to have the Throne.

"My brothers are as strong as I," he told the demon. "The Sovereign gained nothing in putting me here."

The demon wouldn't quite meet his gaze. There was a stretch of silence before he let out a long sigh and said, "Teman has agreed to change your House name from Romerac to Marakel."

Canaan felt as if he had been sucker punched. It was worse than the betrayal to him. This was a betrayal to the entire House of Romerac. "The Sovereign has no family, no heirs. His House will die with him, but with Teman's agreement, it's my House that will die out and the House of Marakel will live on."

"Now you're getting the big picture."

"There's more."

The demon smiled slyly. "Isn't there always?"

"Tell me."

"Once you get us out."

Canaan slowly walked the length of the cell while covertly looking around. Across the way, Canaan watched as some white-skinned creature sat huddled in the corner with its back to them, talking to itself. On either side of it were demons who were chained and lost within their minds.

Whether anyone heard anything, Canaan couldn't be sure. The stone side and back walls gave the prisoners some privacy, but sound carried well in the jail.

Canaan wished the demon had been put in the lower dungeons where he had been. There, a select few were kept isolated from everyone except their torturers.

"Canaan?" the demon urged in a whisper. "What do you say? Shall we break out and take revenge?"

He swung his head to the demon. "You were part of what put me here. What revenge do you have?"

"I can help you get close to the Sovereign."

Canaan refused to put all his hopes on a demon who helped betray him. He would do it on his own, as well as take back his rightful place as the Master of House Romerac.

"Where is the wall the thinnest?"

"I can show you," the demon said.

Canaan didn't waste another minute. He walked to the demon and gripped the chains. Just like the entrance to the cells, the chains recognized him as a torturer and released the demon.

When the demon's arms dropped, Canaan grabbed him by the back of the neck and kicked him behind the knees, sending the demon on all fours. In an instant, Canaan had the demon's arms behind his back and chained.

"So you betray me now?"

Canaan jerked him to his feet and pushed him out of the cell. "I promised you nothing."

"It's been nearly five hundred years since you were dumped in the Oubliette. Many things have changed in the world."

Canaan sincerely hoped so, because he planned to use everything and everyone to his advantage in his quest.

"Where is the wall the thinnest?" he asked a second time.

"At the top on the left hand side."

That was Muriel's office, but even that didn't stop Canaan. He had found a way out. And he was getting out, one way or another.

By the time they reached the top of the prison, Canaan wished he had taken a moment to feed off a human. He was weakening, and he needed his strength. Once he was back on Earth, he could have his choice of women.

The Alp demon hadn't shut up since they had left his cell. Canaan wished he had something to stuff in his mouth. He was tired of hearing about all the ways the demon could be useful.

Yet in that short walk, Canaan learned about cell phones, cars, planes, and trains. He wouldn't walk into the world completely ignorant of its changes.

"Canaan," Muriel said when he walked into her office. She rose awkwardly from her chair and looked from him to the demon he pushed in front of him. "What's going on?"

"There," the demon said and pointed to the wall on Canaan's left.

The more Canaan looked at it, the more it seemed that something was off with the stones, as if someone had painted over them with a color that didn't quite match their darkness.

"What is the meaning of this, Canaan?" Muriel

demanded.

Canaan swung his gaze to her. "I'm leaving."

"Leaving?" Even with her grotesque features he could tell she frowned, her confusion evident. She slammed her tail down. "How do you propose to do that?"

"I'm going to walk through those walls."

He had taken but three steps, the demon pulling him toward the wall. Canaan couldn't believe he was about to be free. Suddenly, the Alp demon let out a startled cry and fell face forward with a large dagger protruding from his back.

Canaan whirled around to find one of the guards—a goblin—with a dagger in hand. Canaan bent to grab the dagger from the Alp demon's back the same instant he slammed his fist upon the ground.

The walls began to shake, causing the goblin to lose his balance. Just as Canaan was about to make a run for the wall, he was knocked off his feet by something hard slamming into his side.

He rolled nimbly and hit the ground again. Large stones began to fall from the ceiling. One landed between him and Muriel as she was about to attack again.

"You're dumber than I thought if you think you can escape this place," Muriel said over the rumbling of the Oubliette. "You'll be back."

Canaan knew he should probably kill her, but he didn't want to waste the time and chance not getting out. Instead, he darted to the wall and dove through.

# CHAPTER TWO

The silence that assaulted Canaan was deafening. Gone were the screams and moans that he had become accustomed to in the Oubliette.

He was down on the balls of his feet, his legs bent, his fingers upon the ground, with his head lowered. Darkness surrounded him, but it wasn't oppressive and crushing. This darkness was...soothing. Peaceful.

Comforting.

Canaan moved his hand and felt grass beneath his fingers that had him remaining in his current position. Grass. He couldn't remember the last time he had touched it, felt it. Smelled it. He drew in a deep breath, inhaling the rich, moist air. There was a hint of coolness in the air, a signal that fall would soon arrive.

Canaan slowly straightened and lifted his head to look around. He was deep in the middle of the woods, the trees standing like silent sentries. Unable to stop himself, he glanced behind him and saw the very air ripple between two trees. Within the ripple he caught a glimpse of Muriel standing in her office, her gaze angry and narrowed.

He was more than surprised that she didn't

come for him or send her army after him immediately. No doubt he would be hunted soon enough.

Not that it mattered. He had some hunting of his own to do.

Canaan sniffed the air and caught the unmistakable scent of females. His body instantly came alive, desire pounding through him. He needed to feed, to feel pleasure and replenish his strength before he could begin his retaliation.

It wasn't long before he stepped out of the woods and found himself on a road, but it was unlike any road he had ever seen. It was hard and dark with bright yellow lines painted on it.

Just as he was about to take his first step on the odd road, something roared past him so quickly it sent him stumbling backward. His gaze followed the object glowing red.

That's when Canaan saw the lights down the hill. A city of some sort. And the perfect place to...reenergize himself.

~ ~ ~

Rayna Averell was reaching for a bottle of vodka when she felt the heat slide over her. It was sensual, erotic. Like little charges of electricity gliding over her, making her flesh rise with bumps of...anticipation.

She didn't need to look in the long mirror before her to know that an Incubus had just walked into the bar. There was no mistaking the stimulation of her body that a sex demon could evoke.

Rayna swallowed, knowing every other woman in the bar was feeling it as well. The difference was that Rayna knew exactly what caused it. She also knew the last thing she wanted was to be near one of the creatures.

Her hand shook as she wrapped her fingers around the neck of the vodka bottle. In her mind flashed an image of herself, naked and crying out in breathless pleasure as her body was brought to a fever pitch.

She nearly dropped the bottle when the electrical charges increased and her sex throbbed. Rayna turned the vodka upside down to fill three shot glasses while trying to ignore the sweat now covering her skin.

"Rayna, is everything all right?" Leo asked.

She forced a smile and looked into the hazel eyes of her handsome co-worker and owner of the bar, Leo Anderson. "I just need a bit of air."

His eyes held a wealth of concern as he gazed at her. More than once he had made it clear he wanted to be something other than friends, but Rayna hadn't wanted to take that next step. Especially since she would eventually have to explain just what she was. There were no easy words to tell someone she was a Nephilim—half human, half angel.

"Of course," Leo said. "Take all the time you need."

She had to put her hands on the bar in front of her to keep her balance as her knees grew weak from the tide of desire that swallowed her. The Incubus had noticed her. His gaze bore into her, as if daring her to face him.

Which she wouldn't do.

"Thank you," she mumbled and pushed past Leo.

She hastily walked out of the bar through the storeroom door. Even as the door closed behind her, she could still feel the heat of the Incubus's gaze, the promise of pleasure she could only dream about.

With her breaths coming in great gasps she pushed through the stack of boxes in the storeroom and banged open the door that led to the alley outside.

As soon as the night air hit her, she stumbled to the side against the outside wall. She bent over, her hands on her legs, and dragged in mouthfuls of air.

She jerked when the door slammed shut. How long would the Incubus stay in the bar before he found a human female and left? How long would she have to remain in the alley hiding from him?

A shiver raced over her bare arms. She rubbed her hands over her arms as she stood upright. Rayna concentrated on drawing breath into her body and slowly letting it out. Eventually she could feel the calm once more fill her.

She gave a shake of her head, not quite believing the odds of an Incubus showing up in the small town bar hours away from New York City and her powerful Nephilim family.

Since her birth she had been raised to believe that lying with an Incubus was not just her birthright, but her destiny. It had been a constant lesson she and her twin, Anya, had heard daily.

Except it had been Anya chosen by the Three.

Chosen. She wasn't even sure how the three Nephilim priestesses came up with the names of the women chosen to go to the Harem to have at least one child with an Incubus.

After Rayna watched her sister leave, she swore then and there never to have sex with an Incubus. Moving away from the city and her family had helped. There were few Incubi in the suburbs. They tended to congregate in the cities, especially when one of the powerful Incubi Houses ruled it.

Which was the case with New York City. The very ancient and powerful House of Romerac ruled not just New York but the entire United States with an iron fist. Or at least they used to, based on what she had learned growing up.

Rayna closed her eyes and leaned her head back against the wall. It had been eight years since she had seen an Incubus. And frankly, she wanted to go the rest of her life without seeing another.

It was the sensual heat, the foreshadowing of mind-boggling, world-altering sex a second before the heart-stopping voice reached her that sent off a mental alarm.

"Do you fear me, Nephilim?"

*Don't look. Don't look. Don't look.*

But oh, did she ever want to see the Incubus. Was he fair-haired and blue eyed? Or was he as dark as his seductive voice?

Her body trembled. Not because she knew what it was to have sex with an Incubus, but because at that moment, she was ready to get on her knees and beg him to have his way with her.

*Anya.*

Rayna needed to remember that her sister had been taken from the family. She was in the Harem, a palace in Morocco that was considered neutral ground. How many children had her sister birthed and been forced to give up?

To think that at one time she had wanted to be the one to lie with an Incubus. That was until she learned just what it meant to be chosen and taken away from the family.

"Are you ill?"

Rayna bit back a gasp. He was standing in front of her, probably close enough to touch. He moved without making a sound. And the closer he got, the more her body trembled for his touch.

It wasn't fair that an Incubus could affect her this way. If he could do this with his nearness and his sexy voice, what would he do to her when she finally looked at him?

Rayna didn't want to find out.

"Yes," she said, still refusing to open her eyes. "I'm ill. You should leave before I get sick all over you."

There was a pause. "Your skin is flushed, but not from illness."

Conceited prick. Of course a sex demon would know when she was aroused. "I know you won't force me, and I'm not interested. So go away."

She waited for his response, waited to hear the charm and seduction she knew was coming. Except there was nothing. Rayna counted to fifty before she opened her eyes.

And promptly gasped when she found herself

staring into eyes of blue-green as fathomless as the sea.

Rayna tried to look away, but only managed to move her eyes to his chiseled chin and jaw that sported a shadow of a beard, making him even sexier. If that was possible.

She caught a glimpse of coal black hair against his shoulder and saw it hung loose, the waves begging her to slide her fingers into the thickness. A lock of that hair fell over his wide forehead to fall against the corner of his eye.

Once more she was caught in his gaze. A woman could drown in such brilliance. Between the brightness of his eyes, the long black lashes, his midnight hair, and his olive skin, he wasn't just handsome. He was striking, breathtaking.

Magnificent.

"Not interested?" he said, a hint of a smile upon wide, full lips. Lips that no doubt kissed as heavenly as he looked.

Rayna had to try twice to get enough wetness in her mouth to swallow. Even then her voice wouldn't work so she shook her head.

He leaned forward and ran his index finger softly down the side of her face before pushing her hair over her shoulder. "Say it again."

Was he insane? Didn't he realize she was barely holding it together? Or perhaps that was the point. He did realize exactly what kind of precarious situation she was in.

It wasn't as if she hadn't known pleasure. She'd had her share of lovers, but not a single one of them had heated her blood like the Incubi before her. And he hadn't even kissed her.

Victory shone in the Incubus's beautiful eyes, and the resulting anger was enough that she could remember just why she didn't want him. She refused to be a pawn in the game played between the Nephilim and the Incubi.

"I don't want you," she said. It might be a hoarse whisper, but the words had come.

To make her point even more clear, she shoved past him. It was a mistake as soon as her hand landed on his chest. The resulting heat, the primal need that thrummed through her veins, halted her.

He moved behind her, his warm breath fanning her neck. Unable to stop herself, her eyes closed and her head fell to the side. Soft lips touched the place where her neck met her shoulders. It barely registered before his hot, wet tongue flicked over her skin.

"You're correct, Nephilim. I won't force you," he whispered into her ear. "Your kind is normally so willing to couple with us. What makes you so different?"

Rayna turned to face him, wondering if she was a masochist. Why else would she willingly face someone so damned gorgeous again?

"I walked away from that world. I want nothing to do with it."

Before she could get in another word, his lips were on hers. There was nothing soft or romantic about the kiss. It was all heat and desire, need and passion.

Lust and longing.

It sent her world spinning. Her body was

scorched from the intensity of the kiss.

As suddenly as it began, the kiss ended. Rayna blinked up at him, unsure why he stopped. She licked her lips, liking the taste of him altogether too much.

"Farewell," he said and disappeared into the night before she could utter a single syllable in response.

# CHAPTER THREE

It took less than a day for Canaan to realize he had to get accustomed to the world much more than he had comprehended. It had taken a lot for him to walk away from the beautiful Rayna, but walk away he had.

He might be a sex demon, but no was no. The next block over he found just the woman he needed to feed off of and restore some of his strength.

As usual, people were eager to share useless information, but he did manage to glean facts he did need. Like the name of the town—Traders Hollow—and that New York City was five hours away by car.

Canaan had expected the human race to make advancements, but he hadn't expected such bold leaps as the computer, cell phones, and weaponry. Then again, the humans were rather gifted in killing themselves.

As the day faded to night, Canaan knew he couldn't leave Traders Hollow just yet, even though he was more than ready to begin his trail of revenge.

If the human world had changed so much, what

of the Incubi and Nephilim? He needed to know every detail before he set out for the city. There would be no mistakes, no oversights. No missteps.

Few would see him coming.

Fewer still would know what ended their lives.

But in the end, he would right the wrong done to him.

Canaan glanced down at the black boots he wore. It had felt good to bathe and change clothes. He felt more himself, but there was no denying his soul was gone.

The Sovereign feared him enough to throw him in the Oubliette. Canaan was going to give the bastard something to fear. Right before he ripped the Sovereign's head from his body.

Canaan could feel his anger grow, and he quickly tamped it down as he reached the door to The White Sail Bar. Thankfully, with the town being small, he had learned quite a bit about Rayna.

He pushed open the door and stepped inside. His eyes found her instantly. Once more she was behind the bar, except this time she didn't have her back to him.

She was talking with a customer, but Canaan saw her flinch, the not-so-subtle tightening of her body. Her dark brown locks were pulled up, showcasing her long, slender neck.

He let his gaze take in the sight of her. In all his centuries as an Incubus, he couldn't remember a woman—human or Nephilim—that had ever remained in his mind after meeting them.

Her oval face was flawless, her skin smooth as cream. She had high cheekbones, a stubborn chin, and lips that could bring even an Incubus to his knees.

He had savored those luscious lips, had sampled a taste of her, and only craved more.

Canaan flexed his hands as he recalled how her lithe body had felt against his, how her hands had splayed upon his chest before her arms wound around his neck. She claimed not to want him, but their kiss had proven otherwise.

It was too bad his mission at the bar that night was for information and not to woo the lovely Rayna.

When her walnut-colored eyes finally lifted to him, Canaan walked to a table and sat. She didn't try to hide her sigh as she came around the bar toward him.

"I thought you were gone," she said sharply.

Canaan merely smiled. She was peeved, but was it at the fact he was still around, or that she wanted him? If only he had the time to find out. "I was hoping you could share some information."

"On?"

He raised a brow, waiting for her to comprehend what he asked.

"Ah," she said with a knowing nod. "I thought your kind knew all there was to know about my kind."

"I've been...gone...for awhile. I want to get my bearings before I leave." Canaan hoped his explanation would suffice. The fewer people that knew who he was, the better.

Rayna licked her lips. "What can I get you to drink?"

"Whatever," he said, uninterested in anything but the woman before him.

"How about your name, then?"

"Canaan."

They stared in each other's eyes, the heat between them growing, expanding until it was an undercurrent, charged and waiting. Desire licked at his skin, urging him to pull her against him for another kiss.

He knew it would take the slightest push to send her over the edge and accept him. Yet Canaan refused to do that no matter how much he longed to slide into her body. She didn't want him, and there were other willing females.

Still...how he yearned to have her skin to skin against him, to hear her sighs, to see her peak in his arms.

"I'll get you your drink. My break is in twenty minutes. You'll have to wait until then," Rayna said in a rush before she spun around and all but ran to the bar.

Canaan leaned back in the chair and looked around. There were crowds of younger humans milling in groups by the pool tables and dartboard. Some were seated at tables, laughing and carrying on as if they didn't have a care in the world.

He had been like that at one time. It had been a short period, but while it lasted it had been the closest thing to paradise that he had known.

Then his father died and he became the Master of Romerac House centuries before he had expected it. He didn't just take on the role as Master of his House, but as more father than brother to his two younger siblings.

It hadn't gone easy with Teman since they were merely days apart in age, but Levi was a full century younger. Canaan had filled the role of father to Levi as best he could.

The days of fun and play had ceased in a split second. Canaan might have chafed at the responsibility placed upon him at the time, but it was his by right.

And it would be returned.

Rayna placed a mug of amber liquid in front of him and hurried away before he could respond. Canaan took a drink and realized it was beer. While he sipped the beer, he found his mind drifting back to the night he had been yanked from the bed of some human he had found.

Canaan had fought them, but he hadn't been able to stop them from killing the female. He had been shot with silver bullets multiple times, weakening him enough that the group had subdued him. When he next awoke, he was in the Oubliette.

That's when the real nightmare had begun.

He was setting his mug down when Canaan heard the door of the bar open. A glance at the entrance showed three men, all wearing black leather jackets. And all Incubi.

Canaan went on instant alert. He wasn't surprised when their gazes turned to him. Instead of approaching him, the group took a seat at the bar.

Rayna, for her part, kept away from them, letting the other bartender, a male, take their order. A ripple of unease ran through the bar as others took notice of the three Incubi.

Conversation lagged, laughter ceased until nothing but the sound of the music filled the room. Canaan didn't think it was a coincidence that Incubi just happened to stroll into the very bar he was in.

Had Rayna told someone about him? That was the only explanation. As far as he had learned, there were few Incubi in the area, and none living in town.

If they wanted a fight, he would gladly give it to them. Canaan rose, the sound of his chair scooting back on the floor so loud that it drew everyone's attention.

Good. He wanted the men to see him leave so he didn't have to wait around for them. Just as Canaan started for the door his gaze skimmed over Rayna at the cash register.

Was the furrow of her brow because she felt bad that she had spoken about him to others? Or was she concerned with the humans being injured?

Canaan supposed it was the latter. He didn't much care who got hurt, but it was better for him if few witnessed what he was about to do. He had the advantage. A driving revenge often did that. Besides, Canaan had nothing else to lose.

He leaned back against the outside of the bar in the alley with one leg bent, his foot propped against the bricks. As he predicted, the three didn't take long to follow him.

"I suppose you're here for me," Canaan said. "I'll give you one chance to walk away. Alive. Forget you even came here."

One of the Incubi in the back with bleached

blond hair laughed. "Do you know who we are?"

The fact was he didn't, but he could guess. There had been rumors swirling before he was betrayed about a group of Incubi akin to the mob. Canaan had learned firsthand just how true those rumors had been.

"Why are you here?" he asked.

The leader rolled a toothpick in his mouth. "There were reports of an Incubus in Traders Hollow. We came to move you along."

Interesting. Why would the Incubi want to keep other Incubi out of the town? The answer came to Canaan like a blow – Rayna. "I'll be leaving soon."

"You'll be leaving now," the leader said.

Canaan smiled coldly as he pushed off the wall. "I make my own decisions."

"Who are you?" asked the third of the group who had been looking as if he recognized Canaan. "Shit. You're Canaan Romerac."

Canaan didn't wait for the others' reaction. He attacked, ramming his shoulder into the gut of the leader, knocking him off his feet before he grabbed Blondie's head and broke his neck.

He dropped the body and turned when a bullet slammed into his chest, the silver spreading like wildfire. Canaan let out a roar and raced for the leader who managed to get off two shots from his gun before Canaan reached him.

With every bullet, Canaan's rage grew. He was focused on killing the two Incubi, making it easy to push aside the pain of the silver.

~ ~ ~

Rayna rushed out into the alley even as she knew the danger that awaited her. As soon as the three Incubi walked into the bar she realized they had come for Canaan.

She looked skyward at the rumble of clouds that seemed to form right over her as if someone had called to them. Thunder rolled an instant before lightning split the sky. She stumbled to a halt, her mouth open as she watched in helpless awe as Canaan left carnage in his wake. His strength was incredible, his speed inconceivable, but it was his blinding fury that held her immobile.

Blood coated the ground and walls of the buildings. Two lifeless bodies lay nearly torn apart, the savagery making her stomach turn.

The retort of a gun made her jump and look to Canaan. He stood over the last Incubus who had just fired the pistol. Canaan swatted the gun out of the weakened hand of the Incubus just as another bolt of lightning hit. Canaan reared back his hand and sent a killing punch to his jaw.

Over and over Canaan hit the dead man. With each punch the lightning became more extreme, the thunder deafening. Rayna debated what to do. She had seen men lose themselves in anger before, but what she witnessed with Canaan was different. He was untamed, fierce, and ferocious in his attack.

She took a step around one of the dead bodies toward Canaan and saw the front of his white tee covered with blood and...was that silver?

He was kneeling on the dead Incubus now, and his punches made the face unrecognizable.

Someone was going to have to step in, and since she was the only one out there, it was left up to her.

Rayna called out his name, but her voice was carried away by the growing wind. She drew closer. "Canaan? It's over. They're dead. Can you hear me, Canaan?"

When she reached him, she tentatively touched his shoulder, ready for him to turn and strike her. Instead, his hand that was lifted and ready for another hit dropped to his side.

He turned his head to her and she saw the rage begin to fade from his blue-green eyes. Blood was all over him, and his hands looked like he had hit bricks instead of flesh.

The wind began to die down. She glanced at the sky to see the clouds begin to disperse. No longer was there thunder and lightning.

"It's over, Canaan," she repeated.

He gave a shake of his head and got to his feet. "It's just beginning."

"Easy," Rayna said when he staggered, and she slid against his side to take some of his weight. "You're wounded."

"Just need...to rest," he said, his words slurring.

She glanced at the three dead men and continued walking Canaan to her car. Once he was inside, she got behind the wheel and started the car. It never entered her mind to leave Canaan there.

As she pulled out onto the road, she dialed Leo to let him know that she was on her way home because she was ill. It wasn't a total lie. She had lost her mind. What other explanation was there for helping an Incubus?

# CHAPTER FOUR

Canaan was being tortured again. There was a beautiful woman, her sensual voice stirring him, her touch tempting him as she wiped a cool cloth over his face and chest.

His strength was completely drained. If Incubi came for him now, he was no better than an infant. They would either kill him outright if they caught him, or toss him back into the Oubliette.

He was on fire, his body in turns raging and so cold he thought he might break into a million pieces. Canaan had no idea how long he suffered before blessed sleep began to finally claim him. He tried to turn, to reach for the siren beside him.

"Easy," the woman whispered. "You need to rest, Canaan."

It was the use of his name that made him recognize Rayna. Why was she helping him?

That was the very question in his mind when he woke. He lay still, listening for...anything. When only silence met him, he chanced to move his head and look around the room. He was in an upper floor of some kind, based on the slanting roof.

Shutters were closed over the windows but light still filtered through, allowing him to see the dust swirling in the sun. The house was old, but in good order. More than he could say for himself.

Canaan clenched his teeth as he sat up and swung his legs over the side of the bed. He raised a brow when he saw he had been divested of his clothes. Had the lovely Rayna been the one to strip him?

His body stirred just thinking about it. It was too bad he hadn't been aware of it. He'd have liked to see her face as she bared his body.

"You shouldn't be sitting up," Rayna said as she walked through a doorway, a tray in her hands. She looked tired, weary.

A part of him wanted to comfort her since he knew it was Rayna who had remained up with him most of the night. Had she sat by his bed while he slept?

Canaan glanced down at his chest to see his wounds had stopped bleeding, but until he fed, the silver would remain inside him, thereby weakening him. "I'm better."

"Better perhaps, but certainly not well." She set the tray down and moved her hair out of her face to tuck it behind her ear.

He liked it when she wore her hair down. It was longer than he remembered though. Then again, it hadn't been her hair he had been focused on when they had shared their kiss.

"You're staring."

And he had no intention of stopping. "Did you alert someone that I was here?"

Her lips parted, an affronted look hardening her face. "No. Before you ask again, let me be clear. I walked away from that world eight years ago. I don't have contact with my family or any Nephilim or Incubi."

"That's not entirely true, now is it? You've had contact with me."

She crossed her arms over her chest and regarded him with a chilly look. "I told no one that you were an Incubus. I've no one to tell."

Canaan didn't exactly believe her, but at the moment his choices were limited. He would keep a close watch on her. He had learned the hard way that he could never trust anyone.

"Why did you help me?"

Her gaze shifted away as she shrugged. "I've been asking myself that same question since I put you in my car."

"For that I'm thankful."

"So," she said into the quiet. "Silver, huh?"

He frowned. It was a secret the Incubi kept from the Nephilim specifically so they could never use it against them.

Rayna threw up her hands, her eyes wide. "Hey. Didn't you hear me a second ago? I don't have contact with that world anymore."

"Someone knew I was in town." He paused as he thought over his exchange with the Incubi who attacked. "Actually, they didn't know who I was at first. They thought I was just a lower level Incubus."

"And you're not?"

Damn. He really was going to have to remember to keep his mouth shut around her. Canaan ran a hand down his face before he braced both hands on either side of him. "It's better if you don't know who I am. I'll be leaving soon anyway."

"I assumed as much. Last night you wanted to talk. I'm not sure I can tell you anything more than you already know."

Canaan grunted. "Ah, but I'm sure you can."

"How long have you been gone?" Her gaze was focused, as if gauging his response.

How much did he tell her? He needed information, information that she had. In order to get it, he might have to tell her a bit about himself. There was nothing wrong with that. She would never know exactly who he was.

"Five centuries."

She blinked and took a step back. "You've been gone for five hundred years?" Her gaze swung away as she rubbed her jaw. A moment later she faced him again. "Where were you?"

"Kept against my will."

"That's all you're going to tell me?" She rolled her eyes and let her hands slap against her thighs. "I should've known."

"It's all you need to know. In the end, it might very well save your life." Canaan motioned to a chair. "Sit, Rayna, and eat some of the food you brought up."

"I brought it for you," she mumbled, but she pulled out the chair and sat. "What do you want to know?"

"Everything. Who is in power in the Nephilim world?"

"The powerful families are still, well, powerful. Nephilim are still being chosen by the Three to be taken to the Harem."

She fairly vibrated with anger as she said the last part. Canaan kept the sheet covering his nakedness as he leaned back against the iron headboard. "I take that to mean you know someone chosen? It's a great honor, Rayna. They are immortal while on that sacred land."

"With no choice about going," she argued. "And yes, I know someone. My twin was taken."

Ah. So much made sense now. No longer did he need to ask why she had left her world behind. "I take it she didn't want to go?"

"No. Anya wanted to go. She was so happy."

"Then you should be happy for her."

"Happy that she'll be there for God only knows how long, producing babies for whatever Incubus comes in and chooses her? Happy that she'll give her children for the good of our people and yours?" She shook her head. "I can't."

"She's only required to give one child. After that, she can leave. It's up to them whether they wish to remain and produce more children for us."

For long moments Rayna stared at the floor silently. "This wasn't the first place I went when I left my family. For two years I was on Long Island. Silly me thought I could remain close but distanced from them. They found me. My mother sent a letter, elated, to announce that Anya had given birth to a little girl who would be given to us in a few weeks. My mother wanted me to take my niece and raise her as my own."

"It's always been the way, Rayna. The female offspring of a Nephilim and Incubus goes to the

Nephilim, while the male offspring remain with the Incubi. That arrangement was set up long ago to help both of our kind survive."

"The Three are supposed to step down in the next five years as their three-hundred-year time as priestesses has come to an end. The entire Nephilim world is in a frenzy because the Three have yet to find their replacements."

Canaan let the abrupt change in topic go as he realized the implications of what she was saying. "The next priestesses should have been chosen already to begin their training."

"I know. This is a first, from what I understand. No one knows what will happen if the Three don't find more priestesses."

"There is a temple where Nephilim would go to be trained and considered as priestesses," Canaan said, a niggle of worry beginning.

Rayna met his gaze and shook her head. "That really exists? I thought it was something else that was made up."

Canaan was beginning to comprehend that the goings-on in the Incubi and Nephilim world were much worse than he first thought. "What about the Incubi? What do you know of us?"

"I know the Sovereign sitting on the Obsidian Throne is still from the House of Marakel. I also know that he has no heirs to be considered when it comes time for him to step aside."

"And the other nine Houses?"

"House Akana is no longer. Something about him unable to father a child."

That was impossible. Incubi had never had a

problem fathering children. "What about the other Houses?"

"All is fine, as far as I last heard."

"What about the Sovereign? You said his House has no heirs to be considered as next in line."

Rayna shrugged and rose to hand him a mug of coffee. "He's done nothing. Before I left my family, I remember that everyone expected him to visit the Harem, but he chose not to."

"Were women brought to him?"

"Maybe," she said with a shrug.

The mug he was holding cracked as he squeezed it in anger. If he was at full strength it would have shattered. It was just another reminder that he was in no condition to move forward with his plans.

Canaan set the mug on the table next to the bed and put his feet on the floor. Then he stood, letting the sheet fall away. "Where are my clothes?"

"Unwearable. I did find you some more," Rayna said, looking anywhere but him. "What do you think you're doing?"

"I need to gain my strength. The only way to do that is by having sex. Are you offering?"

There was a beat of silence, and to his delight, Rayna glanced at him twice before she closed her eyes. "No."

As he thought. "A pity. I liked the way you tasted."

Rayna swallowed and quickly rose so that she faced the doorway. The entire night and most of the day that she had stood over him she had been admiring his body. He was impeccably built, his muscles solid and his skin warm. "I'll just go get your clothes then."

She wasn't entirely sure he was fit to go out. He moved well enough, but the strength she had witnessed the night before was gone. The fire within him, however, burned brighter than ever. He was looking to start something.

"Or finish it," she said to herself as she raced down the stairs and grabbed the pile of clothes at the bottom before she went back up.

As she came through the doorway she saw him with his hands braced on the windowsill with his chin to his chest. He looked so lonely, and she could relate to that.

If she didn't know how his kiss could turn her inside out, or how hard his body was, she might have been able to look away, to ignore the splendid, glorious sight before her.

Canaan was perfectly formed, in every way. From his wide shoulders to his tapering torso, down to his trim waist and narrow hips. Thick sinew corded every inch of him from neck to ankle.

He shifted, bringing her gaze to his butt. She had no idea an ass could look that good or be that tight with muscle. His dark good looks combined with his olive skin and body honed out of her wildest dreams was an intoxicating combination.

If only she was brave enough to give in. For the rest of her days her lips would never forget the feel of his kiss, how he expertly took her, giving her a glimpse of the bliss that could be found in his arms.

"Do you give a women only pleasure?" She wasn't sure where the words had come from, or why she kept wanting to help him.

His head swung to her as his blue-green eyes seemed to pierce her very soul. "Only pleasure. Don't you know? As a Nephilim you'll have been with at least one Incubus."

"I've refused every Incubus who tried. Not that there were that many. Just a handful over the years. At first I saved myself to be considered for the Harem, because that was what we were taught. After, it was because I wanted no part of that world."

"There is only pleasure, Rayna. We feed off the energy created by sex. If we don't feed, we grow weak. If we continue without sex, we die."

She held out the clothes to him, unable to have him walk around nude any longer and not touch him. "Then I'll bring a woman to you."

# CHAPTER FIVE

Canaan looked at her with surprise he didn't try to hide. What was it about Rayna that caught his interest – and held it? She had touched him when he was in full rage, battling his attackers. With just a hand on his shoulder, his fury had abated.

No one had ever been able to do that to him. Though to be fair, few got close when he was in such a state. Still, Rayna had not only dared it, but remained with him.

He hated the weakness of his body. If he had his full strength, she wouldn't have had to watch over him all night. It was his pride that brought him to this. He hadn't fed off the humans in the Oubliette because he had already slept with each of them once.

That choice had left him weakened. It was the silver, however, that was taking the last of his strength. It was all he could do to remain standing. Yet he refused to let Rayna know just how vulnerable he was.

"You're bleeding again," Rayna said as she set aside the clothes and moved to him.

Canaan bit back a hiss at the feel of her hands on his chest. Being this close to her was too much.

He craved the pleasure he knew could be between them, longed to hear her scream in release and see her body flushed with satisfaction.

He looked down at her hands to see her trying in vain to stop the trickle of blood. She had no idea how her touch set his blood aflame.

How having her so close made him ache to pull her into his arms.

How he longed to push her against the wall and ravage her mouth until she clung to him.

It was no surprise that his cock answered by growing hard, straining between them. Rayna, for her part, tried to ignore his arousal. It was the shaking of her hands and the rapid beat of her pulse at her throat that gave her away.

"You've lost too much blood," she said in a breathless, husky whisper.

Canaan couldn't hold back his moan. Her voice sent his body into overdrive, his heated blood beginning to boil with need. He was a sex demon, and yet it was a Nephilim who stimulated him beyond anything he could imagine.

Time stood still when she raised her brown gaze to him. Her large eyes were wide and dilated, her lips parted, and her breathing harsh. She had no idea of her appeal or how she could have him on his knees, begging for another taste of her.

It was a good thing, too. An Incubus who lost control with a woman? That wasn't a good sign.

She had refused him, and yet he had sampled the fire in her kiss. If he pushed her, she would relent. But that wasn't his way. Rayna would have to come to him.

Just when he thought she would turn away, she rose up on her tiptoes and kissed him. Canaan wrapped his arms around her and turned her so that she was pressed against the wall.

He couldn't get close enough, couldn't kiss her deep enough. She was a balm to his shattered life, a calm to the turmoil he was in.

And she fired his blood like no other.

Her hands smoothed over his shoulders to his back, the caress slow and at odds with their frantic, fiery kiss. Canaan fisted his hands in the thick strands of her dark locks, loving the cool texture.

He ground his aching cock against her and felt satisfaction fill him with her answering moan. Every fiber of his being urged him to continue, to release the pleasure that restored his strength, but he couldn't. Not until Rayna told him she wanted him.

Canaan ended the kiss and looked down at her swollen lips and her glassy eyes. She clung to him, her face a mask of confusion.

"What?" she asked.

"I'll not force you."

She shook her head and tried to kiss him again. "You're not."

"I have to hear you say it," Canaan said as he pulled back his head. "I need to know you want this."

Rayna stared at him for several seconds before she gave him a soft push and took a couple of steps away. Then she turned to face him, her head cocked to the side.

"You want me to say it even though I just threw

myself at you?"

He might be an Incubus, but he did have standards. "I do."

If Canaan thought his body was on fire, he didn't know anything until she slowly, seductively began to unbutton her shirt.

All the moisture left his mouth as he watched her lovely breasts exposed, bit by bit. When the shirt fell to the floor and she stood in her plain beige bra, one side of her mouth lifted.

"Minx." She knew exactly what the sight of the globes of her breasts and her toned abdomen did to him.

She didn't retort as she unbuttoned her jeans and gave them a shove over her hips and down her legs. With the jeans divested, she stood in her bra and neon green panties with "Sexy" written across the front.

Canaan got a look at her long, lean legs and her gently flared hips. Despite her undressing, there was a thread of uncertainty in her gaze.

She feared being with an Incubus, of giving in to what she had been told was her destiny. Canaan couldn't find it in himself to walk away from her.

"I want you," she whispered as she stood before him, waiting.

He took a step to her. "Canaan."

Her lips softened into a smile and she unhooked her bra to let it fall from her shoulders to the floor. "I want you, Canaan."

That's all he needed to hear. Canaan forgot about his wounds, forgot that his body hurt. All that mattered was having Rayna in his arms, hearing her sighs and cries of pleasure.

He had her on the bed, his body atop hers, in a split second. There was no holding back for either of them. Their kisses ignited a firestorm of passion.

His hand moved between them to cup her breasts and stroke his thumb over her nipple. She moaned, her hips grinding against him.

Canaan ended the kiss to take her turgid nipple in his mouth while his hand skimmed down her stomach to the juncture of her legs.

With a yank, he tore off her panties, exposing her. He raised his head to look at the patch of brown hair neatly trimmed around her sex.

He couldn't remember ever needing sex so desperately, but if he was only going to have the one time with Rayna he wanted to take it slow, to savor her.

"Please," she begged, her hand on his wrist.

Canaan slid his fingers into her curls and felt her wetness. She moaned, her eyes closing as her legs parted. He sank his fingers inside her and once more wrapped his lips around her nipple.

He moved his fingers slowly in and out of her at first, and gradually quickened his tempo. When her nails dug into his arm, he swirled his thumb around her clit.

A cry burst from her lips as her back arched. She was a vision, a temptress who was unraveling him at the seams. His body shook from the need to fill her, take her.

Claim her.

Canaan," she whispered.

He lifted his head and saw the sheer need in her

gaze. She was on the edge, the desire ruling her as it did him. Canaan pulled his hand from her sex and hooked it beneath one of her knees as he positioned himself.

With their gazes locked, he thrust inside. The pleasure was absolute, unadulterated. It was fire and energy, an inferno of hunger and yearning.

It went beyond anything Canaan had ever experienced, leaving him reeling. He pushed it aside as he began to move within Rayna's body.

Her walls were tight and slick. She wrapped her legs around his waist, sending him sinking deeper inside her. They were soon locked in a dance as old as time, carnal and physical.

Canaan pushed deeper, harder as the pleasure filled them. With each moment he could feel himself growing stronger and his wounds healing. But none of that mattered with the beauty in his arms.

Her moans became soft cries as she barreled toward her climax. A sheen of sweat glistened over them, allowing their bodies to slide.

Canaan drove inside her, taking them higher and higher. Pleasure was there waiting, but he refused to reach for it yet. It wasn't until Rayna came apart in his arms, her scream echoing around the room, that he gave in.

The orgasm seized him, and the euphoria was blinding, the rapture dazzling.

He opened his eyes to find Rayna watching him. This was normally when he would make his excuses and depart, and yet there was a contentment that filled him. It was so strong he wasn't ready to leave her. From the first moment he had seen her, he had known Rayna was special.

He just hadn't anticipated how much.

She lifted her hand to his chest where his injuries had been. "The wounds are almost completely gone."

"You did that," he said and bent to kiss her.

To his surprise, the kiss was soft, sensual, altogether too sexy. And yet he couldn't bring himself to end it as he knew he should.

Rayna smoothed her hands over the warm skin and hard muscle of Canaan's amazing body. Her head was still spinning from the climax that had rocked her world – literally.

Now, after having such a strong orgasm, she wanted more of him. He was still hard inside her. Unable to stop herself, she lifted her hips.

Canaan's hiss brought a smile to her lips. She had done that to him, she had brought him pleasure. It was heady, that satisfaction.

She pushed against his shoulder and rolled him onto his back until she straddled him. Rayna sat up and rotated her hips once, twice.

"You're playing with fire, minx," Canaan said in a tight voice, his hands on her hips, guiding her.

"Take me just once more." She was prepared to beg if need be.

With her hands braced on his chest, she began to rock her hips faster and faster. Canaan's blue-green eyes were riveted on her and filled with desire.

It made her shiver, that look. She had known giving in to him would alter her world. She just hadn't expected to be knocked off her feet in the process.

Her skin tingled, her blood pounded—all for Canaan. He had breathed life into her gray existence, and she feared she would never look at the world the same again.

How easily he brought her to the brink, but this time he prolonged the torture, keeping her on the precipice of pleasure and taking her higher and higher.

The world fell away, leaving just the two of them and the passion that wouldn't be denied. Rayna had never been so unreserved or unrestrained. Canaan brought that out in her, creating a wanton that couldn't get enough of him.

"Now, Rayna," he urged.

The climax was soul-shattering and overwhelming. It left her dazed and searching for something to hold on to. She latched on to Canaan as he joined her in her orgasm.

She screamed his name as his fingers dug into her hips, but she didn't care. She was in the arms of an Incubus, a man who had taken her to the gates of paradise.

With her body sated, sleep pulled at her. To her surprise, Canaan turned her onto her side and curled his body behind her.

There was so much she wanted to say to him, but sleep weighed heavily upon her. She took comfort when his arm draped over her that he might stay.

She woke instantly when he caressed the underside of her breast. It didn't matter that she had dozed for a short time. She turned toward him, opening her body as he once more slid inside her.

Again and again they found each other. Sometimes she reached for him, sometimes it was he who came to her.

Pleasure centered them, cocooning them in a bubble that the outside world couldn't penetrate.

# CHAPTER SIX

Canaan woke with a smile. It had been a long time since he had felt so hale and refreshed. His smile grew as he thought about Rayna. He hadn't been prepared for just how good she would feel in his arms.

He sat up and swung his legs over the side of the bed. Sunlight filtered through the slats of the shutters. He had lost another day and an entire night, but it had been worth it.

Below he could hear the sound of water running. Curious, he rose and walked to the doorway and then down the narrow stairs until he found the source of the sound.

Canaan leaned a shoulder against the doorframe and regarded the sight of Rayna's silhouette through the glass door as she showered.

The shower – as well as the entire bathroom itself – was one of the many inventions he was pleased to find.

All that was forgotten as his body responded to the sight of Rayna. She fired his blood unlike any other. Canaan pushed away from the door and stalked into the room. He opened the shower just as she turned off the water.

"Canaan," she said with wide eyes, surprise making her jerk.

"Turn the water back on. I want to join you."

Instead of doing as he asked, she put her hand on his chest to stop him from entering the shower. "I don't think that's a good idea."

He gazed at the water droplets covering her skin, but it was the pebble of water hanging from the tip of one nipple that made him want to lick it all away.

"I know how to make you scream in pleasure," he whispered and pulled her against his nude body.

Her eyes darkened. "I know. That's the reason I don't think it's a good idea."

Canaan thought back over the night. "We only had sex six times."

"Seven," she corrected. "You're forgetting the chair."

He smiled slowly. "Ah. The chair. How could I ever forget that?"

"You want to smile at the fact we've already had sex seven times?" she asked in disbelief.

All Incubi took precautions never to have sex with the same woman more than once, especially when that woman was a Nephilim. Women became addicted to the Incubi, but if an Incubus and a Nephilim had sex eight times, then the Nephilim became immortal and they were bound together.

But it tied both the Incubus and Nephilim into a relationship that kept the Incubus needing her and only her to survive.

A few Nephilim managed to gain immortality before the Incubi discovered what they were doing.

It then became imperative to keep their mating to once only.

And here Canaan had engaged in sex with Rayna seven times. While wanting another. He knew he should walk away, but he couldn't. He craved her like he yearned for revenge.

"Why remind me?" he asked Rayna. "Don't all Nephilim long to be immortal?"

She grabbed the towel off the rack and held it in front of her while her gaze shifted away. "It didn't seem right not to tell you."

"So you do want to be immortal." He should've known. Though Canaan had to admit, he was disappointed in her.

"Am I afraid of dying? Yes," she finished in a whisper. She paused to lick her lips and hurriedly dried off. "However, I'm not the type to take advantage of someone like that."

Canaan stepped back to allow her to exit the shower. Rayna was never what he expected. She surprised him at every turn, keeping him off kilter.

"I don't work today. I can drive you wherever you need to go."

He frowned. How could he have so easily forgotten what he was after? Not to mention someone had alerted the others that an Incubus was in town. More would come looking for him. It was time to leave.

That also meant leaving Rayna behind. He didn't like the thought, but the only other option was keeping her near, which meant keeping temptation within arm's reach.

Not a wise move when he was going to war and

needed his mind focused on discovering the truth.

"New York City," he said and spun around to get dressed.

~ ~ ~

An hour later they were in Rayna's Camaro, leaving the quaint town of Traders Hollow behind. She hadn't told Canaan that she would rather chew off her own hand than get anywhere near New York City, but then again, she had said she would drive him wherever he needed to go.

The easy exchange of words had all but halted after she reminded him how close to that dreaded number eight they had come. Eight.

The number itself meant very little. Other than its link to infinity.

Rayna could almost hear her mother's shrill voice screaming about how she had let a prime opportunity slide through her fingers.

She had thought Canaan was also keeping track of how many times they had been together. It hadn't been easy, and she had gone over the night five times just to be sure. Immortality didn't really appeal to her, perhaps because it was something her mother desired more than anything else.

That's the real reason she'd told Canaan. She hadn't been able to choose her family or how those blood ties bound her, but she could choose how she acted and the choices she made.

No matter what, she wouldn't become her mother.

The hours and miles steadily ticked by, broken

only by the sounds of music playing through the speakers as Canaan searched through her CDs and even her MP3 files.

His gaze was constantly seeking, ceaselessly searching. He soaked up everything like a sponge, from the music, the billboards they passed, and even the commercials on the radio. It was like he couldn't get enough.

Much like she couldn't get enough of him. She hated herself for turning him away that morning when all she wanted to do was pull him in the shower and have her way with him again. But he would think she tricked him into their binding.

Was it true, the whispers she used to hear? That the more a Nephilim had sex with an Incubus, the more that Nephilim needed the Incubus?

Was that what was wrong with her? Had her desire turned to...need? Oh God, she hoped not. She'd be in real trouble then.

Not only would Canaan never make love to her again, but being this near to him was a torture she hadn't known existed until now.

If she wasn't already tense enough, the horizon filled with the skyscrapers of New York City – the home she had run from.

"You don't have to drive me into the city," Canaan said after he muted the music.

"I drove you this far. What's a few more miles?" she said with an indifference she didn't feel.

"Your family, for one thing."

"They'll never know I was even here."

Canaan settled in his seat, one hand on each leg as he stared with narrowed eyes at the city. "It's gotten bigger."

"New York is the hub for...well just about everything. I imagine it's changed quite a bit in five hundred years."

"More than you can imagine," he said through tight lips.

Rayna shivered. Whoever had incurred Canaan's wrath was about to suffer the hammer. She should feel sorry for them, but from the time she had spent with Canaan she knew he was a fair man.

Whoever he was after had it coming.

"Where am I going?" she asked.

"Romerac Consolidated."

She jerked her head to him. "Are you insane? You can't go in there."

"I can." His head slowly turned to her. "Especially since it's mine."

Rayna pulled her car over onto the side of the road and threw it in park before she put her head on the steering wheel. "Dear God. You're Canaan Romerac."

"At your service."

She had gotten into bed with the Master of one of the most powerful Incubi families that ever existed. So much for everyone thinking he was dead. He was very much *not* dead.

And she should know.

Rayna straightened and once more looked at him. His blue-green eyes regarded her with no emotion, as if he were distancing himself from her.

"Everything you've done makes sense now. Your family doesn't know you're coming, do they?"

"No." The word was as cold as his voice.

"They betrayed you."

He gave a single nod.

"I know about betrayal." She glanced at the city, wondering if she would ever be brave enough to face her family the way he was. "Where should I let you off?"

"There's a secret entrance only my brothers and I know about."

Rayna put the car in drive and pulled back onto the road that would take her into Manhattan. She was returning home only to help someone else get revenge. Too bad she couldn't do the same. But then again, her family was best forgotten lest she be pulled back into the web.

"What will you do when you leave?" Canaan asked when they were stopped at a traffic light, surrounded by skyscrapers, yellow taxis, and deafening noise.

"Return to Traders Hollow. It's my home now."

"Be careful, Rayna. I doubt your family allowed you to leave as easily as you think."

She frowned at his words. "Meaning what? That they'll try to bring me back home?"

"More likely that they're watching you and know everything you do."

"That does sound like my mother," she said through clenched teeth. "She did say she would never let me go."

Which meant, they knew she was in New York. She grew sick to her stomach at the thought.

Canaan's hand suddenly covered hers on the steering wheel. "I know. It means they saw me with you. More importantly, they know you're back in the city."

"I can't," she said while trying to keep her breathing under control. "I can't go back there. Now that she knows I'm connected to the Romerac family, she'll try her best to sink her claws in you."

Canaan's brow lifted. "She can try. I'd offer for you to come with me, but it's the last place you'd want to be, Rayna. It's a war you should stay far away from, especially since I don't know its consequences or just how far the reach is."

"I know." Still, she was disappointed. If there was one person who could keep her mother away it was Canaan. With him, Rayna felt safe, secure.

Canaan dropped his hand, but there was a smirk on his lips. "If I know my brother, Teman, he'll have lots of cars. And I know where he would keep them. You can leave your Camaro and take your pick of his. It'll throw your family off your scent so you can make your escape."

"For them to find me back at Traders Hollow?"

"For you to go anywhere you want."

She looked into his eyes before the car behind her honked. Rayna cleared her throat and drove through the intersection and the now-green light. Canaan had given her something to think about.

All these years she had thought she was free of her family. It had been a false sense of security. Canaan, however, was offering her the real thing.

There was no way she was going to pass it up, no matter how much she might like Traders Hollow. She could find a new home, a new job.

A new life.

She could leave everything of her old life behind. Well, everything but the memories of Canaan. Those she would hold onto forever.

"Take a left up here," he told her.

Rayna frowned, but did as he bade. "Are you sure? It's been several centuries since you were here last, and things have changed."

"Not as much as you might think. Take the third right. After that there will be an alley between buildings."

Rayna followed his directions until she saw the alley. "The car will never fit. Nothing can fit through that."

Canaan's response was a smile as he said, "Trust me."

Rayna shrugged and turned into the alley, expecting to hear the crunch of metal. In the next second, she found herself driving through a lighted tunnel.

Her quiet life had been turned upside down, but she couldn't wait to see what was around the corner next. Especially with Canaan by her side.

# CHAPTER SEVEN

Canaan should have been excited to be returning home. Instead, all he felt was a coldness that seeped into his very bones. He had been betrayed by the people who should have watched his back – his family.

"You don't have to do this. You can just go on and live your life as you want it."

Rayna's voice broke through his fog of growing rage, just as surely as her touch had calmed him during his fight with the other Incubi.

Had the Oubliette changed him so very much? Or was it Rayna who managed to reach him as no other had ever been able to?

He kept his gaze straight ahead as she drove slowly through the winding tunnel. "I do have to do this. It's my duty as the eldest to lead my family. More than that, retribution is mine."

Canaan knew how heartless his words were, but he didn't care. After all he had been through for five hundred years, including giving up his soul, exacting his revenge on his brothers was the only thing that was holding him together.

Rayna's soft gasp when the tunnel opened into a huge garage full of cars, SUVs, trucks, and motorcycles almost made him smile.

"Take your pick of whatever you want," Canaan told her when she parked her white Camaro next to a red Porsche. "The keys will be inside. No one will stop you."

He opened the door and stepped out of the car, his mind already fixed on a plan of attack.

"Good luck, Canaan Romerac."

He turned and looked at Rayna as she stood between the car and her open door, her dark brown hair falling about her shoulders and her walnut-colored eyes trained on him. Instantly, his body heated as desire burned through him.

For a heartbeat, he was tempted to forget his revenge and take her in his arms again. He knew they could never have a future together, because that wasn't what an Incubus did.

But he was thinking about it.

Hard.

Seven times. It would take just once more and he would be bound to her – and she to him. The idea was so appealing he was about to go to her, but he was able to pull himself back under control before he could make that mistake.

He began to count how many times he had taken her the previous night.

"If you ever need anything, let me know," Canaan said.

Her smile barely tilted her lips. "You're so sure of winning."

"I am. I have to. My only other choice is being returned to the Oubliette. I'd rather die."

"Your brothers just might give you that

option."

He shook his head. "They would've done it the first time had they been able."

"You make it sound as if you're invincible," she scoffed.

Canaan ran a hand down his face. "Not invincible, just smarter than my brothers. Take care of yourself," he said and turned away.

Each step away from her was like someone was squeezing his heart. Any moment it would shatter. He couldn't believe he was letting her go, not when every fiber of his being screamed for him to keep her by his side.

Canaan focused on the pain of his heart and let the rage begin. He would give no quarter, show no mercy to those who betrayed him.

~ ~ ~

Rayna watched Canaan walk up five steps and open a steel door where the sigil of House Romerac – a bull – was etched in the door. She couldn't believe he was really gone. It seemed as if he had been in her life forever, not just for a few days.

How could someone leave such a mark on her in so short a time? It didn't seem fair. Then again, that was her life. There was no way she would ever be able to be with a human again, not after a night in Canaan's arms. Nor would she turn to another Incubus.

"Great. The rest of my life celibate. Doesn't that sound fun?" she asked herself with a roll of her eyes.

Rayna closed the door to her Camaro and gave the hood a pat. "It's time we parted ways, Mabel. I've got to get me a new ride, but I think you'll find Canaan will take care of you."

She turned and surveyed the plethora of vehicles to choose from. Rayna walked up and down the long aisles. She bypassed the super cars and motorcycles until she came to a black Mercedes E350 coupe.

A look inside after opening the door showed the key fob sitting in the cup holder, just as Canaan had said. She might not have any clothes or money, but she had a vehicle her family wouldn't be able to track.

A noise startled Rayna so that she ducked next to the car. She peeked over the hood to see two women making their way to the door Canaan had gone through.

"Shit," Rayna murmured as she recognized them. They were distant cousins, trying to make themselves worthy of being chosen for the Harem.

And bringing home evidence of Rayna with a Romerac would be just the thing.

It would be so easy for her to walk away and let Canaan and the Romeracs deal with the fallout, but that just wasn't her way.

Rayna waited until both women had walked through the door before she kicked off her wedge boots and ran after them. Her heart was pounding when she gripped the door handle and slowly opened it. When nothing attacked her, she quickly slid inside and blinked at the darkness.

After the bright lights of the garage, she was

blinded. With nothing else to do, she remained against the wall and hoped her eyes adjusted rapidly.

It was the sound of footsteps quickly moving away from her that got her into action. There was no way her family was going to put her or Canaan in the middle of anything just so that her mother could further the family name.

Rayna ran silent as a ghost along the corridor toward the beam of a flashlight. When she reached her cousins, she kicked the first in the back of the knee, sending her crashing to the floor as the flashlight bounced on the ground and rolled away.

When the second turned around, Rayna punched her in the chest before kicking her in the face. The second fell while the first jumped to her feet.

With only the glow of the small flashlight, Rayna faced off against her opponent.

"I knew it," Sally gloated. "You always thought yourself above us. But not this time, Rayna."

She didn't bother to respond. Instead, Rayna ducked a swing at her jaw, only to miss the uppercut that nearly knocked her senseless when it landed on her chin.

Rayna stumbled backward into the wall that helped to hold her up. She blocked another punch and stepped aside when Sally tried to knee her in the stomach.

With a leg hooked around Sally's, Rayna pivoted until Sally was up against the wall. She was unable to avoid several punches to her abdomen by Sally. Rayna waited until Sally thought she had the advantage before she jerked her legs out from underneath her.

Rayna winced at the sound of Sally's head hitting the floor, but at least Sally didn't move again.

Pain exploded in her side as she was hit by Judith. Rayna tried to turn around, but Judith pushed her face first into the wall with her forearm at the base of Rayna's neck.

"It's time you came home, Rayna."

"Kiss my ass, Judith."

Her cousin chuckled and leaned close so she could whisper, "Always with the smartass."

Rayna slammed her elbow back into Judith. As soon as her cousin released her, Rayna swung around and punched her in the face once, twice. The third time knocked her out.

"Well, I didn't expect to see that."

Rayna yanked her gaze up to find Canaan standing not five feet from her. "What are you doing here?"

"I could ask the same of you," he said.

"Neither of you move," came a male voice from behind Canaan.

The corridor was suddenly ablaze with light. Rayna blinked as she looked at Canaan. His face was set in hard lines, as if he were preparing for war.

The sad part was, that's exactly what he was doing. It was also exactly what she had been doing a few minutes ago.

The big male behind Canaan moved to the side so he could see Rayna. He was in a black suit, but there was no tie against the crisp white shirt open at the neck. His dark blond hair was cut short but couldn't hold back the waves. It was his bright blue eyes that held the promise of pain. "How did the two of you get in here?"

"Because it was my idea to build the damn thing," Canaan retorted.

Rayna watched the Incubus's forehead crease in a frown. "That's not possible."

"It is, Asher."

"Canaan?"

Canaan shifted so that he faced Asher. "It's me."

"I'll be damned," Asher said, a smile upon his face. "Where have you been? Teman told us you died. Had I known you were still out there I'd have come looking for you."

Rayna's heart broke at the doubt she saw in Canaan's blue-green eyes. He didn't know who to trust, and she didn't blame him. Once part of your family betrayed you, it was easy to think others could as well.

When Canaan didn't respond, Asher glanced at her, his smile dying. "Canaan? What is it?"

"Tell him," Rayna urged Canaan. "I don't think he was part of it."

Canaan didn't so much as look at her. "You could be mistaken."

"Perhaps I am. If so, he already knows where you've been, so why not just say it?" she asked.

Asher's face fell into grim lines. "I'm the captain of the Watchman for House of Romerac. You disappeared on my watch, Canaan. Tell me what happened."

"Teman and Levi, along with the Sovereign, betrayed me. I've been in the Oubliette for five centuries."

The air charged with fury as the two men looked at each other. A muscle ticked in Canaan's jaw as Asher's blue eyes became as cold as ice.

"You think I was part of it," Asher said.

Canaan simply lifted a brow. "As you said, you're the Watchman for the House of Romerac. You and your men are the security – my security. How else would my brothers get to me?"

"Teman sent me out to get a bottle of that special wine you liked for when you returned home. He told me it was a gift for you, so I didn't hesitate. When I got back, the House was in an uproar because no one could find you." Asher fisted his hands at his sides. "I wanted to go looking for you, but Teman wouldn't allow it. He said he needed to be protected since he was acting Master of the House while you were missing."

Before Canaan could respond, Rayna stepped over her cousins. "We have bigger problems right now. My family followed me, Canaan. Those two are distant cousins, and they came to be witnesses to me being here."

"Thereby forcing us together," he said with a sneer. "I didn't think they would dare follow us in here."

Asher blew out a breath. "Many things have changed while you've been gone. Teman has let security become lax and no longer cares who comes and goes. With the Sovereign's time on the

Obsidian Throne coming to an end, this is when the House of Romerac should be the strongest, not the weakest."

"There's a reason my brothers aligned with the Sovereign," Canaan said as he held out his hand to Rayna.

She eagerly took it. "You're not sending me away?"

"You took down two of your family to protect yourself."

"To protect us both," she corrected.

He shrugged. "Either way, you'll be safer with me."

Asher punched a few numbers into his cell phone. "I'll get the Nephilim out of here and secure the area."

Rayna had gone only a few steps before she found herself against the wall and Canaan's hard body. She looked into his eyes, but before she could ask what he was thinking, he was kissing her.

She melted against him, her body coming alive as only he could command it. Her hands went to the edge of his shirt as she thought about ripping it off. A low moan rumbled through his chest when she touched the bare skin of his stomach.

Canaan ended the kiss and pressed his forehead against hers. No words were needed. Each knew what was coming, and both were prepared to face it.

After a moment, Canaan straightened but didn't release Rayna's hand. She couldn't contain her pleasure at that simple act.

"Asher," Canaan called as he ran a hand

through his black hair. "Get your men to do that. You'll need to come with us."

To battle, Rayna thought.

To right a terrible wrong.

# CHAPTER EIGHT

Canaan wanted to believe Asher hadn't been a part of the betrayal. If he wasn't, then he would keep Rayna safe and have his back.

If he was...then Canaan wanted all his enemies in one room.

He hid his surprise at the opulent building his family used for business. The shiny dark gray floors, the walls in a lighter shade of gray, and paintings and other works of art everywhere. It had always been his dream to have something tall and impressive with the family name attached. Yet, he hadn't gotten to build it. His brothers had.

At least the family hadn't been eradicated or run into the ground.

"This isn't seen by the public, is it?" Rayna asked as she followed Asher.

Asher glanced over his shoulder at them. "No. This is for the Romerac family and guests only."

Canaan stopped next to a wall where the doors slid open. Asher stepped inside and Rayna quickly followed, but he hesitated.

"It's an elevator," Rayna explained. "It'll take us to the upper floors. It's better than climbing stairs."

There was much Canaan still needed to learn

about this modern world. An elevator that raised them upward. What else would he find? He thought the best had been computers and the internet. How wrong he was.

He stepped into the elevator beside Rayna and watched as Asher punched a button with 55 on it. There was a small jolt, and then the elevator began to move.

"I don't think Levi was a part of your betrayal," Asher said into the silence.

"What makes you think that?"

"Teman. Over the last few centuries, he's pushed Levi out, more and more."

Canaan leaned a shoulder against the wall. "Possibly. Or it could be that Teman got a taste of being in charge and doesn't want to share now."

"Then," Asher continued as if Canaan hadn't spoken, "there's the fact that Levi tried to find you. He went out looking himself. Why would he do that if he was part of it?"

"A very good question," Rayna said and cut her eyes to him.

Canaan couldn't look at her. If he did, he was liable to take her right there in the elevator with Asher looking. It had been a mistake to kiss her, and an even bigger mistake to stop.

His hands itched to touch her, to feel her against him. To run along the silky smoothness of her bare skin. Especially since he had counted exactly how many times he made love to her the previous night. And it wasn't seven.

"Canaan," Asher called.

He blinked and focused on the slate tiles at his

feet. "You may have a point, Asher. I wouldn't have imagined either of my brothers betraying me."

"The Sovereign is part of it," Rayna said. "Too much has been happening lately with the Three unable to find new priestesses, and now the Sovereign."

Asher gave a nod of agreement. "Instead of preparing to step down, he's been putting off the Council getting together to figure out which family will take his place."

"And it won't be another Marakel. His line will die out with him. No matter what he's convinced Teman to do," Canaan added. Asher cleared his throat, bringing Canaan's gaze to him. "What is it?"

"Were you really in the Oubliette?"

"Yes."

To Canaan's surprise, Rayna's hand touched his arm. "You never said how you escaped."

"I gave my soul to the Warden so she would stop torturing me. A prisoner told me that the Sovereign put him there for helping hatch the plan to betray me. He told me how the Oubliette constantly moves, but every so often aligns with this world and the walls become thin. He was killed before he could escape with me."

"Your soul?" Rayna repeated. "You gave up your soul?"

"Instead of being tormented, I was the one tormenting. Try to spend five hundred years being tortured and tell me you wouldn't give up your soul."

A soft ding sounded just before the elevator doors opened. Asher stepped between them to hold them open. "I stopped us a few floors down. Teman rarely leaves his rooms anymore. He hired extra men to guard him."

"Extra?" Canaan repeated. "You mean he's not using your men? Men who have guarded our family for generations?"

Asher shrugged. "What was I supposed to do? Quit? He's Master of Romerac House. He gets to make the decisions."

"Not for much longer," Canaan whispered and walked off the elevator into a dimly lit room.

Rayna joined him as she looked around. "What is this place?"

"It's five floors below him. This was where the family would gather for meetings and special occasions, but Teman stopped doing that about a hundred years ago."

"There's a lot he hasn't been doing, apparently," Rayna said.

It was time Canaan faced his brothers. "Where are the stairs?"

The words had barely left his mouth when a door on the opposite side of the room opened and Levi appeared. Canaan was struck with how haggard his youngest brother looked.

His black hair was trimmed short, and it stuck out at odd angles everywhere, as if he had been running his fingers through it. Levi's red plaid shirt was buttoned, but only half tucked in, and his light denim had a large stain on his left leg.

Levi suddenly stopped and looked up as if just now realizing he wasn't alone. His gaze moved over each of them before jerking back to Canaan. "Is it really you? Have you finally come home, brother?"

Canaan didn't get a chance to respond as Levi started toward him, his pale eyes suddenly alight and a large smile on his face.

"You were always the adventurous one, but I did go looking for you. Several times. I kept it a secret from Teman, because he's happy being Master of House. But it's rightfully yours, Canaan." He paused when he reached Canaan, the smile melting away as a frown took over. "Why did you leave? It's not like you to toss aside your duties, and certainly not for so long."

Asher folded his arms over his chest and said, "I told you Levi wasn't part of it."

"Part of what?" Levi asked as he looked between both men.

Canaan didn't want to talk. He wanted to confront Teman and use his fists to convey all the agony and misery he had endured for five hundred years.

The fury must have shown in his gaze, because Levi took a step back. Suddenly, Rayna was beside him again, her hand on his arm. Just as before, the rage dissipated to a simmer, allowing him to think clearly again.

"He was in the Oubliette," Rayna explained. "He only recently escaped."

"And returned here to exact his revenge," Levi said. He met Canaan's gaze. "You may not believe it, but I had no part in your imprisonment. I'll do whatever you need to prove it."

As the youngest, Levi had been the free-spirited one of them, the one who always did his duty only to return to his pleasures. He was honest to a fault, and just as when they were children, Canaan could always tell when Levi was lying. The truth shone in his eyes now.

"You've already proven it," Canaan said and embraced his brother.

Levi slapped him on the back, his smile returning as they separated. "It's so good to have you back, Canaan."

"What's next?" Rayna asked. "Do we confront Teman?"

Canaan grabbed her by the arms and faced her. "You're not going to do anything but remain here, out of danger."

"There's something else you need to know," Levi said as Rayna's lips parted to speak.

Canaan was grateful he wouldn't have an argument with Rayna. "What is it?" he asked Levi.

"Teman is dropping the Romerac name."

Canaan let out a deep breath. "I know. I was informed of that in the Oubliette. I'm going to make sure Teman fails in that endeavor."

"Dear God," Rayna whispered as she covered her mouth with her hand.

Canaan heard Asher let loose a string of curses. Everything was beginning to make sense now. Teman betrayed him because the Sovereign had managed to talk him into believing Teman would be the next to sit on the Obsidian Throne.

"Part of the deal must have been that he change the family name," Levi said.

"So the Sovereign's wouldn't die out," Rayna finished.

Asher stripped off his suit jacket and rolled up the sleeves of his dress shirt to reveal intricate tattoos. "I'm not going to let this happen."

Canaan looked at the three people surrounding him. He had returned to the world thinking he could trust no one, and yet he had discovered three who stood beside him in the midst of a coming war.

"Oh, no you don't," Rayna said when she caught him looking at her. "You think you're going to leave me behind? Need I remind you that I can take care of myself?"

Canaan knew that all too well. "You still have a chance to live the life you've always wanted, away from your family. Take it, Rayna, and don't look back. For if you stay, I can't promise you'll remain unhurt."

"I'm not leaving," she said and rose up on her tiptoes to give him a quick, hard kiss. "I know how it feels to be betrayed. I want to help."

Asher grunted. "In a room full of Incubi? I don't think that's wise."

"I don't think that'll be a problem," Levi said.

Canaan narrowed his gaze on his youngest brother. "What do you mean?"

"She's been next to Asher and myself this entire time, and yet she can't stop looking at you. Tell me, just how many times have you two bedded each other?" Levi asked.

Asher began to laugh when neither Canaan nor Rayna would answer. It was Asher who said, "This could play into our hands. I think I have the perfect plan."

"It better not include putting Rayna in danger," Canaan stated.

Rayna rolled her eyes. "If it will put Canaan back in the seat of power, then I'll do whatever necessary."

"Don't be so quick to say that, Nephilim," Levi said cryptically.

Canaan squeezed his eyes shut. Rayna was supposed to be long gone from here and away from all danger. She was supposed to live out her life free of the duties her family forced on her, free from the life of a Nephilim who was bound to an Incubus.

"Wait," Rayna said. "Canaan has returned. Can't he just resume his seat of power? No one can deny that it's him."

Canaan opened his eyes and tucked a strand of her hair behind her ears, just now noticing that she was without shoes. "It could work, but who's to say Teman and the Sovereign wouldn't try again?"

"He's right," Levi said. "Canaan must take his seat by force."

Asher rubbed his hands together. "My men are loyal to the family, to you – as well as to me. None were too thrilled with Teman adding different security. They'll do as I ask."

Canaan took a deep breath. He was about to engage his brother in a battle that could possibly end with one of them dead. Their father would be appalled, but in the end it was about protecting the family.

Teman hadn't done that. He had sought his own agenda, his greed for power overruling the teachings of their father. Canaan really did have no other option. He would take Teman down, and then he would turn to the Sovereign.

It was time that bastard left the Obsidian Throne, once and for all.

# CHAPTER NINE

In all her imaginings, Rayna never thought she would be helping an Incubus or conspiring to take down the Sovereign. Yet here she was in only a dress shirt that left her feeling...bare.

She prayed their plan worked. It had to work.

It would work.

"You don't have to do this," Asher said as the elevator climbed to the sixtieth floor.

She looked at the handsome Watchman and smiled. "I do."

"You're putting yourself in the way of danger for an Incubus who you'll never see again."

Rayna swallowed past the lump in her throat. She didn't want to think about the future, especially when she knew it wouldn't include Canaan. "I've spent years running away from my family. Canaan has shown me that there is another option out there if I'm willing to reach for it."

"How many times have you two really slept together?"

His eyes were too shrewd, too clever for his own good. The doors dinged before slowly opening. "How did you know?"

"The way Canaan looks at you. The way you

look at him," he whispered as he took her arm and led her off the elevator. He nodded to Teman's two guards as they walked to the left. "I know you care for him or you wouldn't be here. Why not take him to your bed for as many times as needed for you to be immortal and the two of you to be bound to each other?"

Rayna tugged on the hem of Asher's dress shirt that barely reached her thighs, even as the two guards watched her with lust in their eyes. "I do care for Canaan. A lot. He's been betrayed enough already."

Asher remained silent as they walked down a long hallway lined with a thick Oriental runner that seemed to stretch for miles before them.

When they came to a set of tall wooden double doors he stopped and faced her. "If I found someone like you, I'd seriously reconsider the only once rule. You'd be good for Canaan."

It was the best compliment she had ever received. "Keep him safe during all of this, but especially afterward. He's going to have a difficult time trusting again."

"You have my word. Are you ready?"

No. She wanted to run the other way and never stop, but she had the chance to help right a wrong. Not to mention that if the Sovereign didn't give up his Throne to the next Incubus as he was supposed to, there was no telling how the ripples of the Sovereign's decisions would affect the Nephilim. She could help stop it all before it began.

Her throat tightened as anxiety coursed through her. She nodded, and was rewarded with a crooked smile from Asher that she was sure had most women throwing themselves at him.

"Remember to fawn over him," Asher said under his breath as he opened the doors.

Rayna's gaze was immediately drawn to the floor-to-ceiling windows that overlooked Manhattan, the lights from the other skyscrapers illuminating the night.

"I've found something for you, Teman," Asher said.

Rayna hastily looked around as she stumbled over her feet when Asher dragged her to the right. The room was sparsely furnished with modern furniture in white against the dark slate floors. It made the room seem cold and emotionless.

Asher's fingers tightened on her arm. Rayna pulled her gaze away from the room and found Teman at a sideboard where he was pouring himself a glass of wine.

Teman paid them no attention as he swirled the red liquid in his glass before bringing it to his nose so he could inhale deeply. Only then did he take a sip.

"What is a Nephilim doing at Romerac Consolidated?" he asked Asher.

"It appears one of my men thought she would be a nice gift for you."

"Me?" Teman said and faced them.

Rayna was taken aback at just how much he looked like Canaan. The same dark features, the same full lips, the same square jaw. But there were differences as well. Teman's hair might be the same color, but it was kept shorter.

His eyes might be the same blue-green, but they held no warmth, no...life.

No passion.

"She's never been with an Incubus," Asher explained.

Teman chuckled and walked over to them. His expensive dress shoes made no sound on the solid white rug he stood on. His attire was much like Asher's, except the suit was dove gray and his dress shirt was burgundy.

"A Nephilim who hasn't been with an Incubus," Teman said as he looked her up and down. "Why is that?"

Asher roughly dragged her closer to Teman. "She's from the Averell family."

Teman's eyes darkened with desire. "Is that so? Interesting. She could very well bring about my first son."

Rayna wanted to punch him. Instead, she softened her eyes and smiled. Then she ran her hands over her breasts, causing her shirt to rise up.

"You can leave, Asher," Teman said. "And be sure we're not disturbed."

There was the barest of pauses before Asher gave a nod and turned on his heel to walk away. Leaving Rayna alone with a man she was supposed to want.

"The Averells are particularly fertile," Teman said as he walked around her, letting his finger trail over her hips and her butt then to her other hip, until he stood in front of her again. "Between you and my visit to the Harem next week I could have two sons in a matter of months."

She placed her hands on his chest. "Yes. Anything. Just please take me. I had no idea being around you Incubi would cause such a...need...within me. Can you ease it?"

"I'm not a sex demon for nothing, sweetheart." He set aside his wine glass and pulled her against him. "I'll have you screaming in pleasure in no time."

~ ~ ~

"Easy," Levi said.

Canaan didn't like to see anyone with their hands on Rayna, but especially not Teman. "It was a bad idea."

"It's a good idea. Teman will never see you coming."

Canaan wanted to burst from his hiding spot behind a huge potted plant and tackle Teman when he began to unbutton Rayna's shirt.

"Asher is here as well, remember," Levi said. "Rayna will be fine."

She better be. Canaan would never forgive himself if something did happen to her. They were supposed to wait until Teman was completely occupied, but Canaan couldn't stand to watch him touch Rayna another minute.

Without a word to Levi, Canaan stood and walked around the plant. Rayna saw him first, her eyes opening and going straight to him. The small smile turning up the corners of her lips was all that kept him from ripping Teman off her.

"What's wrong with you?" Teman asked when

Rayna dropped her hands.

She disengaged herself and walked to stand beside Canaan. The gratification Canaan felt when Teman's eyes grew round as he spotted him was the first step in his revenge.

"Ca...Canaan," Teman stuttered. "Where have you been? We've looked everywhere for you."

Canaan glanced at Rayna. "Not everywhere. You didn't look in the one place you sent me – the Oubliette."

"I don't know what you're talking about," Teman hedged.

"I know about your deal with the Sovereign. I know how you plotted with him to betray me. I know that he plans to remain on the Obsidian Throne and name you heir as long as you give up the Romerac name."

Teman let his false façade drop as he took a deep breath and clapped. "Bravo. I never expected to see you again. Tell me, brother, how did you escape your prison?"

"With difficulty. It'll be much easier sending you there."

Teman laughed, the sound bouncing off the walls. "That'll never happen. I've got powerful friends who will ensure I'm never touched."

"If they're so powerful, why aren't they here now? Why aren't they saving you?" Canaan asked as he moved closer to his brother.

"I can save myself."

Canaan smiled when he saw the fury in Teman's eyes. Just as when they were kids, Teman could never control his rage. He launched himself at

Canaan with a low growl. Canaan wrapped his arms around him and grunted when Teman's shoulder slammed into him.

Teman got off two good shots to Canaan's kidneys before Canaan kneed him in the face. Teman staggered backwards and jerked off his suit jacket. Buttons went flying when he grabbed his dress shirt by the collar and ripped it off.

Canaan knew from childhood fights how easy it was to send Teman into a fit of anger so great that he lost all common sense, forgetting basic rules of combat.

It seemed nothing had changed. Canaan held out his arms, waiting for Teman to make a move. That simple action had Teman bellowing in fury as he rushed Canaan.

Canaan easily stepped aside from Teman's attack, but at the same time held out his foot so Teman tripped. He went sprawling across the floor. His growl was the only sound he made as he gained his feet and grabbed the chair nearest him and flung it at the windows.

Glass shattered as the chair went flying into the night. Wind howled, and noise from the city filled the space. Then Teman began to laugh.

"You'll never be the Master of House again!" Teman yelled over the racket.

Canaan didn't have a chance to answer as Teman attacked again. This time, he aimed a punch at Canaan's head, and when Canaan tried to duck it, he got elbowed in the jaw.

The assault didn't stop there. Teman landed punch after punch. Blood poured into Canaan's left eye and his lip was busted. He let Teman have his fun until he'd had enough. Canaan raised his arms to block the next assault.

"Enough!" Canaan glared at his younger brother and pushed him away. "You betrayed me, Father, and the family. I hereby banish you from our House. No longer can you use the name Romerac. Go find the Sovereign and take his name as you intended."

The doors burst open as Teman's private security entered. A heartbeat later they were surrounded by Asher and his men who had been waiting for just such an action.

Canaan never took his eyes off his brother. "What did I ever do to make you want to betray me?"

"You were born first. By two damn days," Teman said with a sneer. "This all should've been mine."

"But it isn't."

Teman threw back his head and laughed. "Ah, you'll soon understand that there are more things coming, brother."

Canaan had managed to contain his temper during the entire fight. It's what had always given him the upper hand in his battles with Teman, whether they were with fists or words.

"Take him to the Oubliette," Canaan said and started toward Rayna. He needed to hold her, to know that everything was going to be all right.

Levi was all smiles as he walked to Canaan. "I knew the plan would work."

Asher and one of his men each grasped

Teman's arms. Out of the corner of Canaan's eye he saw Teman twist away and turn as he raised his arm, a pistol in hand, aimed at Levi.

"No!" Canaan yelled at the same time Teman fired the gun.

Canaan watched, helpless, as the silver bullet slammed into Levi's chest. Levi glanced down before he looked back at Canaan, confusion on his face.

The rage Canaan had held at bay exploded. He pushed Rayna away from him and charged Teman. He collided with his brother, sending both of them crashing to the floor.

Canaan started landing punches immediately. It was one thing for Teman to betray him. But Levi was the best of them, the one who wanted to be happy and experience everything.

It didn't matter how much Teman tried to fight back. Canaan was past the point of any control. He wanted the pain to stop, needed the hole inside him to be filled with something good and decent instead of betrayal, greed, and dissent.

Dimly, he heard someone shouting his name, but he couldn't stop. He had to protect his family, had to protect Rayna. And that meant Teman had to be eliminated.

"Canaan."

He paused, his fist in mid-swing when he heard Rayna's voice. Then she touched him. He squeezed his eyes closed and fell to the side, his hand over his eyes.

To his surprise, Rayna wrapped her arms around him from behind and rested her head on his shoulder. "It's over now."

That's when Canaan realized the building was rocking. When his rage got the better of him, he never knew how it would affect the world around him. There were times he did cause earthquakes on purpose, but when he was too out of control to know what he was doing was when the worst could occur. Thankfully, Rayna had stopped him.

"Levi is being seen to. Asher thinks he'll make it," she said as she continued to run her hands over him.

Canaan couldn't look at Teman. He knew what his rage could bring. He didn't need to see it again. "I killed my brother."

"You had no choice," she whispered and placed a kiss on his neck. "Teman gave you no choice. You're once more Master of the House of Romerac, Canaan. Just where you were always supposed to be."

Was it? He wasn't so sure anymore. All he could think about was the dusty attic and a night of exquisite pleasure he feared he would never feel again.

# CHAPTER TEN

Canaan looked over the land that had been his family's to rule for thousands of years. The days of the Succubi were gone, though no one knew what caused all the female sex demons to die.

The Incubi hadn't died out, however. In stepped the Nephilim, which allowed the Incubi to continue to procreate. There had been so much upheaval when the last Succubus died, and it had taken hundreds of years for the Incubi to sort things out. Yet they had.

Now, another upheaval was around the corner. Canaan knew the Sovereign wouldn't stop now that Teman was dead. The Sovereign didn't want to give up his throne, and he would do whatever necessary to keep it.

The real battle had yet to begin. Canaan might have resumed control of his family, but it was a small battle in a coming war.

The silence was broken by the sound of Asher's approaching footsteps. Canaan turned from the wall of windows to the now empty room. All evidence of Teman had been erased, from the furniture to the blood.

"Rayna is getting ready to leave," Asher said.

Canaan drew in a deep breath. "I'm in over my head with her."

"You've had sex with her seven times. It was bound to happen."

"Nine."

Asher blinked, his body gone completely still. "Nine?"

"Nine," Canaan repeated. "I could've stopped at seven. I should've stopped at seven, but the need to claim her as mine was too strong."

"You did it without talking to her? And how the hell didn't she know?"

Canaan shrugged, unable to define his emotions during that long, ecstasy-filled night. "I have to convince her to stay."

"After you've told her repeatedly to leave? Being in the Oubliette must have made you lose your mind, as well as your soul."

His soul. He'd forgotten all about that. It was a small price to pay to return home and find someone like Rayna. "Where is Rayna now?"

"A floor below."

So many things were running through Canaan's mind about how he would tell Rayna that he needed her, that he...cared. He didn't want to think about just how deeply his feelings went, not now. Not when she could be walking out of his life forever.

Canaan knew that if he let her walk away, it would mean he would starve since they were now joined. Still, he wouldn't force her to stay.

Nor would he give up on her.

~ ~ ~

Rayna folded Asher's shirt and laid it on the table. She was back in her own clothes, but she no longer felt like herself. There was no reason to remain at Romerac Consolidated, no matter how much she wanted there to be.

Her mother would love the fact that Rayna had spent so many years running away from the connection to the Incubi, only to fall – hard – for one.

She turned around and came face to face with Canaan. How did a man grow more good-looking each time she saw him? It was the case with Canaan. She couldn't get enough of him

Her lips tingled just thinking about his kisses.

Her body heated just imagining his hands running over her.

Her soul stirred just dreaming about a future together.

Rayna swallowed and tried to look away from his blue-green eyes, but she couldn't. She was trapped, ensnared. "Say something," she begged.

"Don't go."

She couldn't be more surprised if he said he wanted to return to the Oubliette. "W...what?"

He took a step toward her then halted. "Look, I know you want away from your family. I can offer you protection here."

"Protection?" Wow. Was she ever disappointed. For a moment she had thought he was asking her to stay because he wanted her.

Rayna ground her teeth together as her heart

began to break. She should've known better than to fall for an Incubus. They didn't stay around longer than one night. And they rarely tied themselves to one woman.

How silly she was for even thinking that she meant anything to him.

"Yes, protection," Canaan said. "Your family won't be able to touch you here. You'll be able to do what you want."

While seeing him every day? Unable to touch him, all the while remembering the beautiful night they had. It would be a special kind of torture she inflicted on herself. No, thank you. The memories would be enough.

"Thanks for the offer," she said and swallowed around her breaking heart. "But I think it's time I leave."

She started to walk off when he stepped in front of her. Rayna squeezed her eyes closed for a second before she lifted her gaze to him. A frown marred his forehead while his gaze seemed to search hers for something.

"I didn't think I'd ever be able to trust anyone again." Canaan ran a hand through his hair. "You showed me that I could."

If only she had touched him more deeply. She didn't regret her time with Canaan. She just wished that she had shielded her heart better. It wouldn't have been easy against someone like him, but she still should have tried.

She forced a smile she didn't feel. "I'm glad. Good luck with everything."

Rayna once more started around him, and this

time he didn't stop her. Tears gathered in her eyes, tears she hated and refused to shed until she was miles away from Canaan. She didn't want him to know just how deeply she felt for him.

"I lied to you," he said as she reached for the door handle.

The admission stopped her cold. She dropped her hand and turned to him. "Lied to me about what?"

"We didn't have sex seven times."

Rayna's heart began to pound – with excitement and nervousness. "How many times, then? I thought I counted all of them."

"It was a long, passion-filled night."

"It was." It was also the best night of her life. She couldn't believe she was silently hoping it was eight. It would mean they were irrevocably tied together for eternity. She barely knew him, but her body and her heart did. "How many, Canaan?"

"What if I told you that it would take only once more for us to be bound?"

Was that hope she saw flash in his eyes? "Are you telling me you...want to be bound to me? It would mean you could only have sex with me. It would mean that I would be the only one who could keep you alive."

"You aren't telling me anything I don't already know," he said softly. "I'm asking if you would agree to sleep with me again. It would mean you could be immortal."

"I don't care about immortality," she said with a shake of her head. "The consequences are far-reaching. You can't possibly mean you want to be bound to me. You're an Incubus."

"I know precisely what I am."

Rayna rubbed her hand on her forehead as confusion muddled her brain. "You have sex with different women almost every night just to stay alive. Why would you give that up to be bound to one woman?"

"Because I care for you."

It took her a moment to realize that he actually spoke the words and they weren't just a silent wish from her. "Stop," she said and backed away. "It's just cruel to say something like that and not mean it."

"How do you know I don't mean it?" Canaan asked as he tracked her. Gone was the ambivalence he'd displayed before. There was a touch of anger in his face now. "Why do you think I lie? Because I'm an Incubus, and we can't possibly tell the truth?"

"No, of course not." She had hurt him. It hadn't been her intention, but she had to protect herself.

"Am I so bad? Is it because of what you've seen me do this night?"

"No. No," she said louder to emphasize how wrong he was. "You tried to let your brother live. Teman made his own choices. You were acting in defense of your family."

Rayna leaned against the door and sighed as they stared at each other. She couldn't imagine returning home after being tortured for five centuries. Canaan was a natural-born leader, a man who would continuously put others before himself.

DONNA GRANT

She had always shied away from Incubi, but not because she didn't like sex. She was beginning to think it was because she had been waiting for Canaan to find her.

For too many years she had run away from her family, herself, and her true feelings. It was time to stop running and face everything head on, regardless of the outcome.

It was time to put everything on the table.

"Yes," she said into the silence.

His brow furrowed deeply. "Yes, what?"

"Yes, I would be with you again. Whether it was the eighth or the eight hundredth. I would always walk into your arms. I did that first night because of the way you made me feel. I continued to turn to you that night because I couldn't deny you. I don't care about immortality. All I care about..." She paused to lick her lips and gather her courage. "Is you. I know it's foolish to fall in love with an Incubus, but you can't stop the heart."

In the next second, Canaan stood before her, his body pressing hers against the door. "Did you just say you loved me?"

"Yes," she admitted, amazed at how free she felt after telling him. No matter what happened next, she had spoken true.

"Say it again."

Rayna smiled and reached up to cup his cheek. "I love you, Canaan Romerac."

The smile on his face was beautiful to behold. "And I love you, Rayna Averell. I don't care that I'm an Incubus and you're a Nephilim. All that matters is our love. Stay. For me. For us."

"Gladly," she said and threw her arms around him.

Every window on the floor shattered, followed immediately by the light bulbs. A strange glow suddenly filled the room. Rayna could only watch as it drew closer and closer to them.

Canaan shoved her behind him and faced it. The glow zoomed directly at Canaan before it went through him. Rayna screamed as Canaan jerked, his arms spread wide as the glow consumed him.

As quickly as it came, it vanished. Canaan fell to his hands and knees with his head bent. Rayna knelt beside him and ran her hands over him, feeling for injuries.

"Canaan? Canaan, are you all right?" she asked worriedly.

He lifted his head up at her and smiled. "It appears my soul has returned."

"What?" Would the strangeness of this day never end? "I don't understand."

"Me either, but I'm not questioning it." He gathered her against him and held her tight.

Rayna returned his embrace. Who knew how a drop-dead gorgeous Incubus would change her life? "You're going to have to replace more windows."

"I'll replace every damn one of them if it means I get you," he said as he pulled back to look at her.

"You have me for as long as you want me."

"Then that's for eternity."

"Not until you make love to me one more time." Canaan looked away, causing Rayna to scowl. "What are you keeping from me?"

He smoothed her hair away from her face.

"Sweet Rayna, we've been bound since our first night together."

She started laughing, because she wasn't surprised. No wonder she had fallen for him so quickly. It was also why she kept finding reasons to stay.

She was still laughing when Asher came running into the room. He slid to a stop when he saw them.

"Do I even want to know what happened?" he asked them.

Canaan got to his feet and held out his hand for her. "Rayna is staying. She loves me," he said with a wide grin.

"And Canaan got his soul back," Rayna said as Canaan pulled her up. "That's what blew out the windows."

Asher chuckled and kicked at the broken glass that littered the floor. "I'm happy for you both."

"I want to celebrate my return and Rayna."

Rayna entwined her fingers with Canaan's. "Before or after you confront the Sovereign?"

"Before," Canaan said.

Asher held the door open for them both. "I'll get the festivities started. How does tomorrow night sound?"

"Wonderful," Rayna and Canaan said in unison.

Asher closed the door behind them and followed as he said, "There's someone I think you should consider joining forces with, Canaan. The two of you could make quite the showdown against the Sovereign."

"Who?" Canaan asked.

"Devil Gravori. He's still the Master of House

Gravori, and could be a good ally."

Rayna watched as Canaan nodded. There was much planning that would need to come, and she would be a part of it. There was no way she would lose Canaan after just finding him. Even if she had to kill the Sovereign herself.

Asher, the upcoming war, and the world were forgotten as Canaan pulled her into a room and shut the door as he began kissing her.

~ * ~

# ABOUT THE AUTHOR

*New York Times* and USA Today bestselling author **DONNA GRANT** has been praised for her "totally addictive" and "unique and sensual" stories. She's the author of more than twenty novels spanning multiple genres of romance.

Her latest acclaimed series, Dark Warriors, features a thrilling combination of Druids, primeval gods, and immortal Highlanders who are dark, dangerous, and irresistible.

She lives with her husband, two children, a dog, and three cats in Texas. Visit Donna at **www.DonnaGrant.com**.

# SHAMELESS
## House of Vipera

# Laura Wright

# CHAPTER ONE

Fire licked at Rosamund's ankles. Wet, rough, fire that moved tantalizingly up her calves to her knees, then slowed as it settled between her thighs. A groan of desire escaped her throat. But she did nothing to try and quell it.

She needed this.

Him.

Like one needed air and water.

"Rosamund, wake up…"

The words were a distant whisper. Unwelcome. Irritating. She pushed them away and focused on the man before her. He was poised over her sex now, spreading her thighs wide with his long, thick fingers, his insistent palms. Though her eyes were closed, she could see him. Fierce, hungry, his smile invitingly wicked.

"Is she ill?" It was another voice now, once again female and worried.

"No, no," came the first voice, her tone threaded with false concern. "She is still sleeping. Poor, sweet Rosamund. Perhaps she is dreaming of what she can never have."

The man's smile morphed into something sexually sinister, and Rosamund's insides went instantly liquid.

"Don't be cruel, Eva," said the second female.

"It is not cruel to speak the truth," the first female returned, her voice slightly muffled.

"If she would just allow us to see to her. Bathe her. Rub her skin with salts and oils. Do her hair. Dress her. Perhaps one of the males would notice her."

Rosamund's heart beat furiously against her ribs. Gone was the male's gaze. *Oh yes!* His head was between her trembling thighs now. She lifted her hips in anticipation.

"You say this as though it would be the easiest task in the world," answered Eva. "One cannot turn a tuft of esparto grass into a rock rose no matter the efforts."

"She is tall and slender, and has beautiful eyes."

"Indeed," Eva conceded. "Like the golden desert sands. But her face and teeth, hair and posture…"

Rosamund gasped as the man ran his nose along the seam of her sex. Why couldn't they go away? These stupid, silly Nephilim? Their opinions meant nothing to her. All she wanted was this male. His mouth on her. His tongue inside her.

"Rosamund, you must wake!" called the second female, more urgently this time. "Constance is on her way. There is to be an announcement."

Rosamund drove her fingers into thick, soft hair in response. *Yes! Yes! Right there, male,* she urged, squeezing his scalp. He groaned, the sound vibrating against her heat as he nuzzled his way to her swelling clitoris.

The sound of a doorknob rattling entered her consciousness, but she pushed it away. It was the click of a lock being breached that truly yanked her from the rising pleasure, cutting into her dream like a guillotine to the neck. She came awake with a start, eyes flying open, body jackknifing upward into a sitting position. Breathing heavy, she glanced around, blinked. It was pitch black in her little anteroom—the space she'd claimed when she arrived in the Harem nearly one year ago. The space that was all hers. Every other Nephilim in residence lived in shared accommodations—very gratefully and happily. But Rosamund had wanted to be alone.

No. She'd needed to be alone.

"Rosamund, Constance will give you a week in the kitchens if you're not in attendance," Eva persisted, inching the door open.

Panic seized Rosamund. She couldn't have them see her. Not like this. "I'm up," she called, scrambling off her pallet and rushing to the door. She pressed herself against it, blocking their entrance. "I'm up. I'll be out in a few minutes."

There was a momentary pause, then a sigh. "All right," Eva said. "We will see you in the courtyard. And Rosamund?"

"Yes?" she said with a touch of irritation she wasn't quite awake enough to hide. Sleep still clung to her mind. Wet heat still claimed everything south of her navel.

"Good morning to you," the female called.

*Oh great Goddess, it had been*, Rosamund thought with a groan as she listened to the females' retreating footsteps. *Or could have been.* She heaved a sigh and let her head fall back against the wood. She was truly dying to know how her dream ended. She'd been having it nearly every night of her three hundred and sixty one nights in the Harem. And each time, the intensity grew, the need intensified. Granted, she could never see the male's face clearly, but she knew it was Roger. The human man she'd met and fallen for three months before she'd been called to the Harem. The human man who believed she was away on a yearlong animal research trip in the Australian bush.

The human man who had held her in his arms the night before she left and sworn that he would wait for her forever. But Rosamund knew forever was a relative term—and that waiting wasn't easy for anyone. Normally a letter from him came once a week, forwarded from a post office box in Sydney. But in the past couple of months she'd received nothing at all.

Her heart squeezed as she pushed away from the door. Just four more days, she reminded herself, setting about lighting the three lamps that lined her tiny bookcase and clothing rack. Four more days until she was back in San Francisco, back to Roger—back to creating the life, the home, the family, she'd always dreamt of having.

With quick, seasoned hands, she performed her daily routine. Tying down her breasts and padding her middle. Applying powders to her face to make her appear sallow and tired, and oils to her long, pale blond hair to make it appear unwashed. And the one last accompaniment that was a guarantee to her continued success—the one she'd had made before leaving San Francisco nearly a year ago—a dental prosthetic that made her teeth look almost rotten.

After slipping on the large pumpkin-colored day robe, she made a quick inventory of her appearance in the cracked half mirror. She looked as she did every day. A younger version of the witch who'd sold Snow White her poisoned apple. She heaved a great sigh of relief. Perfect. No male on Earth would choose her over the stunning Nephilim females of the Harem.

After turning off the lights, Rosamund exited her converted closet and headed down the flagstone hallway toward the courtyard. A cool, salty breeze from the sea nearly five miles south lapped over her heated skin. She groaned at the sensation. Would Roger come to her again tonight? Would he finally take her to completion? Or was he to ever torment her until she returned to him?

Sand surrounded the sumptuous Moroccan palace that had been the Harem of the Nephilim, and neutral ground to both Nephilim and Incubi, for centuries. But inside its sandstone walls, lush, fragrant gardens and pools carved out of rock reined. As Rosamund came into the courtyard, brilliant sunlight assaulting her vision, she saw that one of those pools was occupied. Ten or so Nephilim were swimming and splashing about, naked and bronzed and laughing gaily. Rosamund felt a pang of envy, of loneliness, in her heart. It was the same every day. Relaxing in the sun or the pools, dining on all sorts of lovely concoctions as the eunuchs fanned their heated skin. Friendships were being created out of leisure and decadence, and a shared understanding that being called up to the Harem by the Three was a great honor. One almost every female hoped would end in a full womb and a healthy baby.

Rosamund heard her name being called and turned to see Eva waving at her. The young and very beautiful redhead was standing with a group of three Nephilim who were gazing up at a marble statue of Demeter, the goddess of fertility. The statue was positioned on a small raised dais to the right of the rock pool. Rosamund hunched her shoulders and started forward in a slow, awkward manner befitting someone with an ever-present backache. As usual, a few females glanced her way and offered her a tight smile. Though they would never admit to it, they didn't like having her around. Not just because she didn't fit in with them socially, but because everything in the Harem was beautiful and seductive and immortal. And she reminded them that outside these walls ugliness and pain and mortality existed.

"I like that color on you, Rosamund," Eva said, unconsciously running her hand over the silk skirt of her lovely, formfitting blue takchita.

Rosamund smiled. "Thank you."

Facing the rotten teeth up close, the beautiful Nephilim blanched and turned away—just in time to see an attractive older female with thick dark hair knotted at the top of her head walk into the courtyard and over to the dais. She was flanked by two eunuchs, who wore serious expressions and little else. She climbed the four steps, stood in the center of the dais and called to the group of thirty, "Good morning, Nephilim."

Laughter died down and chatter ceased as every female turned to give the woman her attention.

"For the next two nights, we welcome a most honored guest." Her black eyes glittered with excitement and a broad smile curved her full lips. "The Incubus I speak of has not been to our Harem in nearly five years."

A few startled gasps rent the desert air. It was unheard of for an Incubus to go longer than a few months without visiting the Harem. Unless they were bonded to a female, of course. Though they could engage in sex elsewhere, pull their power elsewhere, the Harem was purported to give an Incubus the ultimate power surge.

"He is of most ancient blood," Constance continued. "And a strong, decided personality." Her black eyes moved over the crowd. "I have been told that unlike most of his Incubi brethren, there will be little preamble. No introductions. No voicing your interest. He will simply look on each of you and make his decision."

How strange, Rosamund mused. Not that there was a great deal of chit chat between an Incubus and the Nephilim he wished to bed. But a touch of hands, a few words spoken, eye contact—these were always utilized. Except when it came to her, of course. Incubi didn't even notice her, much less try and touch her.

"Who is it, Constance?" a Nephilim named Anya called out from the edge of the rock pool.

"Do not keep us in suspense."

The woman's chin lifted a fraction, and Rosamund noticed that her hands trembled slightly at her sides. "Scarus Vipera."

A wave of excited whispers moved on the air, through the crowd. Rosamund glanced from female to female. They were smiling, eyes wide and eager.

"The Master of the House of Vipera himself," Constance went on, her voice taking on a husky quality. "It would be a great honor to carry his seed." Her eyes once again moved over the crowd. "I suggest you prepare yourselves. He will be here at sundown."

Rosamund watched as the woman and the two eunuchs moved down the dais steps and left the same way they'd come. Oh yes. She would prepare herself. Most carefully.

"I wonder who he will choose for his first night," called a petite, pale-eyed Nephilim who was climbing out of the pool.

"I hope it's me," replied her friend, who was still in the water, her large breasts bouncing on the surface.

The petite woman toweled off her wet, naked skin. "I hear tell he is the most handsome of all the Incubi."

"I hear he is the most dangerous," called Eva, who was still standing beside Rosamund.

"Barbaric is what I was told," replied the woman in the pool. "And stoic."

A tall, stunning Nephilim reclining on one of the outdoor chaises laughed. "And I hear he is the most shameless."

"Whatever do you mean by that, Cleo?" the petite woman asked, wrapping the towel around herself.

The woman's light blue eyes, expertly lined in kohl, flashed with heat. "Just that he cares little for modesty in his bed."

Feminine giggles and trills of anticipation erupted from the women. They could hardly wait to meet this male, lie beneath him. Rosamund didn't blame them. Once upon a time, she too had been excited to come to the Harem and be taken by one of the handsome and virile Incubi of the nine Houses. But that was before she'd met Roger. Before she'd realized that she wanted to give herself and her womb—and her heart—to one male.

Leaving the gaiety and plans for dress and hair and scent behind, Rosamund headed out of the courtyard and back to her room. She didn't know Master Scarus Vipera, had never seen him, and didn't expect even a glance her way when he walked the line of exquisitely painted and perfumed Nephilim this eve. But she would take no chances. She would prepare herself, as Constance had suggested. Make herself even more hideous than usual.

Four days.

That was all she had left until she was back in Roger's capable and comforting arms.

It was the ancient clause—the one she had found after getting her call from the Three, the one no Nephilim had ever spoken of. Yes, a Nephilim remained at the Harem until she bore one child. In exchange, she was granted immortality for that time. But if she was not chosen by an Incubus in one year's time, she must leave. Rosamund wondered if the Three believed that an Incubus could tell that a female wasn't good stock, couldn't produce a healthy babe.

Whatever the reason for the clause, she was grateful.

In just four days, she would be on her way home. To America. To her tiny apartment over the veterinary clinic. To Roger. To a chance for a real life, a future, and the family she had always wanted.

# CHAPTER TWO

Scarus Vipera, Master of the House of Vipera, was growing weaker by the day.

He needed sex.

Power-rich sex.

But not just any female would do. If he was to gain back his strength, he needed one of the Immortal Nephilim of the Harem.

He exited his private plane and moved down the steps toward the waiting limousine. The heat of the desert clime invaded his custom gray suit and attacked the skin, muscles and bones beneath. He despised the weakness spreading unchecked inside of him. Despised that it forced him to revisit the place that had, only five years ago, caused him both stunning pleasure and the deepest pain.

Walking out those ancient doors framed in the finest gold, he'd sworn never to return. He would find his pleasure, his power, his repast, elsewhere. He would forget. About the Nephilim who'd birthed his son—his only child—then run away. He'd forget how he'd bonded with the boy. Watched as his mother nursed him. Oh, he'd been a strong little male. Scarus should've seen how the Nephilim was doting on him, how she'd held him all through the night as though she hated to be parted from him. It wasn't something he'd ever seen before. Normally, if the child was male the Nephilim would be only too happy to be rid of it. But not Daya. She'd taken the boy and run, both of them meeting with an accident just two days later.

The pain that had swarmed Scarus like a thousand angry wasps was both surprising and debilitating. He hadn't been able to forget, and had lost any good nature that he'd been blessed with. Barking orders at his servants, not attending any celebrations or holidays with his family, refusing to meet with the Masters of the other Houses. He could not care for what was happening outside his palazzo in Ravello. Whether it was how the Sovereign was closing in on the end of his reign and had not been seen in far too long. Or how Devil Gravori believed that the Three were destroying all human/Incubus pregnancies to ensure that the Succubi remained extinct. He only cared about staying alive and strong for his House, and for all of those within it who relied on him.

As he approached the sleek black car, whose doors carried the Vipera House sigil of a coiled serpent, the desert wind whipped around him. To regain his strength he needed the power of the Harem.

With a clipped nod to the chauffeur who held the door ajar, Scarus slipped inside the limousine. Already seated and tending bar was his Watchman, Fausto. The male was a distant cousin, which was evident in his dark features. Most of the Vipera line was blond, light-eyed and built like a Viking, all thanks to those Norman knights who came to Italy and settled in as mercenaries.

"A drink, Master Vipera?" he asked, his black eyes glittering with humor.

Scarus settled into the backseat and took out his Blackberry. "No. *Grazie.*"

"They have a very good Brunello."

"Enjoy it." He frowned as he read a text from his art advisor. They'd lost the van Dongen. He returned the text with a five million dollar bump. He wasn't losing the Rockwell, too. He enjoyed how those humorous depictions of everyday American life mocked him from the walls of his home.

"I think you should have a drink, sir."

Scarus glanced up from his phone and uttered through gritted teeth, "*C'e un problema,* Fausto?"

The man took a healthy swallow as they raced toward the coming sunset. "No problem. I just know this will not be easy for you."

The splinter that had resided in Scarus's heart for the past five years twisted. "You know nothing."

"*Bene, bene.*" The male shrugged. "But I could carry the burden for you. At least for one of the nights."

"How generous," Scarus replied dryly. "But weren't you at the Harem only a few weeks ago?"

"*Sì,*" Fausto said with a wicked grin and an incline of the head. "But I would happily fall on my sword for you, sir."

A twitch of amusement curved Scarus's lips. "I appreciate the sacrifice, Fausto. But I must feed.

You and your overworked sword will stay in town."

The male laughed. "*Molto buono*, Master Vipera. You know I am at your service."

The buzz of his Blackberry shifted Scarus's gaze. A slow, satisfied grin moved over his features as he read. The Rockwell was his.

"We have arrived, Scarus," Fausto announced as the car whisked past the open gates and down a stone drive. "Do you wish me to take in your things?"

"No. The eunuchs will see to it."

The sun was a giant ball of orange fire in the sky as Scarus unfolded from the back of the gleaming car. Once again, heat surged into him. But it wasn't from the desert winds or the anticipation of settling himself between a pair of willing and wet thighs. It was the kind that spoke of torture and grief and soul-deep pain. His head lifted and he eased the sunglasses from his eyes. Acres of the most stunning Arabic architecture in the world stared back at him, beckoning. *Come in. You know you wish to take what we so willingly give. But beware, we also take.*

Scarus turned and motioned to the driver, who was opening the trunk for one of the Harem eunuchs. "When you're done here, drive my servant back into town. I will call when I need you again."

The man nodded. "Yes, sir."

The tie at Scarus's neck pressed hard against his Adam's apple, but he ignored it. Just as he ignored the weakness spreading like wildfire through his blood. He moved up the steps just as the doors opened and a woman with dark hair and a nervous smile emerged. She was dressed in a dark purple takchita, the typical dress of the Harem. The modest of the Harem, that is. As some Nephilim chose to be bare at all times.

"*Benvenuto*, Master Vipera," she said, using his native language. "My name is Constance. What a pleasure to have you here."

"Where is Anacia?" he inquired.

"Anacia left the Harem three years ago. I am Head Female now."

He gave the woman a nod. He didn't require further information about the female who had been here when Daya birthed their child. In fact, he wanted no personal connection whatsoever. Nothing that endeavored to tempt his heart from the cage it resided in.

"Please follow me," she said graciously. "I trust your trip was a pleasant one."

"It was acceptable." As he walked into the compound beside her, he asked, "Am I the only guest?"

"Of course. As requested, Master."

As always, the Harem was startlingly beautiful with its zelij-covered walls, colorful tiles, fountains, lush gardens, and polished cedar ceilings. Every carved wooden doorway one walked through brought on another visual treasure, and the air…it was heavily scented with spices and warmed sand and oiled skin.

Scarus felt the muscle between his legs pulse with desire and hunger. He needed to feed. And he knew that once he was within a few feet of the Nephilim he would no longer be thinking clearly.

No longer be hyperaware of his vow to not create another life.

His House, all the Vipera line, had the gift of knowing when a female, Nephilim or human, was fertile, and he would use that gift tonight as he choose his first meal.

The Head Female, Constance, led him into a room he'd never seen before. Though dotted with dozens of tropical plants it was very formal, with ancient furnishings, floor to ceiling windows, a walk-in fireplace and intricate carvings on the walls.

"We have thirty unclaimed Nephilim," she announced. "All are excited to meet you, Master Vipera."

Scarus knew there were more Nephilim in residence at the Harem. The twelve-acre property boasted over one hundred rooms and ten suites. As was custom, Nephilim stayed, as Daya had, for the duration of their pregnancy and afterward.

Granted, a Nephilim was only required by law to produce one child, but some chose to remain. To have more young and to remain immortal.

Scarus's chest tightened, but he cursed it away. He was not here to think on the past. He was here to feed and to grow in strength once again.

"Where are they?" he said, his tone cool and fierce. "These thirty Nephilim? I do not appreciate being kept waiting."

The woman blanched, pressed her lips together.

"Perhaps they weren't informed of my arrival?" he continued, knowing he was acting the brute, the barbarian.

The Incubus.

And yet he stared imperiously at her.

"I… Of course…" she stumbled.

The doors to their right opened abruptly, and two eunuchs entered.

An audible sigh of relief escaped the woman before Scarus and she turned. She exclaimed weakly, "You see." She gestured to the wave of females coming into the room. "They come, Master Vipera."

# CHAPTER THREE

Late. Late. Late.

*Stupid female.*

Forgetting about her usual, hunched over gait, Rosamund ran though the Harem. Constance would have her working not in the kitchens as was the usual punishment, but in the baths. Washing toilets as well as the hair and skin of the Nephilim.

Back in her anteroom, she'd meant to close her eyes for only a moment, but had used up a good three hours. She'd had very little time to make sure her appearance was grossly on point. And to make matters worse, her dream male—Roger, of course—hadn't even shown up.

Spotting the two eunuchs standing sentry outside the Garden Room, Rosamund slowed and hunched. Four days left. She wasn't blowing it with something as foolish as a change in posture.

Eyes down, she entered and hastily made her way to the line. Two Nephilim she didn't know very well made room for her with an irritated sigh. *Not to worry, females. I will only serve to make you look better to Master Vipera.*

As nervous, excited energy pinged off the walls, Rosamund wondered who the shameless Incubus

Master would choose for his first night in the Harem. Her money was on Beatrice or Cleo. They were definitely the most beautiful, and though they had been chosen before had yet to produce a child.

Hair falling in her face in a greasy mass, she ventured a glance upward. It was a mistake. All she saw before the earthquake hit her was thick blond hair, massive shoulders encased in a perfectly tailored gray suit and thick-fingered hands flexing out from a fist.

Wave upon wave of the most intense shocks of desire she'd ever experienced slammed into her. She felt like she was drowning. It was glorious. Her hips started to swing and she moaned. Gods, she wanted to take off her clothes, wanted hands on her body, in her body—and she didn't care whose hands they were.

Her eyes lifted again, and this time connected with gold orbs so fierce, so sexually powerful, she felt a rush of moisture leave her sex and trickle enticingly down her leg.

*Me. You want me.*

His nostrils flared and he breathed in. Sweat broke out on Rosamund's forehead and neck and the backs of her knees, and she realized she was panting. In her peripheral vision she saw that the females on either side of her had dropped to their knees. They were rubbing their breasts and moaning. One was trying to take off her dress.

*Will that be me soon?* Rosamund's mind queried softly, weakly. *Standing before the gold-eyed Incubus naked and glistening with sweat and arousal?*

The question did something to her. Slapped her

face and pulled her just a few inches out of the sexual earthquake that was continuously erupting inside of her. *Naked. No. No. I...can't be naked.* Those gold eyes narrowed. *No, Incubus. I belong to...whom? Whom is it I belong to?*

Someone was speaking. To her?

"Rosamund!"

It was one of the Nephilim. No...no...it was Constance.

Rosamund didn't take her eyes off the Incubus. She had to fight back. It wasn't uncommon for these males to turn on their power, their thrall, during selection. But not like this. Never like this.

*Fucking barbarian.*

His expression changed in that moment to one of cruel determination, and Rosamund realized through her sexual haze that she'd said the words out loud.

And suddenly she was a nerve, a violin string. And this Master was playing her body like it belonged to him—like he knew it intimately. Like he'd watched her every day and every night. How she moved, how she breathed, how she touched herself.

A gasp escaped her throat. Goddess, what was happening to her? It was too much... It was too delicious...

It was the dream.

She cried out as her body flooded with wet heat and gave in to the climax it so desperately craved.

And then it was over.

Sucked from her marrow.

Though she still breathed deep and rapid, and

though her heart beat like a hummingbird's wings, and though her underwear was soaking wet, the intensity—the command—was gone.

She glanced around. The Incubus wasn't there anymore, but twenty-nine pairs of eyes were glued to her person. And each was filled with a different emotion:  shock, irritation, jealousy, interest and rage.

She turned to Constance. "What happened?" she panted.

The woman looked perplexed. "He has chosen you."

"What?" She didn't understand. Couldn't have. Clearly, her brain was still in a fog.

"He has chosen you, Rosamund," she repeated. "I find it impossible to believe as well."

Rosamund turned to the Nephilim, her eyes running down the line of sweating, pissed off females. Maybe she was looking to them for clarity. Or maybe to start laughing at what Constance had said. But all she received was a curt nod from a narrow-eyed Cleo.

"No." Her head whipped back to the woman, and she managed another, "No…" on a panicked gasp.

But Constance was looking elsewhere, her arm outstretched. She was calling to the eunuchs at the door. "He waits for her in the Desert Suite."

Fear and anger coursed through Rosamund as she felt fingers enclose her upper arms. She stared at Constance. Waiting. For something. Anything.

This couldn't be real. She was four days from freedom…

But the woman only uttered a stern, "Take her to him," before the eunuchs yanked her back and led her from the room.

# CHAPTER FOUR

He could have fucked her right there. In front of the others. It mattered not. It was a feeding he craved, and she had great power.

But the Nephilim of the Harem had *rules*.

As the night wind off the desert blew cool and dry through the thin, white curtains near his massive chair, Scarus surveyed the plush suite that was to be his feeding ground for the next two nights. It was a small private villa set apart from the main compound, and boasted one massive room and an equally sizable marble bath. Everything about it—from the Persian rugs to the mosaic walls to the moonlight shining in through the stained glass windows around the central dome in the ceiling, and the four poster bed surrounded by sensual, shimmering purple bed curtains—was seduction for the eyes.

Not that he needed it. Maybe the Nephilim he'd chosen did. Scarus hardly remembered her. She'd just been the first in the line who'd lacked the scent of fertility. But the one thing he did recall were eyes the color of glistening sand, fringed with long amber lashes. And power within her blood. So much power.

Saliva pooled in his mouth and his fingers twitched reflexively as they hung over the arms of the chair. He hoped she would come to him unclothed and ready to be taken—ready to receive the pleasure of his mouth, his tongue and his cock, as those in the past had done.

It would make for an easy transaction.

A knock on the door across the room brought his head up. "Come," he called, his tone thick with restrained hunger.

The two eunuchs from the Garden Room entered, pulling something behind them. The female? His eyes narrowed. Why were they handling her as though she were a prisoner?

As she moved into the room, Scarus was truly able to take in her appearance for the first time. She looked unwashed, unkempt, and though she was tall, he could barely see her shape through the thick, faded orange robes she wore.

But those eyes...he remembered those eyes. They captivated him still, enflamed his already palpable hunger. They gleamed with the color of the desert sand at dawn, a pale, erotic golden brown. They were stunning, fearsome, soulful eyes that didn't match the rest of her, but spoke of her sensual power.

"Are you going to say something, Incubus?" she demanded in a strong, clear voice that went straight to his groin. "Or are you just going to look me up and down like a hog at market?"

Scarus stared at her, surprised. Her appearance may have been lacking, but her tongue was sharp as a blade.

"You could ask my name," she suggested. "Or are manners in the House of Vipera as nonexistent as they say?"

He sat back in his chair. He had never been spoken to in such a way, not even by his advisors, and the urge to have her brought to him, have her sink to her knees before him and find some better use for her mouth pulsed in his blood.

"No words, no introductions?" she continued, trying to pull herself away from the eunuchs holding her. "Perhaps you would just like the males here to turn me around and lift my skirt."

The suggestion entered his gut and slithered lower. *That is an idea.* Though he sincerely doubted she meant it. He turned to regard the males on either side of her. He didn't like their hands on his meal. "Release her."

The eunuch on the left only gripped her tighter. "Master Vipera, it is unwise. She is a hellcat—"

"Release her," Scarus replied in a deadly cold voice. "And do not speak again, male. Unless you wish me to cut out your tongue."

Both eunuchs paled and not only freed the woman but backed up until they reached the shadows near the door.

Scarus shifted his gaze to the female once again. She stood in the center of the room, those lovely pale brown eyes surveying every inch of the suite. When they caught and remained on the massive bed with its waves of purple curtain, her nostrils flared and her lips thinned. Curious, he mused. And unprecedented. This Nephilim's sharp tongue stemmed from either nerves or a desire to be

221

anywhere but here.

"*Come ti chiami?*" he inquired.

Her head whipped around to face him. "He speaks. And it's in Italian."

Her voice had a power of its own, utterly separate from the female. Scarus couldn't help but wonder how it would feed him as he fed from her, brought her to orgasm with his lips and tongue.

"What is your name?" he said.

"Rosamund."

A brow lifted over his right eye. A name befitting a queen. "And are you angry, Rosamund?" he asked.

"Yes," she answered plainly.

"Why is that?"

Her chin lifted a fraction, but she never dropped her gaze from his. "What you did to me out there... To all of us."

Confusion moved through him. "Out there?"

"In the Garden Room," she ground out.

Scarus leaned forward, one elbow on his thigh, his hand supporting his chin. "Pray do not tell me that was the first time an Incubus has released his power, his thrall, on the Nephilim of the Harem?"

"You didn't just release it, sir," she fired back. "You flooded the entire room with it!"

"So you haven't felt the thrall before?"

She sighed with irritation. "Of course we've all felt the great and wondrous power of the Incubi. But it was always contained, respectful." She pointed behind her to the door. "What you did back there was degrading."

Curiosity trumped his lack of enthusiasm for

this subject. "How so?"

"You made females drop to their knees," she said as though it should've been obvious.

"Not you," he pointed out.

When she didn't say anything right away, he continued, "In fact, you were the only one who remained standing." He cocked his head to the side. "Why is that? Or how is that?"

"Are you asking how I could possibly resist you?"

His lips twitched. "*Sì, signorina.*"

"Because in your experience no one ever has?" she continued with a mocking grin of her own.

When he nodded that her assessment was in fact truth, her grin promptly faded. "Listen, I might not have fallen to my knees, but I was humiliated just the same. You made me…" Her cheeks flushed. It was a lovely sight, considering her strange gray pallor.

"Come?" he supplied easily.

She turned her head away and groaned. "Oh, sweet Goddess."

"I do not see the problem, Rosamund. You are Nephilim and I am Incubus. I take power and give pleasure. You give power and receive pleasure."

To demonstrate this, he released his thrall. Not full force, but enough to make her eyes close, her cheeks flush and her lips part with a hungry moan.

Lovely. She was exactly what he craved. What his insides were screaming for. What would make him strong.

"Stop. That," she ground out, her eyes bursting open.

Scarus felt her push back, and released his hold on her. Confusion swam in his blood. "I don't understand, Nephilim. You resist me?"

"Yes, you asshole," she said through gritted teeth. "I resist you. Let me go and find another. There are twenty-nine other females out there who want you. Want this."

Both eunuchs broke from the shadows and headed for the female.

"Wait," Scarus commanded. He'd never experienced anything like this—like her. He would not take her against her will. But he would not give her up, either. As well as not being in her fertile time, she contained great power. He'd seen it in the line and now as she pushed his power back at him. He licked his lips. He would taste that magnetic force on his tongue.

"Pray, take her to your mistress," Scarus instructed the males.

Rosamund's eyes widened with hope. "You're letting me go?"

He took out his Blackberry and started typing. "I believe you've been treated harshly here. Perhaps it is because of your strength, your sharp tongue. I have just texted your Head Female, Constance. You will be pampered, treated as the jewel you are, then returned to me." He stood and placed his phone back in the breast pocket of his suit.

"I don't want this," Rosamund shouted as him. "I don't want to be pampered. Look at me, you viper."

Scarus did.

"How could you want this? I'm nothing

224

compared with the other Nephilim. Can't you see that?"

His eyes never left hers. "You give yourself too little credit, Rosamund. In the Garden Room, I saw no one but you. Standing tall and proud and defiant as you took what I gave." He turned to the eunuchs. "She is to be treated like a queen. Anything less and I will know."

# CHAPTER FIVE

"You told him we mistreated you?" Constance demanded as she paced the terracotta tiles before the large bathing pool.

"No. God, no," Rosamund insisted, feeling as though her world—her carefully constructed world—was falling apart around her. "It was him doling out all the mistreatment."

The woman stopped and glared at Rosamund. "What do you mean? What did you say?"

"That he was a barbarian who came in with his sexual guns blazing and forced every Nephilim to their knees."

"Oh dear Goddess," Constance moaned, glancing around the Nephilim's main bathing chamber, which was glowing with the light of the dual fireplaces on the opposite side of the zelij-tiled pool. "What you fail to understand—clearly, what you have never understood—is that the females in the Harem want to lie with an Incubus. They want to have their wombs filled. They want the pleasure of his thrall."

Fine. Rosamund would give her that. She'd give them all that. Frankly, if she wasn't promised to Roger perhaps she too would find Scarus

Vipera…what? Attractive? No, that was too dull a word. Irresistible? Absolutely not. Tempting, perhaps? Alluring, definitely… But she had to believe that was only because her body still vibrated from the climax he'd given her in the Garden Room, and the one he'd nearly given her earlier in his suite.

"I only chastised him for releasing his power so fully," she said at last. "Causing that reaction in every female. He is a brute."

"You are impossible. You should be feeling grateful. Honored." Her eyes skimmed down Rosamund's body. "That male chose you for Goddess knows what reason—you continually look like something that has been wandering in the desert for far too long."

"Exactly. So please go and convince him how unsuitable I am. Bring Zoe and Eva with you. They're always walking around naked. He won't be able to resist them—he'll forget all about me."

She sighed. "How I wish that were true."

"It can be."

"He wants you, you silly girl."

"Well, I don't want him," Rosamund returned almost petulantly.

Constance was crossing to her, standing before her, nostrils flaring with fierce irritation. "Listen to me. Whether you know it or not, the world outside these walls is in turmoil. The Sovereign is nowhere to be found, the Three have revealed that they destroy any human who gets pregnant by an Incubus, and just as of late an Incubus was killed by a Temple Blade."

"What?" Rosamund exclaimed on a soft gasp. She had known about the mystery surrounding the Sovereign. But... "They kill humans who are pregnant by Incubi? Why would they do that?"

"I don't have the answers. The balance that the Three were so capable of maintaining is starting to crumble." Her eyes appeared weary and fearful. "We need to help them and ourselves—make sure our world stays in balance by standing by the old ways. I know you do not wish to be the catalyst for a war between the Incubi and Nephilim by rejecting one of the Masters."

"Of course I don't," she said in all seriousness.

"Then we must sustain this delicate balance between the Incubi and Nephilim. The traditions of the Harem will be upheld. Do I make myself clear?"

Rosamund's heart was pounding so hard she worried it might explode inside her chest. She wanted to belong to Roger. He was light and easy and simple and kind. Like her, he wished for a family, a home and normality. She'd never known her father, and her mother had died when she was only two. Roger represented everything she'd prayed for growing up alone in the Nephilim world.

She had to figure out a way for Scarus Vipera to retract his choice. Only then would she be free. Could she reason with him? Tell him the truth? Beg him to choose another? Could she do that without disrupting the delicate balance Constance spoke of?

Two Nephilim she didn't know entered the room. They were both wearing thin, white bathing sheets that glowed in the light of the fires. One was obviously pregnant, though her belly didn't extend farther than four or five months along. The other was a little older than Constance and carried a basket of soaps and oils, brushes and shaving implements. Without a word they walked down the steps into the pool.

"Remove your clothes, Rosamund," Constance commanded.

Panic flickered inside her belly. She'd thought she would be able to bathe alone.

"He believes I am to blame for your appearance," Constance continued with a humorless laugh. "Who knows? Perhaps he will change his mind once you are brought to him. Once your personality and figure have been revealed to him. After all, how much can clean hair and a proper shave change reality?"

Rosamund's breath was held captive inside her lungs. This was it. She couldn't hide herself any longer.

One dark brow lifted over Constance's left eye. "Shall I call the eunuchs in to assist you?"

Without a word, Rosamund lifted the pumpkin robes over her head and let them fall to the terracotta tiles below. Then she quietly and quickly untied the belly padding covering her flat stomach, and unwound the binding that hid her full breasts. When she was completely naked, she lifted her gaze to meet the older woman's.

Shock and ire glittered in the depths of Constance's eyes. She shook her head. "What have you done?"

"I want a life of my own choosing."

"You are Nephilim," she answered blackly as if

this was all the answer that was required. And maybe it was. "Do you hide anything else, Rosamund?"

Her shoulders fell. It was foolish to try and keep up this ruse now. The woman would give her a cavity search if she felt Rosamund was further deceiving her. Opening her mouth, she slipped out her rotten teeth and handed them over. Then without another word to the furious and flabbergasted den mother before her, she walked to the pool's edge and descended the steps.

# CHAPTER SIX

Scarus stood on the private terrace between two stone columns heavy with red bougainvillea and surveyed the blue-tiled swimming pool, which was bordered by olive trees, hibiscus bushes and brightly lit torches. Hunger raged inside of him. Not for the meal that was to be served at the table to his right. But for the sharp-tongued Nephilim who he couldn't seem to get out of his mind.

In the past two hours, he'd attempted to work. The Vipera line had dealt in art, ancient currency and manuscripts for centuries, and had amassed a great fortune, but Scarus had been the first to bring their prizes public, both at galleries and museums. Tonight, he was attempting to discuss details for the Vipera Gallery opening in his home town of Ravello—which was just a few days away. But his concentration and creativity had waned early on. The female invaded his thoughts. *Rosamund.* There was just something about her. Granted, she was no beauty. But that didn't matter to him. She carried deep power within her, and the way she'd spoken to him, with such resolve, such fire, had made his insides come alive again.

He stalked to the edge of the pool and stared

out. Beyond the villa, moonlit sand stretched for miles. It had been many years since he'd felt such a stirring. Five years to be exact. And he didn't know if he should be intrigued or concerned. If he should grab hold or turn away.

His nose caught her scent on the desert breeze and he inhaled deeply.

"I didn't know Incubi consumed anything other than sexual energy."

Her voice snaked through him and brought his head around. "We don't need to. We are—" The words died on his tongue. Or perhaps they died in his mind. Whatever it was, he was rendered mute as he stared at the female who occupied the very same spot he'd vacated only a few moments ago. Bracketed by columns of wild, ruby red bougainvillea, she was a stranger to him, this tall, slender goddess in white. And yet, she had the same defiant lift to her chin. The same brilliant sandstone eyes that connected to his without fear. And the same vibrating power that broke from its stunning cage, traveled the seven feet to the water's edge and wrapped around him—not once but several times, until he felt squeezed by it.

"You were saying?" she asked, one perfectly manicured eyebrow lifting.

"That Incubi don't need food to survive," he forced from his throat, taking note of the growl in his tone. "We are sustained by a female's climax."

Her eyes widened at that, and her cheeks flushed pink. Scarus took note that it wasn't just her cheeks that held this healthy glow now. Gone was the ugly orange costume, and in its place was a strapless white caftan that showed off her full breasts and cinched her small waist with gold roping and beadwork. The stark white fabric made her long blond hair glow gold, and displayed smooth, pink skin that looked as though it had endured a hard scrubbing. Irritation bit at him. Who had been granted the honor of performing that task? Whose hands had rubbed oils into her shoulders and back? Who had helped her dress?

His eyes cut to the eunuch hovering near the French doors behind her, and his lip curled. "Go."

The male went ashen and he stammered, "Lady Constance has asked that I...that I remain, sir." He cleared his throat. "To make certain the Nephilim pleases you."

"She more than pleases me."

"My lady means for her to do her duty, Master Vipera—"

"Do you wish for this eunuch to stay, Rosamund?" Scarus cut off the male coldly, his eyes shifting to the Nephilim. "Do you want him here? Do you want him watching your every move?" His brow drifted upward. "My every move?"

She didn't answer right away, but he could see her pulse pounding at the base of her long, soft neck. His hands twitched as he imagined running his fingers over that furious tattoo.

"I don't want him," she said at last.

The words, however they were meant, enflamed Scarus's blood. He started toward the male. "You heard her."

The eunuch's eyes grew wide with unease and he started to back up. "But sir—"

Scarus kept coming, his strides purposeful and predatory. "Tell Constance we need no chaperone, no witness, no interference or assistance."

The male nodded, stumbling back into the suite. "Yes, sir."

"Go, then." Scarus stopped at the French doors. "And Goddess help you if there are any more interruptions tonight."

Without waiting for a reply, he shut the doors with a little too much force, then turned back to face Rosamund. "Sit," he growled, gesturing to the table heavy with food. By the look on her face, he knew he sounded like a bastard, a barbarian, and quickly amended gruffly, "Please." Even walked over and pulled the chair out for her.

Her eyes went to the chair, then to him. "If the eunuch is gone, who's going to serve dinner, Master Vipera?"

Scarus knew what she was asking, and what she was thinking. His expression calmed and he said, once again, in a far gentler tone, "Please."

This time, she walked toward him, her hips swaying attractively inside the white silk. When she sat down, he poured wine into her glass, then his own.

"Are you sure you should be doing this?" she asked.

"What? Seeing to your needs?"

The pale hair on the back of her neck lifted at his words, and Scarus felt the reaction deep in his gut.

"Waiting on me," she clarified. "Masters should be treated like royalty. Or so I've heard."

"It's true," he said, dropping into the seat across from her. It barely contained his large frame. "But that doesn't mean I can't offer the same treatment to the very beautiful Nephilim before me."

Her gaze slipped and she reached for her wine.

"Which leads me to ask," he continued, lacing his fingers and dropping his chin. "Why would you hide such beauty?"

She took a sip of wine, then placed it back on the table.

She looked uncomfortable, but Scarus was not about to pull back. She was hiding something, and he wanted to know what it was. He wanted to know her.

"Rosamund?" he pressed.

She released a weighty breath. "I don't want to be here. In the Harem."

"Why not? Isn't it an honor to be chosen?"

"Yes." She reached for a slice of brown bread.

"An honor to lie with an Incubus," he added. "A blessing to carry his young?"

"I'm sure for some it is," she said cautiously. "But for others, it's not necessarily the choice they'd make if a choice was offered."

Scarus stared at her, dumbfounded. In all his years on this Earth, all his days and nights in the Harem, he'd never heard a Nephilim speak so. It had never even occurred to him that one might not wish to accept the honor of bedmate and... His mind slowed, then suddenly whirled back in time. Could this have been the reason for Daya's defection? Had she not wished to lie with him? Bear his child? Had she punished him by taking their son?

No. He refused such an idea. Refused to believe it. Incubi and Nephilim had engaged in this exchange of power and peace forever. Perhaps the woman before him was merely making excuses to cover up feelings for another male.

Scarus's eyes narrowed on her. Just the suggestion made his insides pulse with a primal fervor.

He watched as she took a bite of the succulent lamb in plum sauce. "Can I ask you something, Rosamund?"

She glanced up and her eyes held a touch of humor. "Do you really need my permission, Master Vipera?"

A shiver moved through him. His name on her tongue... Her wet, pink tongue... "Did you give yourself to any of them? The other Incubi who came here?"

That humor died. "No." She didn't even hesitate. "No other Incubus chose me."

Relief moved through him. "I'm glad of that. And I'm glad you wore that disguise." His eyes traveled over her face. "Although they were fools if they couldn't see the jewel beneath it."

Her eyes softened at his words. "I appreciate what you say. I appreciate your position here, and the connection our two worlds have forged in the name of peace and endurance. But I can't sleep with you."

Scarus stared at the woman, once again astonished. "You find me unsatisfactory?"

"No," she said.

"Does the idea of coming to my bed repulse you?"

"Of course not." Her cheeks flushed with embarrassment. "But that's not why I can't be with you. I have a man waiting for me. Outside of these walls. It's why I donned a disguise in the first place."

Scarus's jaw flickered with tension. A male? So, he'd been right. He regarded her intently. "You are bonded to another and yet the Three called you here. I've never heard of such a thing. What is happening in our world? Perhaps the whispers are true. The Three are not ruling properly."

"No," she said, passion in her tone. "That's not it at all—"

"I was turning a blind eye to the unrest," he continued. "To the Sovereign's abandonment of the Obsidian Throne. I didn't want to acknowledge that this balance we share could be in trouble. But clearly, it is not just happening on the Incubi side." He reached inside his jacket for his Blackberry. The Master of the House of Xanthe was a distant, but trusted, acquaintance. He was also one of the best spies ever born. Scarus would retain Jian's services. Find out what was truly happening with the Sovereign, then take it to the other Masters for review.

"Please, this has nothing to do with the Three," Rosamund insisted, her tone heavy with panic. "This is all about me. What I want. What I never had and always wished for."

Scarus glanced up from the text he'd just sent. Rosamund's lovely face was grave. "What do you mean?"

She looked as though explaining further was the last thing she wanted to do. "I grew up with nothing and no one," she said begrudgingly. "No family. My mother abandoned me a few months after I was born. And as a Nephilim, I was told only that my father came from Romerac House and that he died when I was three. I never even took a last name because I didn't really know where I belonged. I was shuffled around the High Chamber, but as soon as I could manage it—as soon as I was old enough—I moved away and started a life of my own."

"Where?" Scarus asked, his surprise at her history evident. Shuffled around? It was not how things were done in the Incubi families.

"San Francisco." She placed her fork on her plate with care. "I met this man when I applied for a job at his veterinary clinic. Dr. Roger Young." She smiled softly, sadly. "He's so kind and calm and stable. After our third date he told me that he wanted to settle down, have a big family. It spoke to my heart because that was the one thing I wanted. I wasn't looking for romance or—"

Fury roared through Scarus and he interrupted with an explosion of words, "You belong to a human?"

She drew back an inch or two. "Yes. Well, no," she stumbled. "I don't belong to him exactly. We're not engaged or anything. But he told me he cares about me. And when I went away, he promised to wait for me."

The urge to hunt down the human male and rip

his limbs from his body was strong within Scarus. He sat back in his chair, folded his arms across his chest and attempted to be calm. "I don't understand any of this."

"I know it's unusual."

"Very. That any male would wait for his female to bear another's offspring shocks me. Your Roger sounds like an imbecile."

Every shred of color in her face vanished. "He's not an imbecile. He doesn't know. He thinks I'm working in Australia... And he wasn't supposed to wait for long. There's a clause in the rules of the Harem. If a Nephilim isn't chosen by an Incubus within a year, she must leave."

"I have never heard of this rule," he ground out.

"Most haven't. As you said, Nephilim consider it an honor to be here." Her eyes implored him then, the meal before her all but forgotten. "You could choose one of them, Master Vipera. Now. Right now. I could fetch her for you. Cleo or Eva, these two Nephilim are stunning, and have a much more suitable personality."

"I chose you, Rosamund," he said evenly.

She bit her lip. "I know that. But what does it matter to you, Scarus?"

Again the shiver rushed through him as she said his name, and he inhaled deeply.

"You came here for sex and to spread your seed. Does it matter who lies beneath you?"

It shouldn't, he thought darkly. As long as the female wasn't in her fertile stage. And he was fairly certain there were other Nephilim in the Harem who fit this criterion. But he was immovable. He stared at the woman across from him with predatory and possessive menace. "I chose you."

Her eyes narrowed and her nostrils flared slightly. Wrath looked very well on her. "With everything I just told you, you're going to keep me here?"

"You aren't promised to that male," he answered as though it was the simplest thing in the world. "Therefore you belong to me."

"I don't belong to you," she returned hotly.

"While we are in the Harem—" he began.

She cut him off. "It's one night."

"We'll see."

She went pale. "What does that mean?"

He leaned forward, his eyes pinning her where she sat. "Perhaps I will forgo selection and keep you. It would be considered a great honor, Rosamund."

"For whom?" she ground out.

He inhaled deeply. Heat and power were radiating off her body and he wanted to lap it up with his tongue. "Let's say for us both."

"You are a barbarian," she accused, pushing back her chair and coming to her feet.

"I am," he agreed.

"And an unreasonable, uncaring, take-whatever-he-wants-no-matter-what asshole!"

"I believe that is the very definition of an Incubus."

She tossed her napkin onto her plate and stormed past him. Scarus remained seated, breathing in her scent. She was right on all accounts. He was a terrible, lecherous barbarian with the moral compass of a tarantula. He'd never strived to be anything else. It was his nature. His birthright. But now…

He rose from the table. She had already passed the torch-lit pool and was stepping off the edge of the terrace into the sand. Now he wanted her. This female who seemed to have forgotten the ancient ways. A fact that both stunned and attracted him. It had been many centuries since his line had needed to stalk their female prey.

He followed her, but when she started running into the moonlit desert, white silk and flaxen hair billowing out behind her, he cursed and took off after her. About twenty feet out, he caught up to her, took her by the shoulders and turned her to face him.

"Let me go," she demanded, struggling in his arms.

Darkness spread out around them. The only illumination coming from the moon above, the torches around the pool and the muted light spilling out from the windows of the suite.

"Why are you acting this way?" he asked, holding her still. "You are Nephilim."

"So the hell what?" she shot back.

"We are meant to mate, to breed, Rosamund. It is how things are. How they have always been."

"As you said, Vipera, things are changing." Breathing heavy, her eyes were fierce and glowing under the moonlight. "I'm meant for whoever I wish to be meant for."

"That's a child's fairy tale."

"No, that's a woman's choice."

"You are not a woman," he growled, pulling her closer. "You are not human. And you should not being mating or setting up house with one."

Her face was inches from his. "He is good and kind and cares about me. He wants to make me happy."

"Good and kind," Scarus uttered blackly as the desert wind picked up around them. "What would you do with such a male? Share your day's events while braiding each other's hair?"

She looked like she wanted to hit him. "You can't understand because you don't have a kind or generous bone in your barbarian body!"

Right now the bones in Scarus's body were humming against the tense, ready muscles. "Tell me something, Rosamund. Does this male create a fire inside of you?"

She fell silent, except for her ragged breath. Her eyes flickered to his mouth.

"When he touches you, do you melt?" Scarus continued.

She shook her head. "Stop that."

"When he kisses you, does your sex weep?"

"It's not like that," she said on a whimper.

"*Cazzo*, Rosamund," Scarus cursed. He leaned in and brushed his lips against hers. "It should be like that," he whispered. "Don't you understand? When a male holds you, kisses you, touches you, every inch of your body should erupt. Like a volcano. Like this." He captured her mouth on a growl. He kissed her so intensely, so fully, his tongue slipping past her lips to play, that when he pulled back an inch, she went with him.

"*Sì, bella Rosa*," he uttered on a growl, taking her face in his hands.

This time, when he captured her lips again, she groaned and plunged her tongue into his mouth. *Merda*! She tasted of spiced honey. So sweet, so hungry. She matched him in her need. Pressing herself against him, moaning when he changed the angle of their kiss to go deeper. Heat infused him, wanted to overtake him. The demon magic hummed just below the surface of his skin, begging to be released. He'd wanted this from the moment Rosamund had come to his suite, in her padding and orange robes, her greasy hair and those shockingly beautiful eyes no amount of sallow makeup could hide.

As she dragged her hands up between their bodies and grabbed onto the lapels of his suit, yanking him closer, Scarus's body pulsed with the need to make her writhe and cry out and explode with pleasure. Not just because his existence relied upon it, but because he wanted her to feel that fire, that hunger that was inside of her too—in her nature. He was no sweet, kind, compassionate human. But he knew what Rosamund craved and he could give it to her—for as long as she wanted, as many times as she wanted it.

*That* no human man could ever give to her.

Cupping her face, his thumbs stroking the underside of her jaw, he feasted on her mouth. Every moan, every sigh she released belonged to him and he lapped them up with his tongue, then thrust himself back into her mouth. He was hard everywhere, his cock pressed between them. And she was soft and wet and fragrant. His nostrils filled with her scent and he ground his hips against her.

On a whimper of anger and sexual frustration, she pushed at him. The sudden shift of feeling yanked Scarus from his sensual devotion, and he released her instantly.

Remaining where she was, she stared up at him. Her breathing was ragged, her eyes heavy lidded, and her skin glowed with health and heat under the moonlight. Scarus had never seen anything so beautiful or so tantalizing in his life, and he wanted to consume every inch of her.

"Please," she whispered, her lips trembling. "Turn it off, Vipera."

"What?" he uttered, confused. His eyes were pinned to her mouth. He wanted those lips again. And the ones below her navel. He breathed in deeply, trying to keep her scent within him.

"The power," she said. "The thrall. Stop it now."

His eyes flipped up to meet hers. What was she saying? That their kiss was... He stared at her, nostrils flared, skin pulling tight around rock hard flesh. "I am doing nothing, Rosamund. I assure you." One brow lifted sardonically. "Whatever you're feeling, it's not coming from me. Not in the way you think."

She shook her head, her arms wrapping her body. "Don't do this to me again," she begged. "Don't make me come."

"I am not."

"Liar," she said through gritted teeth.

"You don't believe me?"

"No. You will do anything to create this frenzy inside of me."

His chin lowered and the viper inside of him struck. "The frenzy, *mia bella*, is your body wanting mine."

"No." She shook her head. "No."

"You want to feel what true thrall is once again? Just so you will know the difference, of course?" Ire and sexual hunger, and something he couldn't name—something foreign he'd never felt before— rippled through him, and he flipped the switch.

Rosamund had already been halfway to climax from their kiss. With the demon magic upon her, it only took seconds for her to convulse with shocking pleasure. Power surged into Scarus as she cried out, orgasm rippling through her. But he took no satisfaction in it. Only disappointment.

"Do you see the difference now, Rosamund?" he asked bitterly.

She looked up at him. "You are shameless," she uttered through gritted teeth.

*Yes.* "I am Incubi."

And with that, he used the power she'd just granted him to teleport back to the suite.

# CHAPTER SEVEN

Rosamund was wrecked.

Emotionally, physically, mentally wrecked.

And yet, she wanted more.

Of him. Of what he'd made her feel when his lips had taken hers. It wasn't his thrall that had done it. She knew that, and hated herself for it. If it had been his demon power, she could've blamed the entire wanton mistake on him. On his barbarian nature. But when his mouth had captured hers, when his hands had gripped her face, she'd melted. No. She'd erupted. Never in her life had she felt such desire. Not the false desire of an Incubus's demon magic, but real hunger and uncontrolled need.

She stepped up onto the terrace stones. She'd been outside for more than an hour. Sitting on the sand, staring at the moon, wishing she could turn back time. Wishing she'd gone to the end of the line of Nephilim in the Garden Room. Wishing she hadn't leaned into Scarus Vipera after he'd kissed her that first time.

Wishing he hadn't stopped when she'd pushed him away.

Her hands shook at her sides as she passed by

the pool and headed for the French doors. She was a fool, a hedonist. A breaker of promises. Once she returned to Roger she would tell him everything and hope that he forgave her.

If, in fact, she was able to return at all.

But first she had to get through the night with Master Vipera. Goddess only knew what was waiting for her inside the suite. More thrall? More tantalizing looks? More arguments? More claims of possession? But what she found when she entered the massive and beautifully designed room was a very casual and non-threatening Scarus Vipera on the bed. Not at all like the dangerous, erotic viper she knew him to be. He was propped up on several thick pillows, reading a book. His long, large body clad in only a pair of black drawstring pants.

Like the fool she was slowly but surely showing herself to be, her gaze moved over him. He had very wide, very tan, very muscular shoulders and arms that she remembered feeling almost desperate to run her hands over when he was kissing her earlier. His chest was a solid wall of muscle except for the two dusky nipples and waves of abdominals. But it was the way those black pants hung low on his lean hips, giving her a clear view of his navel and the masculine trail of hair that disappeared into the black waistband, that made her mouth start to water.

Made her entire being flush with unresolved heat and tension.

She swallowed tightly and forced her gaze to lift. It was in that moment that he glanced up from his book and found her standing there, near the edge of the bed.

Gold eyes pinned her. "Can I get you something, Rosamund?"

*Your pants. Off.* "Your approval of my release would be good," she said through tightly clenched teeth.

His mouth curved up into a smile. "I meant wine, fruit…" His eyes flashed with heat. "Dessert, perhaps."

"I don't need to be taken care of, Master Vipera." *I only need to get out of here before I make an even bigger mistake. One I can't come back from. One that won't be forgiven.*

*One I want so badly I ache with it.*

"That's not what you professed earlier," he said, placing his book on the side table. "When you spoke of what you wanted, what you didn't have growing up."

"I was talking about Roger."

He didn't say anything for a moment. He seemed to be mulling something over in his mind. Then, he asked, "You think Dr. Young is going to take care of you?"

Roger's name on this man's lips made her gut ache. "It's the kind of man he is," she returned. "You wouldn't understand."

"Why? Because I am a barbarian who only wishes to fuck you." He said the words without malice.

"Fuck me, fuck any female," she answered. "You know nothing about care or kindness or sacrifice or civility."

"That is quite a judgment."

"As you said, you're an Incubus. I can't blame you for that. How you were brought up. What you were in essence trained to be. I'm willing to bet you've never loved a thing in your life."

His eyes suddenly flashed with heat and ferocity. "Don't speak of love, Rosamund. That emotion colors our vision, makes us see things and believe things that aren't true. Makes us vulnerable to debilitating pain."

"That isn't the love I know, Scarus."

"Oh?"

"No. Love is gentleness and kindness. Love is hope and seeing beyond the physical."

"And your Roger is all of these things, is he?"

"Of course."

"The veterinarian was married six weeks ago, Rosamund," he said evenly, unsympathetically. Without any kind of emotion at all.

Rosamund froze. She stared at him, unblinking. "What did you just say?"

His dark blond brows arched severely. "It took my Watchman five minutes to find him, and another five to see the happy announcement."

Her breath was caught in her lungs. She shook her head. "I don't believe you." Roger wouldn't have done that. Maybe they weren't promised to each other with rings, but there had been words.

Scarus reached for his Blackberry, which was also on the side table, and held it out to her. Rosamund practically dove at it like a hawk hungry for prey. She had to see. The viper had to be lying. He wanted to hurt her because she'd rejected him—because she'd pushed him away...

Tears tightened her throat. There he was, sweet and sensitive Roger, on the screen. She didn't recognize the woman he held in his arms, but she was pretty and smiling. She bit her lip. They were both smiling.

*Dr. and Mrs. Roger Young.*

It was all she chose to read before tossing it back on the bed. Without another word, she grabbed a blanket from the end of the four poster and headed over to the rug on the floor. In her beautiful white dress, she lay down and covered herself. Tears leaked from her eyes. Not because she had loved Roger. She cared for him. He was a good man. But because he had represented the life she'd wanted so dearly. The family she'd never had. Would probably never have now.

She closed her eyes and prayed for sleep. But just as she was about to drift off, she felt hands beneath her, lifting her.

"Wait—" she cried out. "Please don't."

"You will not sleep on the floor like a dog, Rosamund." Scarus carried her to the bed and placed her down on top of the coverlet. "I won't touch you again. Nor will I make you cream or cry out."

She didn't look at him when he covered her with the blanket. But she listened as he walked around to his side of the bed and lay back down. The click of the lamp brought on darkness, save the moon. And Rosamund waited to hear his breathing slow and grow even before she allowed herself to sleep.

# CHAPTER EIGHT

Scarus awoke to the dull, gray light of dawn, and the anxious moans of a dreaming female. It took him only seconds to recall where he was and who slept beside him. He had never shared a bed with a female for anything other than sex, as he believed such an intimate act was reserved for mated couples. Something he was completely uninterested in. Or had been, before last night.

Another pained groan cut through the silence. Rosamund must be having a nightmare, he thought with a pang of what he believed might be guilt. He wasn't familiar with the emotion. But after his callous treatment of her last evening, he wouldn't be surprised if he was the cause of her fretfulness.

In an attempt to comfort her, he turned over onto his side. But what greeted him when he did was anything but a nightmare. Rosamund's moans didn't stem from pain or fear or anxiety. She was dreaming of pleasure. Blood pooled low in his belly as he wondered who her mind was conjuring as she touched herself. His gaze raked over her hungrily. The bodice of her dress was pulled down, exposing one pale breast. A breast she was massaging, squeezing, pulling until the ripe nipple extended fully. Her skirt was up around her waist and she wore no panties beneath it. Her long, smooth legs were clamped tightly together, thigh kissing thigh, and her feet were crossed at the ankles. As she plucked and pinched her nipple, her other hand was busy inside her shaved sex, two fingers working her clit as she pumped her hips furiously.

Scarus felt his cock fill with blood and rise to his navel. He should leave the bed. Before the demon inside of him awoke too. Before it pushed him into taking what it felt it deserved.

The scent of her sweet pussy rose to meet his nostrils and he inhaled deeply. He wanted it. Her *sticchio*. His tongue inside, tasting, making her wake, making her wetter.

Without thought, he leaned down and kissed her breast, the one still covered. Rosamund responded instantly, her back arching, her lips parting in another sensual moan.

"Yes," she cooed. "Kiss me."

Jaw tight, Scarus closed his eyes and fought for control. The demon inside of him was scratching to get out. It needed to be fed, and Rosamund's tight, hot and very wet sex was exactly where it wanted to be.

Just inches away from her skin, he whispered, "Rosamund, you must wake."

Her hand abandoned her breast then and reached for him. "Lick me," she whimpered in an almost desperate tone as her fingers wrapped around his neck. "I have to know. I have to know."

*Merda.* She wasn't awake. True, he was a barbarian, but he didn't take without consent.

"Please," she urged, guiding his face to her breast. "Suckle me. Hard. I have to know what you feel like."

The perfect, pale globe with its tight pink bud was an inch away. It cried out to him. Fuck. He dropped his head and lapped at it with his tongue. Instantly, Rosamund groaned and arched her back further. Scarus lapped at it again, then ran his nose over it, flicking it back and forth gently. Then, when he could no longer stand it, he took the full mound in his hand, squeezed and latched on.

Pure, almost shocking pleasure rippled through his body as he suckled her deep into his mouth.

"Oh Goddess, yes!" she cried, her fingers digging into the skin of his neck.

Feeding his hunger and her need, he alternated between sucking, flicking and biting. It was the biting she seemed to like best. It made her writhe, made the scent of her arousal intensify.

Made her nearly come.

A growl vibrated through Scarus. No matter how desperately his demon desired the power of her climax, Scarus wasn't going to allow it. Not yet. Not until he claimed her with his tongue. Not until he knew her taste.

With one last rake of his teeth to her nipple, he moved down her body, not stopping until he reached the skin of her exposed belly. Slowly, languidly, he kissed her, lapping at her navel. Her hips were lifting and lowering, begging and pleading, and he wanted to accommodate her. Give her what she was aching for. But there was something inside of him that feared it. Not accepting her power. No, that wasn't it. Confusion swam in his overheated blood as he stared at her shaved sex, glistening with the moisture of her arousal. He dipped his head and ran his tongue over the top of her sex. He groaned at the sweet, addictive taste.

"Please," she begged again. "Look at me."

Scarus glanced up, his gut tight, his cock straining to be released. Waves of blond hair bracketed a beautiful, sleep-weary face with parted pink lips and eyes that were very much open and aware. He waited, nostrils flaring as he breathed in the scent he craved.

"Open for me, Rosamund," he uttered fiercely.

Without a moment's hesitation, she brought her knees up, then let them fall to the side. It was all the consent Scarus needed. His gaze dropped and he took in the most entrancing sight in the world.

Rosamund completely bared to him.

"*Bellisima*," he murmured. "So pink. So wet."

He settled himself between her legs, his hands raking up her inner thighs, his thumbs opening her so he could see her swelling clit.

"Oh, yes. It pulses for me, Rosamund," he said, dipping his head, and flicking the bud lightly with his tongue. "Calls to me. It wants to be licked."

Her hips canted. "Yes!"

"It wants to be sucked while I fuck you with my fingers," he added, lowering one hand.

"Yes, please, Scarus."

His name on her lips broke him entirely. Madness claimed him. Or perhaps it was the demon. But all the both of them wanted was her pleasure, her climax, her wet heat. As one finger entered her tight sex, Scarus covered her clit with his mouth.

She cried out, her hands finding his scalp. She fisted his hair and rubbed herself against him.

Scarus slipped another finger inside her and drove deep. Never in his ever-long existence had he wanted something—or was it someone?—so furiously. He sucked her clit gently as he pumped her, groaning every time his fingers were bathed in her arousal. She was his. Right now. This moment. She belonged to him.

And then it began. The exchange of power. Heat and madness, glory and pleasure. But it wasn't the same as it had been before. Even with the climax he'd given her beneath the desert moon last night. This was like the waves of a tsunami. Grand, awesome, terrifying. And all he wanted to do was stand beneath it and be taken over by it— destroyed, if that was its wish.

Shocks of liquid heat convulsed around his fingers and the bud in his mouth swelled.

"Scarus!" she screamed, her body out of control, spasming, electric and fraught with tension as she came.

And then he was pulling away from her clit and latching on to her sex. Sweet, blazing-hot cream cascaded over his tongue and snaked down his throat. He hadn't known how deep his thirst ran until now.

Until her.

*Merda…*

Even though he blazed with the power of a

hundred stars, there was nothing he wanted more in that moment than to bury himself inside her and claim her body for his own. But he wouldn't dare. Sex was for power only. Whatever he was feeling now had nothing to do with a Nephilim/Incubus exchange.

Breathing heavy, his cock straining against his pants, he drew back and covered her glistening sex with her dress. Then he stood up and attempted to gain some semblance of control over himself.

"I apologize, Rosamund," he said through tightly clenched teeth.

She was staring up at him, confused and flushed and unbearably sexy. "Why? I asked you to touch me—"

"I speak of last night. It was not my intent to wound you." The words felt strange on his tongue. The tongue that had only moments ago tasted Heaven. "Or perhaps it was." He looked away. Cursed brutally. "I'm not sure anymore. Of myself or my intentions. Ever since you walked into this suite yesterday, I have felt strangely. Possessive, weak, insecure..." He growled at the word. Hated that he had admitted to it. "I feel compelled to tell you something, Rosamund—whether you believe it or not. I have known love. I have lost love." His eyes lifted to meet hers. She looked enraptured, vulnerable. "A child."

She gasped, sat up. "Oh, Scarus—"

He cut her off with a raise of his hand. He was not used to gestures or exchanges such as these. He had said what he felt needed to be said—what was owed to her—but there couldn't be anything more if he was to preserve his dignity. "I will tell Constance that nothing has happened between us. I will tell her that you are not my choice." He exhaled heavily, attempting to make his tone as consoling as possible. "I know you cannot have your human male. But frankly, he is not worthy of your grief. Any male who refuses to wait for a female such as yourself does not deserve her love."

Rosamund's mouth fell open, and her eyes widened.

"I'm going for a swim now," he announced, formality heavy in his tone even though his cock remained stiff and hungry against the waistband of his pants. "It will give you time to shower and dress. Then I will speak with Constance. It has been a pleasure, Rosamund."

Without allowing her a reply, he inclined his head and promptly left the suite.

# CHAPTER NINE

She was free.

And yet she'd never felt more claimed in her life.

She slipped off the bed and headed for the bathroom. Her legs felt like rubber. Her skin was so sensitive she was almost wary of stepping under the shower spray. Scarus Vipera had owned her this morning. He'd crushed that dream she'd had nearly every night since coming to the Harem and showed her what true desire, true hunger, felt like.

She slipped out of her dress, turned on the water, and leaned against the glass door. He'd said he was going to Constance, said he was going to tell her that nothing happened between them—that Rosamund was not his choice.

It was exactly what she'd wanted. In four days, she would return to San Francisco and... And what? she mused, staring at the droplets of water snaking down the glass before her. Roger was married. He was her boss at the clinic so that would be remarkably uncomfortable if she chose to stay. She could move out, she supposed. Get a different job. Start her life fresh somewhere else.

A flash of dark blond hair, gold eyes, and hot,

skilled tongue erupted in her brain. *Absolutely not*, she admonished herself. *Just because a sexually gifted Incubus made you feel complete and magnificently satisfied for the first time in your life doesn't mean you should just abandon your life's dream.*

Waves of steam started to escape the confines of the stone and glass shower. *Get in there, Rosamund. Wash yourself. Wash the memory of his hands on you, his lips on you, his tongue in you, from your mind, and return to the life you know and understand.*

He was an Incubus. A sex demon. They didn't want normalcy. They didn't want family and children.

*I've known love, Rosamund. I've lost love.*

*A child.*

His words washed over her. Said with such sincerity and vulnerability. Of course, Incubi made offspring. The females went to the Nephilim. The males to the Incubi. But she didn't think the demons came to love them. Hers certainly hadn't. She wondered if Scarus had lost a female or a male? Surely it had to be a female, as males were given over to the Incubus right away. Had Scarus Vipera, barbarian and sex god, actually wanted to keep his female child? And if so, had he truly felt love and loss for her?

With a weighty groan, Rosamund reached for the faucet and turned off the shower. She grabbed one of the white silk robes hanging there and headed out of the bathroom. She felt so mixed up. Her emotions sliced in half. She wanted a family. She wanted her freedom. But she also wanted more of what she'd felt in that bed—and a chance to know Scarus Vipera's Incubus heart.

Crossing to the French doors, she swung them wide and stepped out into the cool desert morning air. Scarus was swimming laps in quick, sharp movements that accentuated his thickly muscled back and buttocks. A small aftershock erupted inside of her. Barbarian or not, this male was stunningly, knee-weakeningly gorgeous.

After nearly five minutes of swimming the pool like a shark in search of blood, he finally came up for air near the steps. He noticed her at once, his jaw clenching when he saw what she was wearing.

He heaved a sigh and rested his massive arms on the edge of the pool. "You haven't showered."

Water droplets clung to his tanned skin. Rosamund's tongue tingled with the need to capture one. "How do you know that?"

"I scent you," he said on a growl. "I scent the cream that still clings to your sex and inner thighs."

Rosamund's legs threatened to give out underneath her. His words. His voice. The way his eyes never left hers when he spoke.

He arched one wet eyebrow. "Coming to me like this will not help me give you up, Rosamund."

"Then don't," she said recklessly, the words spilling from her lips.

A flash of heat crossed his expression. "What?"

"Don't tell Constance you don't want me."

"You've changed your mind?"

"Yes," she said, impassioned. She couldn't hold it back. It was inside of her. This need. This need for him.

"*Perche, bella?*" he asked, then repeated his query

in English, "Why?"

Nerves skittered through her. She descended to the first step of the pool. Cool water rushed over her feet and ankles. She and Scarus were in such a strange, tenuous place. Yesterday, she'd fought him and he'd fought to keep her. Today he was letting her go, and...well, she didn't want him to.

"I was your choice," she said shakily. "Right?"

He nodded, his eyes heavy lidded, his jaw strained.

"Well..." She slipped off her robe and tossed it aside. "I'm choosing you back."

A low growling sound echoed across the water, but Scarus's eyes remained pinned to hers. "Rosamund, you must think. Your plans, your future. What you want—"

"What I want is in this pool," she said, her heart slamming against her ribs. "Leaning against the stones, staring into my eyes instead of at my naked flesh."

"I am trying to control myself. Trying to control my demon." He cursed and pushed away from the stones. "The thing wants to devour you."

She took another step down. "Then let it."

Eyes the color of liquid gold ripped away from her gaze and slowly traveled down her body. "As you stand there, Rosamund, you steal the beauty from everything around you, do you know that? The sky, the sand, the flowers. They pale in comparison."

His words made her heart beat right and true. Possibly for the first time in her life. But before she could say a word in response, he was gone from the center of the pool. Seconds later, he rematerialized—directly in front of her. She gasped as his hands wrapped around her waist, and with a primal growl he dragged her into the water with him.

Rosamund immediately wrapped her arms around his neck and her legs around his waist. His skin was tight and hard and hot, and she melted into him with a deep sigh.

Scarus groaned with appreciation and raked his hands up her back and into her hair. "This is madness," he uttered.

"I know," she returned, feeling his hard cock near the entrance to her sex. "But I want you. So desperately I ache with it."

"And I you, *bella*." His eyes searched hers. "I've never felt like this."

She smiled suddenly. "That's good."

He smiled back.

"Let's not think, okay?" she said impulsively. "About anything outside of this pool, the suite?"

"Yes," he growled, his fingers threading her hair. "Only here and now. You and me."

She leaned in and kissed him. A soft, gentle kiss that made him moan—made him return it with a lap of his tongue.

"I want to feel you inside me, Scarus" she whispered against his mouth. "So deep I can't breathe."

"Oh, *mia bella*," he uttered, then kissed her hard and hungry and long until she moaned and her breasts tingled. Then he dropped his hands to her ass and in one smooth move lifted her up and placed her down on his shaft.

Rosamund cried out, and for a moment just remained still. She felt so full, so deliciously impaled. Scarus was staring at her, those gold eyes blazing into hers, taking in every ragged breath, every tremble of her lips. And then he started to move. Not himself, but her—guiding her hips away, then drawing her back in again. Slow and languid, stretching her, going so deep. Rosamund had only been with one man in her life. And only a handful of times. It had been sweet and gentle and quick. Just like the male himself. But this… Goddess, this connection, this invasion, this utter takeover of her limbs and breath, insides and brain…it terrified her in its wonder.

Nothing would ever be the same after this.

No one would ever come close to making her feel so—

She gasped as he drew her back again, thrust into her and rolled his hips. Water churned and splashed over the lip of the pool.

"Rosamund," he said on a shudder of need. "What is happening?"

She shook her head, her breathing shallow. "I don't know. I don't know."

"You have taken control of me, of this demon inside me. I will do what you say. Whatever you say." His eyes probed hers. "Tell me what it is you want."

"Just you. Deeper. As deep as you can go."

His fingers dug into her backside and he pressed her firmly against him. Then, with a snarl of possession, he drove up into her, hard and shockingly deep.

Rosamund screamed. His name. Out into the desert.

But he didn't stop or slow, wait for her to catch her breath or drift down to Earth. He surged up into her, over and over, the perfect rhythm, and so deep she lost herself completely. She clung to him, trying to hold on as her legs shook and her fingers fisted his hair. His eyes glowed as he battered her womb. He was like a man possessed—a demon—and she loved it. She was meant for it.

For him.

His mouth captured hers again, and he kissed her hard and hungry, stealing her thoughts and only allowing her to feel. And she did. Everything. Heat and rabid hunger, pain and pleasure, want and hope.

But it was too intense to contain. The insides of her body were too small to hold such pleasure captive for long. She needed release, but she didn't want it to end. Not just because the feeling was so amazing. But because she knew that with every climax Scarus took from her, used to sustain his demon magic, a bond was growing. She couldn't allow that. Not with an Incubus.

Even one she knew she was falling for.

"Oh, Rosamund," he growled, pounding into her. "I feel you all around me. So hot and tight, your walls fisting me."

His words...his voice, they drove her over the edge. She couldn't hold on.

"That's right, *bella*. Come," he commanded, his thrusts gaining in speed. "Come for me. I want to feel your body weep, the sweet cream I tasted last night bathing my cock."

Waves of electric pleasure crashed over her and she gasped, her pussy clenching around him. Her eyes filled with tears—beautiful, wonderful, painful tears—and she moaned and cried out his name, coming so hard she forgot everything except the pleasure of the moment.

And him…

Him.

"*Sì*, my beautiful Rosa," Scarus roared. "There it is. That's what I wanted. What I had to have. Fuck!" His groan was guttural as he drove up into her over and over, again and again—until her sex was bathed in hot torrents of his powerful Incubi seed.

They remained like that for long seconds, clinging to each other, Scarus twitching with the power he'd just received, rolling his hips to make her shiver and gasp. Then he started to kiss and nuzzle her neck. The feeling was so divine, Rosamund nearly purred.

"Oh, Rosa," he uttered between kisses, moving up her neck to her ear. "*Ho bisogno di te.*"

She sighed with happiness. "What does that mean?"

He eased back so they were face to face, their bodies still connected. "I need you."

A slow, satisfied smile crept over her features. "Good."

His gold eyes impaled her. "No, Rosamund. I need you."

"But you just had me."

"I know." Though his expression darkened, his hold on her tightened. "*Dea*, I know."

# CHAPTER TEN

Scarus stood in front of the desk in the Head Female's office.

"Master Vipera, I'm not sure I understand," Constance said, her eyes nervous as she stared up at him. "Rosamund has been in your company all night."

"And nothing has occurred," he said coldly.

The female's face went ashen. "Did she reject you?"

Scarus sniffed with irritation. "She didn't get the chance."

"Oh." The female sat back and appeared thoughtful. "How disappointing."

"I made the wrong decision yesterday, *signora*," he explained as sunlight blazed in through the large window to his left. "A hasty decision. I kept the Nephilim for the evening, hoping my desires would change." He lifted his chin imperiously. "They did not."

Constance swallowed thickly. "Where is Rosamund now?"

"Sleeping." Just the word—no, the mental picture—sent a wave of desire running through him. Rosamund was asleep. No doubt still wrapped in the silk sheet he'd laid over her before leaving the room. After their time in the pool, he'd carried her inside to his bed. Made love to her again. Much slower this time. Exploring, tasting... His skin tightened around his muscles as he recalled her cries for release. That was what he craved now.

Not her power.

Her pleasure.

"I will have someone fetch her immediately, sir," Constance said, tearing into his thoughts and reaching for the phone.

"No," Scarus said, his tone so sharp the woman flinched. "I wish to talk with her first. I don't want to embarrass her."

"You needn't be concerned with her feelings," Constance stated evenly. "A Nephilim understands her place here. If she does not suit one Master, she'll most certainly suit another. She will be fine. Trust me."

Scarus's hands curled into fists at his side. Another Incubus? Touching her? Kissing her? Making her moan? Feeling the beginnings of a bond forming as he thrusts inside of her?

Fury coursed through him. He wouldn't allow that. Couldn't.

Not with himself—not with anyone.

"Now," Constance began gently, deferentially. "Would you like the remaining Nephilim brought before you once again? Or would you prefer I choose the female for you? Cleo, Margaret and Absinthe are all stunning creatures. And such gay personalities."

Scarus's lip curled. The idea of even looking on

another female repelled him. It was strange—this feeling. He wanted no other. Craved no other. Only Rosamund. But instead of taking her, claiming her as his body wished, he was sending her away.

No. No. That wasn't right. He was gifting her the life she wanted. Had wanted since she was a child. He cared for her that much.

"I will think on it and give you my decision tonight," he told Constance. "Now. To Rosamund."

"As I said, she will be returned to the Harem."

"No."

Her brows slammed together in a confused frown. "Sir?"

"I want her released. As the Harem's clause states. She was not chosen by an Incubus in one year's time."

A slow, worried expression moved over the female's face. "How do you know about that?"

"It matters not."

"She has told you, hasn't she?" Constance asked, rising from her chair. "How could she know such a—" Suddenly, realization dawned, and the female's eyes sharpened. "That is why she wore the disguise. Oh…she shames us. That wicked girl."

A snarl broke from Scarus's throat. "Never speak of her that way, do you understand me?"

Constance gasped and dropped back down into her chair.

"Now." He leaned down, placed one hand on either side of the desk. "If you want life at the Harem to continue as is," he said coldly. "If you want the Masters to continue to come here, you will release Rosamund in two days' time." He leaned in. "Am I making myself clear?"

As she stared up at him, every inch of her body trembled with either fear or anger. Scarus didn't care which one it was. All he wanted was her acquiescence.

"*Sì, signora?*" he pressed darkly.

She nodded, her gaze lowering. "Of course, Master Vipera."

# CHAPTER ELEVEN

Rosamund rearranged herself on the pillows once again. She was going for casual sexy. Her hair was mussed from bed, and from Scarus's wonderfully greedy hands, and her lips, cheeks and skin were all pink from a morning of energetic sex. Never in her life had she felt so happy, so content and so blissfully confused. This Incubus, with his barbaric nature and caged heart, had come into her life, had shaken the foundation of her carefully constructed ruse and had made her forget about her past and her future and just live in the now.

She grinned and hugged the sheet to her chin. Maybe the now could be stretched into days or a week. She knew he had business to see to—no doubt that's where he was now—but there had to be more time for them.

"Sleep well, *bella?*"

The sensual growl wrapped around her and squeezed. Her eyes lifted and took in the gorgeous Incubus dressed in a crisp black suit, white shirt and muted gold tie. Business, indeed. She nearly moaned looking at him.

"Very well," she replied warmly. "But I'm starving."

He moved to the edge of the bed, his eyes blazing down into hers. "How I wish that I could feed you."

Heat surged into Rosamund's cheeks, and other more intimate places as well. She licked her lips. "You can, Master Vipera. In fact, I've been dying to know what you taste like."

His nostrils flared and his jaw tightened with tension. "I have been to see Constance."

It was as if all warmth, all intimacy, everything they'd created over the past two days evaporated in an instant. Ice water filled her veins and she stared at him, stuttering, "What? Why?"

"I want you to have your chance, Rosamund," he said with passion—passion that almost rivaled his touch, his kiss.

*Oh Goddess, no...* She blinked up at him, feeling lightheaded. "I don't understand. We agreed."

His eyes moved over her, slowly, desperately, as if he was trying to memorize her. "In two days you will be free."

"But that's not possible. I was chosen by you. Taken by you."

"No one will know that."

*No, no, no.* What had he done? She cast aside the sheet, not caring for modesty or foolish thoughts of seduction, and scurried across the bed. "I rejected that choice, Scarus. I made my decision."

A groan escaped his throat as he took in her nude form. "I want you to have what you want, Rosamund. Your life the way you see it—the way you desire it. Not sitting in the Harem waiting to be impregnated." He backed up, growling at the idea.

Rosamund didn't cover herself. She wasn't going to make this easy on him. "I could be carrying your child."

He shook his head. "No. You aren't fertile at this time."

Her eyes widened and her heart started to beat furiously inside her chest. "How could you know that?"

"The Vipera line can scent fertility, Rosamund."

His tone was wicked and cold, but it sounded forced. He was trying to hurt her. Trying to make her detest him. But he only succeeded in destroying the vulnerability, the sweet intimacy, they'd created together.

Her hands shaking, Rosamund reached for the sheet and covered herself. Scarus watched with shuttered eyes. But behind them, she could see his pain.

"Did you know that when you chose me?" she asked.

"I did," he answered.

Tears pricked at her eyes. "Is that why you chose me?"

"Yes."

Without another world, Rosamund scrambled off the bed. She needed clothes. Needed to get dressed. She swiped at a tear rolling down her cheek just as she reached the armoire. She splayed the doors and grabbed a pale blue takchita.

As she tossed it on, Scarus stood behind her and tried to talk to her. "I didn't want a child, Rosamund," he explained, his voice threaded with anger and pain, frustration and desire. "I couldn't go through that hurt again. I was growing weak. What I needed was the power of the Harem."

It didn't matter. His reasons for wanting her. None of that mattered. "I understand," she said. What mattered was that he was pushing her away.

"I know what you want, Rosamund," he continued. "The life you want. Home and family. It is a beautiful thing, but nearly impossible for an Incubus."

And he wasn't going to follow her.

She shook her head. "You don't have to say anything more. I understand."

"Rosamund—"

She glanced up then, knowing her eyes were blazing with a love she had only started to feel—a love that was being obliterated right there. "I won't be here when Eva or whomever you've chosen shows up for round two."

He flinched. "*Merda, Rosa.* Is that what you think of me? That I would welcome another female into my bed tonight?"

She didn't know, didn't care. But in that moment, all she wanted to do was hurt him as much as he'd just hurt her. "You are a barbarian, Scarus Vipera. An Incubus. As you say, it is exactly who you are."

She left him then, walked past him and out the door, her newly released heart breaking.

# CHAPTER TWELVE

The tiny San Francisco apartment felt stunningly large compared to the anteroom she'd lived in for the past year at the Harem. But at least, inside of it and outside of it, she could be herself.

Whoever that was, she mused with a snort as she ran a line of tape across the box that held her dishes. Rosamund had been back home for only a few days, but in that time she'd managed to talk with Roger—whose wife was lovely and perfect for him—quit her job and decide that a new apartment and a new town were in order. She was going to head down the coast, maybe check out Pescadero or Santa Barbara. Nothing was holding her here anymore. Nothing was holding her anywhere, frankly.

Nothing hadn't even tried to contact her in the past two days.

She kicked the box of dishes, then cursed when she heard something break. *Get over it, Rosamund. What happened in the Harem wasn't real. He wasn't real.*

Armed with her tape dispenser, she moved on to another box. That was her go-to mantra now. Pretending that her time with Scarus was a fantasy she'd made up in her head. After all, it could happen. A delusion brought on by those nightly sex dreams.

Leaning over, she placed the tape on one side of the box, and was about to pull it across when she spotted something white peeking up at her. Her heart sank. The takchita. The one she'd come to him as her true self in. The one she'd kissed him in, fought with him in, slept in, and woke up in. Woke up with him between her legs, doing things she'd only dreamt about.

Her throat tight, she reached in and fingered the diaphanous fabric. So soft. Without Constance's knowledge, she'd packed it away with her belongings before leaving the Harem. She'd just wanted something...

Tears pricked at her eyes and she closed them. Oh, no, that wasn't good either. Flashes of him wreaked havoc on her mind, on the insides of her eyelids. Tall, broad, dangerous, soulful, shameless...

So it was real. Him. Them. So what? Hearts were broken every day. Whether they were human or Nephilim or...

Oh, that bastard barbarian.

She stuffed the dress back into the box and was just about to close it when there was a knock at the door. She swiped at her eyes. The movers were here. They didn't need to see another post break-up scenario. No doubt they'd seen plenty in their time.

"I'll be right there," she called.

She finished taping the box, then hurried to the door. "I still have a bunch of boxes to close up," she said, pulling the door wide. "But you can take the fridge down first."

"*Buongiorno*, Rosa."

That voice. It tore her apart. Made her weak and...wet. But that face and those eyes—those eyes that could look straight into her—it wasn't fair. For two days, she'd tried to convince herself he wasn't real. Or at the very least that he was a jerk who had murdered her heart and needed to be forgotten immediately. But here he was. Filling up her doorway. Looking like the ultimate sex demon that he was, in a perfectly cut dark gray suit, black tie and devilish expression.

His eyes shifted to the boxes behind her. "Are you moving?"

"I am," she said, finally locating her voice.

When he turned back to face her, his eyes were like two boiling pools of liquid gold. "Where are you going, Rosamund?"

"Away," she told him nonchalantly, though her heart was beating so fast and painful inside her chest she was afraid she might give herself a stroke.

"That's not an answer. I will know where you are going." His brow arched severely. "And with whom."

*With whom?* Was he serious? Suddenly indignant, she forgot all about being nervous or stunned to see him. "I'm no Incubus, Scarus. I don't leave one male's bed only to jump into another's."

"I should hope not." His mouth twitched with a touch of amusement then, and he gazed down at her through his lashes. "May I come in?"

Her skin tingled. Damn him. Damn that voice and those eyes. She backed away from the door. "Fine." Then watched him as he moved inside, every step a lesson in predatory grace. Goddess, there was no one who could fill out a suit like him. "Why are you here, Scarus?"

Once he'd checked out her very small studio apartment, he turned to face her. "I've come to ask you on a date."

Nothing. She just stared at him. There was absolutely nothing that had prepared her for him to say that. "A date?"

"I realize this is unprecedented for one of my kind," he acknowledged thoughtfully.

"Yes, it is."

He exhaled heavily, even gave her a small shrug. "But so was what happened in the Harem, Rosamund."

Her heart gave a little kick. She tried to read him. Was he talking about her? About them? Or what had happened later, after she'd walked out of the suite. "Yes, how was the Harem?" she asked cautiously. "After I left, of course. Did you get your fill of Nephilim?"

He stared at her for a moment, his eyes soft. Then he walked over and put a hand around her waist. "There were no other Nephilim, *bella*. There was never going to be. You refused to listen to me on that subject." He reached up and touched her face, ran his thumb across her lower lip. "I wanted no other then, just as I want no other now."

Her throat went tight again. His words... Oh, how she wanted them to be real. "Then why did you go to Constance?" she asked. "Why did you tell her I wasn't your choice? We could've been together."

"Yes," he said, his jaw tightening. "And then you would've had to remain at the Harem. I couldn't allow another male to touch you." He leaned in and kissed the lower lip he had just been stroking. "Only me, Rosa."

Melting. Goddess, she was melting. "But you wanted me to have my freedom too?"

"Yes." He looked deeply into her eyes. "Freedom to choose me, as I have chosen you."

"You're an Incubus, Scarus." Her eyes clung to his. "You said you can't give me—"

He covered her mouth then with a hungry kiss, lapping at her tongue, then pulling back and nipping at her lip. "I told you home and family was rarely done," he uttered fiercely. "I told you losing my son nearly broke me."

"A son?" Rosamund said on a gasp.

Grief flickered in his eyes. "Nico."

"Oh, Scarus."

"But I want it, *bella*. I want it with you."

It was as if her heart broke wide open at his words, and a hundred butterflies emerged. Their little, soft wings healing every inch of her heart. She felt light. She felt seen and known and understood.

Scarus gathered her in his arms. "So, *mia bella*, what do you say to our date tonight? The first of many, I hope."

Blinking away tears, she smiled. "I say yes."

He returned her smile broadly, chuffed. "Then come with me now. We must hurry."

"It's nine a.m., Scarus," she said on a laugh.

"We have a ways to travel. My plane is waiting for us at the airport."

A whirlwind of emotions were whipping through her. Fifteen minutes ago, she was boxing up her life, and now…she was running off to… "Where is this date? And please don't say Morocco," she added with a laugh.

He sobered, even growled slightly. "You and I are never going there again. No. We are headed home."

Her heart stuttered. "Home?"

"Ravello."

"Italy?"

He nodded. "The Vipera Gallery opening is tonight. I wish for you to accompany me, Rosa. See where I have come from. See my passions, my land. See that I can not only give you my heart, but provide you and our young a safe, comfortable home." His eyes softened. "You told me you never claimed a last name. I am offering you mine."

Tears flowed freely down her cheeks now. She couldn't believe what she was hearing. But this wasn't a dream or a false memory to protect her heart. It didn't need protecting anymore. "Oh, Scarus…"

"I am a barbarian, true," he said, holding her close, one hand caressing her back. "But I would be your barbarian if you'll have me."

For years, she had lived a half life. Aching for something real, something lasting, something outside of her world. Here he was. The barbarian, the bastard, the master of seduction—and the ruler of her heart. And he'd just claimed her. Forever.

"Will you have me as your mate, Rosamund?" he said, his eyes darkening with emotion.

"Yes, Scarus," she cried passionately, lovingly, truthfully, snuggling deeper into his formidable chest. "I will have you. Your name, your children and your heart."

"Then let us go home, *bella*."

Home.

*Casa.*

It was a dream no more.

~ * ~

# ABOUT THE AUTHOR

*New York Times* and USA Today Bestselling Author **LAURA WRIGHT** is passionate about romantic fiction. Though she has spent most of her life immersed in acting, singing and competitive ballroom dancing, when she found the world of writing and books and endless cups of coffee she knew she was home. To Laura, writing is much like motherhood – tough, grueling, surprising, delicious, and a dream come true. Born and raised in Minnesota, she has a deep love of all things green, wet and grown in the ground.

Laura is the author of the bestselling Mark of the Vampire series, the USA Today bestselling series, Bayou Heat, which she co-authors with Alexandra Ivy, and the *New York Times* bestselling Wicked Ink Chronicles series. Laura lives in Los Angeles with her husband, two young children and two loveable dogs.

She loves hearing from her readers, and can be reached by email at laura@laurawright.com or visit her website at **www.LauraWright.com**.

# RUTHLESS
## House of Xanthe

# Alexandra Ivy

# CHAPTER ONE

Jian, the Master of the House of Xanthe, stood at the edge of the barren, uninhabited island in the middle of the Arctic Ocean. He grimaced as he studied the jagged mountain of blue ice that soared toward the sky.

Despite the weak sunlight, the breeze was edged with a lethal chill and beneath his feet the ground trembled as the ice abruptly split open. Only his swift leap to the side prevented him from tumbling into the deep fissure that formed.

Not the first place anyone would willingly choose to spend the night.

Not even a demon.

Thankfully, Jian wasn't just any demon.

As a powerful Incubus, he could not only compel others with the force of his sexual enchantment, but he was physically impervious to the brutal elements. He also possessed the unique ability to see through magical illusions.

Which was why he was the current Master of House Xanthe.

Unlike other Incubi Houses, Xanthe didn't accumulate their wealth through vineyards, or sprawling hotel chains, or sex clubs.

No, their profitable spice trade had been destroyed, and worse, their lands stripped away, after Jian's grandfather had stood against the House of Marakel and been labeled a traitor by the Council. Now Xanthe depended on their own skills to rebuild their empire.

Two of Jian's younger brothers were expert assassins who offered death for an obscene price. And a handful of cousins sold themselves as mercenaries for other Incubi.

But it was Jian's ability to gather and collect information that was slowly returning Xanthe to its position among the most respected Houses.

There was nothing in this world, or any other, that paid quite so well as secrets.

A wry smile twisted his lips as he recalled the extremely large fortune that had just been transferred into his account from a human politician who preferred to keep his habit of siphoning funds from his elderly donors from hitting the front page.

"This is a bad idea," Taka growled.

Jian turned his head to study the large Incubus standing next to him.

The captain of Xanthe's Watchmen, Taka looked exactly like what he was—a ruthless killer. Dressed in leather pants and a T-shirt despite the frigid air, he was as large as an ox, with bluntly carved features and a smoothly shaved skull. His skin was tanned to a rich mahogany, and his arms, which bulged with muscle, were tattooed with the Xanthe House emblem of a warrior.

Jian, on the other hand, was built along leaner

lines, with the sleek muscles of a trained swordsman.

His skin was a smooth, unblemished honey and his straight blue-black hair was cut short on the sides, with the top long enough to fall over his wide forehead. He had a thin blade of a nose and high, narrow cheekbones that whispered of his Far Eastern heritage. His face was lean, with eyes that were faintly tilted and glowed like melted gold in the sunlight.

At the moment, he was dressed in the traditional white robe that was expected from a petitioner to the Obsidian Throne. Not that he intended to be seen, but it was always better to be safe than sorry.

"So you've said," he drawled. Taka had been bitching about their journey since they stepped into his private jet that had been waiting for Jian in Hong Kong. "With tedious regularity."

"I just want it on the record," Taka insisted, one of the very few who would dare speak to Jian with such familiarity. "This is a very bad idea."

"Duly noted," Jian murmured, his gaze returning to the top of the mountain where a massive stone structure was disguised behind thick layers of demon magic.

The forbidding fortress had been specifically built to protect the Obsidian Throne, the ultimate symbol of power in the demon world. As well as the Sovereign, the leader of the Incubi, who sat on the Throne.

At least…the House of Marakel was the *current* leader of the Incubi.

Jian clenched his hands at his side, a blast of fury searing away the deep freeze.

It'd taken centuries, but at last the rest of the world was beginning to suspect what Jian's grandfather had always known.

The Master of Marakel couldn't be trusted.

"Then let's go home." Taka broke into his dark thoughts, glaring at their bleak surroundings despite the fact he was as impervious as Jian to the frigid weather.

"I've been hired to perform a job, Taka," Jian reminded his guard, his voice soft but filled with a dark power that could make a woman fall to her knees in ecstasy or a man tremble with fear. "To walk away would jeopardize my reputation and put the future of our House at risk."

"You would have your life."

"My honor has more value," he reminded Taka. Xanthe House had been forced to pay a steep price for his grandfather's refusal to kneel before the Throne. He wasn't going to throw it all away because his path had become unexpectedly dangerous. "To all of us."

Taka gave a grudging nod. "Fine. Then at least allow me to go in first."

Jian arched a brow. "You are a formidable warrior, Taka, but you have no talent in seeing through illusions. You would set off any alarm that has been hidden."

Taka's expression hardened, his frustration vibrating through the air.

"Why the hell do you have me as a Watchman when you won't let me protect you?"

"Your charming personality."

"Fuck off."

Jian gave a short laugh before returning his attention to the gray fortress with its thick walls and heavy turrets.

"Do you sense anything?" he demanded.

Taka tilted back his head, allowing his acute senses to scan their surroundings.

"No. It feels…" He paused, as if baffled by the desolate emptiness that surrounded them. "Abandoned."

Jian nodded. He was equally wary of the lack of overt activity.

Surely there should be dozens, if not hundreds, of servants and guests filling the fortress?

"Wait here," he muttered, lifting his arms as he prepared to use his power to travel through the layers of illusion, only to be halted as Taka placed a hand on his shoulder.

"Master, wait."

Jian bit back a curse, appreciating his Watchman's concern even as he wanted to be done with this latest job.

"We have to discover the truth, Taka," he said. "Not just because I was hired by Vipera to track down the Sovereign, but because we have to know if the Nephilim have truly been destroying the Succubi. Not to mention where the newest Council members have been hiding." His jaw clenched with a renewed burst of anger. "And most importantly if the authority of the Obsidian Throne is being used as a weapon against the Incubi."

Taka grimaced. "Marakel might be a power-hungry bastard, but you can't believe he would destroy his own people?"

Jian didn't hesitate. "After five hundred years on the Throne I think he would sacrifice the world to maintain his position as the Sovereign."

Taka reluctantly loosened his grip, his body rigid as he struggled against his instinct to prevent Jian from walking into danger.

"You have twenty minutes," he grudgingly offered. "A second longer and I'm coming after you."

Jian's lips twitched at the rough words. "Remind me again who is Master."

The dark eyes narrowed. "Twenty minutes."

Jian conceded defeat. Why push the issue? In twenty minutes he'd either have found the information he needed or he would be dead.

And just in case it was the latter...

"If I don't return, you'll need to get word to my brother," he warned his companion. "The Sovereign will most certainly retaliate against our House if I'm discovered."

Taka slowly nodded. "Take care."

Without offering the Watchman another opportunity to halt him, Jian gave a wave of his slender hand, disappearing in a swirl of demon magic.

There was the sense of shifting through dimensions before Jian was reforming in an antechamber just off the reception hall that he'd deliberately chosen before leaving his home. The blueprints he'd discovered that revealed the original construction of the fortress might have been old, but he doubted anything had been changed in the past few millenniums.

He swiftly melded into the shadows of the empty room, pressing against the stone wall as he moved to peer out the open door.

Pausing, he absorbed the details of his surroundings.

The lofty echo of the nearby Throne Room. The moist, scented heat from the public baths. The whisper of silk from the private harem.

And...emptiness.

He frowned. He could sense less than a couple dozen servants spread throughout the massive fortress. And none of them had the power signature that would indicate the Sovereign.

So where the hell was Marakel?

Jian stepped out of the small room and moved through the catacomb of hallways that connected the public rooms with the private living quarters.

He wasn't certain what he expected to find. His research had turned up remarkably little information on the Sovereign over the past few decades. There were rumors he was desperately trying to produce a child, and that he'd bribed a younger brother of Canaan to change the name of the House of Romerac in exchange for putting Canaan in the Oubliette—the equivalent of demon purgatory.

But he couldn't discover any accounts of face-to-face meetings with the Sovereign in the past twenty years.

So was the bastard in hiding?

And even if he was, what had he done with the

large staff of Incubi who were specifically chosen from the various Houses to serve the Sovereign and protect the fortress?

He grimaced at the thick silence that hung like a shroud in the stifling air.

Clearly he wasn't going to discover anything by skulking in the shadows. It was time to take a more direct route.

Following the scent of the closest demon, Jian entered a large bedroom decorated with glazed mosaic tiles in brilliant shades of red, black, and gold. In the center of the room was a pile of satin pillows and at the far end was a silk screen that separated a shallow pool from the room.

Just across the floor from Jian, there was an arched doorway that led to a balcony that was framed by heavy pillars.

Or at least...

Jian narrowed his gaze, his breath hissing between his teeth.

An illusion.

Speaking a word of power, Jian shattered the magic, revealing that the doorway didn't lead to an open balcony, but instead into a thick darkness that sent a shudder of revulsion through him.

He couldn't see what was beyond the doorway, but he knew that it was another dimension.

Jian frowned. The Obsidian Throne had been created to block the doorway between Heaven and Hell. Was this the entryway it protected?

And if it was...why was it open?

Dread twisted his gut as he stepped forward, his concentration locked on the doorway even as he sensed the Blade move from a shallow alcove to stand directly in his path.

"Incubus," the female warrior spat out, her hand reaching to pull out a long, obsidian dagger.

Expecting one of the traditional honor guards, Jian narrowed his gaze as he studied the Nephilim dressed in a black linen tunic and loose pants with supple boots.

Her lean face was pretty and surrounded by a halo of pale golden curls, but Jian didn't miss the practiced ease of her movements, or the barely suppressed violence that smoldered in her eyes.

This was a well-trained warrior who was eager for a fight.

"Blade," he said with a mocking dip of his head. "Are you lost?"

The female flicked a dismissive glance over Jian, clearly unaware of his status.

"I was about to ask you the same question," she drawled.

Jian folded his arms over his chest. The obsidian dagger could kill him, but he wasn't the Master of his House simply for his ability to see through illusions.

There were fewer than a dozen demons strong enough to best in him battle.

And this Blade wasn't one of them.

"Why are you here?" he demanded, his voice a low tendril of seduction that brought a flush of anger to the female's face.

There were few things that could piss off a Blade more than forcing her to feel arousal toward her enemy.

"I'm a guard for the Sovereign," the Blade snapped.

Jian's brows snapped together. "Impossible. Only Watchmen serve as protectors to the Throne."

The female tried to sneer, but Jian sensed she was beginning to suspect that Jian was not just another Incubus.

"Obviously the Sovereign no longer trusts the Incubi to keep him safe."

"Careful, Blade." His voice lowered, threading pain with pleasure. "You wouldn't want to imply there are traitors among my people."

The female made a strangled sound, gripping the hilt of her weapon as if it could protect her from the sensations that were making her body twitch.

"Why else would they send an assassin?"

A cold smile curved Jian's lips. It wasn't uncommon for people to assume that anyone from the House of Xanthe was a paid killer.

And he'd dealt his share of death.

"Make no mistake, if I was here to kill you, you would be dead."

The Blade took an instinctive step backward even as she held up the dagger in a gesture of bravado.

"Don't threaten me, demon."

Jian shook his head.

So young.

And stupid.

"Not a threat…a promise." Jian's smile abruptly disappeared, the air sizzling with the force of his impatience. He had less than ten minutes before Taka would be charging into the fortress, stealing away any hope for discretion. "Take me to the Sovereign."

"He isn't here."

Jian clenched his hands, but he didn't argue. He'd already suspected that Marakel was absent from the fortress.

"Then where is he?"

"This is not a prison." The Blade shrugged. "The Sovereign is allowed to come and go as he pleases."

"Without his supposed bodyguard?" Jian taunted.

"I am but one of—"

The words were cut short as there was a sudden movement in the doorway.

Holy shit.

Someone, or something, had been about to step into the bedroom before they'd seemingly sensed that it wasn't empty and retreated back into the darkness.

Without hesitation Jian was moving forward. He didn't know what the hell was going on, but he was done screwing around.

He wanted answers. And he wanted them now.

Starting with the mysterious gateway.

"Stop." The Blade hastily moved to block the opening. "What are you doing?"

"Move aside or die."

"I'm not afraid of you."

"Idiot."

With a nonchalant motion, Jian knocked the

dagger from the younger female's hand. Then, wrapping his fingers around the Blade's throat, he lifted her off her feet and smashed the back of her head into the slender column.

There was a low grunt before the Blade crumpled to the floor in an unconscious heap. She was injured, but she would recover.

Stepping over the Nephilim warrior, Jian leaned down to grasp the obsidian dagger.

He paused long enough to strip off the robe to reveal the black jeans and T-shirt beneath before sending a brief text to Taka, ordering him to return to their homeland.

Then, with a grim determination he moved forward, allowing the darkness to consume him as he stepped through the doorway.

# CHAPTER TWO

Muriel was tired.

Not just physically, although the past days of enduring the abyss had taken a toll on her body. After all, even angels felt pain when they were dropped into a pit of flames that seared the flesh from their bones.

But she was also mentally and spiritually exhausted.

For five hundred and thirty years she'd been the Mistress of the Oubliette, a job forced on her by the Angel Conclave after she'd refused the mate that had been chosen by her family.

It was a punishment she'd accepted rather than being bound to a male who considered her nothing more than a suitable breeder.

Of course, when she'd accepted the punishment, she'd believed the promise that she would be purged of her shame and returned to her family at the end of two centuries.

Now, as the years continued to pass and the Conclave refused to answer her pleas to be released, she was beginning to accept that she'd been well and truly swindled.

Clearly her gig in the Oubliette was destined to

be an open-ended sort of deal…at least until some other angel was stupid enough to piss off the Conclave.

And worse, a week ago she'd allowed an Incubus to escape, which triggered her painful trip to the abyss.

Reaching a small cavern, she came to an abrupt halt, a tiny shiver racing over her skin.

Shit.

A demon had arrived in the Oubliette through the secret entrance.

Incubus.

But not the one she'd been commanded to allow free access to the lower dungeons.

With a low curse, she called on her protective illusion. Suddenly she was no longer an angel, but a creature with crimson skin and leathery bat-like wings that spread behind her. She had a long, slithery tail and eyes that could blind when she unleashed her powers.

If that wasn't hideous enough, she added the appearance of snakes twining around her body and the offensive stench of sulfur.

Flicking out her forked tongue, she tested the air, her claws scraping on the rock as she stood in the center of the chamber.

The Incubus was near, but somehow he was capable of hiding himself from her sight.

Muriel shivered, her mouth dry. Dammit. She was still weakened from her days of torture.

The last thing she needed was yet another Incubus causing her trouble.

"I can sense your presence, intruder. Reveal

yourself."

A brush of acute pleasure slid over her skin, her body suddenly filled with a molten heat.

"Not until you answer my questions." A dark, wickedly beautiful voice filled the cavern.

Muriel's breath lodged in her throat. She was an angel. She should be immune to the raw sensuality that was a tangible force in the air.

So why was her heart racing and her mind filled with images of black satin sheets and a hard, hot body pressed against hers?

"This is my house," she said between clenched teeth. "You don't give the orders here."

"So who does?"

She gave a flick of her imaginary tail. "I do."

"A lie," he whispered from the shadows.

Muriel stiffened, her gaze darting around the chamber in a desperate attempt to catch sight of the demon.

She'd just escaped from the abyss. She'd be damned if another Incubus managed to send her back to the agonizing flames.

"Who are you?"

"That depends," the sinful voice drawled. "Give me what I want and I promise to be your deepest fantasy. Defy me and I'll make you beg for mercy."

The whisper of bliss stroking her skin. A dark, sinful heat flowing through her blood. A flutter of excitement that made her pussy clench in anticipation...

Muriel battled to disguise her shiver of pleasure, even as she accepted this demon was more than a pain in her ass. He was capable of stirring the passions she'd buried centuries ago.

That made him a danger she couldn't tolerate.

Drawing in a deep breath, she ignored the warm scent of cinnamon and luscious male as she began to slowly back toward the opening at the far side of the cavern.

Hopefully he would assume that she was trying to covertly retreat from the blinding power of his seduction.

"I'll give you full credit for your arrogance," she mocked, spreading her wings as the mirage of snakes continued to crawl over her body. She needed to keep him distracted until he'd stepped into her trap. "Your intelligence, however, is obviously deficient."

His low chuckle wrapped around her like a silken caress, making her nipples bead with a sharp-edged longing.

Damn. It'd been so long since she'd been touched in anything but anger.

Too long.

"Trust me, I'm not lacking in anything."

Muriel felt the soft stroke of fingers down the slope of her shoulder.

Incubi magic, of course.

It had to be. She would know if the demon were that close to her.

Still, that didn't halt the searing lick of anticipation that spread through her body.

"Then why are you hiding from me?" she rasped.

"I've told you," the aggravating male murmured. "I want answers."

"Answers to what?"

"Why have you created a gateway into the fortress?"

Her mouth went dry as she continued to back toward the distant wall.

That was a question she had no intention of answering.

Instead she feigned confusion. "What fortress?"

Without warning a pulse of heat sizzled through the air as the Incubus abruptly stepped from the shadows.

"You want to play games, sweetheart?"

Muriel hissed, reeling beneath the impact of his beauty.

He was quite simply…magnificent.

Not the ethereal loveliness of male angels. Or the rough aggression of humans.

He was pure male temptation. A walking, talking invitation to sex.

Against her will, Muriel found her gaze lingering on the glossy darkness of his hair and the lean, finely sculpted features, before lowering to the slender, muscled body that made her fingers twitch with the urge to explore every hard inch.

Her heart raced as her gaze returned to his face, instantly ensnared by his golden eyes.

Oh heavens, those eyes…

They shimmered with the promise of pleasure beyond her wildest dreams.

She unconsciously halted her retreat, grimly focused on the effort not to melt at his feet in a puddle of aching need.

"I'm no man's sweetheart," she forced herself

to mutter. A reminder to herself of the danger of Incubi.

Females often became addicted to the demons.

And as much as it aggravated her, it was increasingly obvious she was not immune to this particular male.

"Not yet," he murmured, a smile playing around his lips as if he was aware of her helpless response to his sensual beauty. "Tell me about the gateway."

She sucked in a deep, steadying breath. "I didn't create it."

"Then who did?"

"The Sovereign," she admitted. Why lie? It wasn't as if the Incubus was ever getting out of this prison.

He frowned, as if caught off guard by her revelation. "Why would he want access to the Oubliette?"

She arched a brow. "He's your king. Why don't you ask him yourself?"

The golden eyes flared with heat. As if he wasn't pleased to be reminded he owed his allegiance to the Sovereign.

Hmmm…

Was there dissent among the Incubi?

"Because he seems to have disappeared."

She shrugged. "Not my problem."

"What does he do when he's here?"

"I don't know."

He stepped forward with a liquid grace, his expression tight with frustration.

"This is your territory. How can you not

know?"

"I was told he was to be given access to the lower dungeons, but it was made clear that I wasn't to interfere in his business."

His eyes narrowed. "Told by whom?"

The question managed to jolt Muriel out of her strange sense of enchantment. Damn, what was wrong with her?

Her skin was still raw and her muscles aching from her days in the abyss.

Did she truly want to risk another round of torture?

"Do you have a death wish?" she demanded, resuming her slow, backward journey across the cavern.

As she hoped, he followed her retreat, grimacing as if he sensed that she had no intention of revealing who gave her orders.

The dimensions between worlds were supposed to be neutral. The demons wouldn't be pleased to discover the angels had regained enough sway over the Obsidian Throne to claim these lands as their own.

"You wouldn't be the first person to ask me that question," he admitted in dry tones. "What's in the lower dungeons?"

"Fire. Brimstone." Another step backward. And another. "The usual."

"Anything else?"

"Caves."

"Are any of them occupied?"

Feeling her wings touch the chilled stone of the wall behind her, Muriel turned to the side so she could angle herself through the narrow opening.

"I can't keep track of every prisoner."

She forced herself to meet his hypnotic honey gaze as she silently willed him to join her in the small cavern.

There was a long pause, as if the Incubus was well aware he was being led into a trap. Then, with a speed that made her gasp, he was through the doorway and standing so close she could feel the heat of his body sear through her thin linen shift.

"Lie," he breathed, his fingers wrapping around her throat, an intense concentration etched on his beautiful face.

Dear heavens. Could he see through her layers of illusion?

No. Of course he couldn't.

It was impossible.

She licked her dry lips. "There are no prisoners that have been given into my tender care."

His thumb brushed the underside of her jaw, lingering on the frantic beat of her pulse.

"Is the Sovereign here now?"

She shivered at his gentle touch. If he'd tried to hurt her, she could have fought him.

But she had no defense against tenderness.

"Are you intending to kill him?" she demanded.

"On the contrary. I wish to assure myself he's alive and well."

"Lie," she retorted, throwing his word back in his face.

Whatever his interest in the Sovereign, it had nothing to do with concern for his welfare.

The honey eyes darkened at her taunt, the air

prickling with a dangerous hunger.

Was he thinking about sex or food?

Not that there was any difference between the two for an Incubus.

"I have questions only he can answer," he husked, his fingers drifting down to touch the sensitive joint where her wing met her shoulder blade. "And I have waited too long for answers."

The pleasure combusted through her with shocking force, wrenching a gasp from her throat.

"Stop that," she breathed.

Seemingly impervious to the mirage of snakes that were now slithering from her body onto the supple leather of his jacket, the Incubus traced the graceful slope of her wing.

"There's something going on." The warm smell of cinnamon filled the air. "Surely you can feel it."

Unable to halt her flare of panic, Muriel knocked aside his hand.

"I feel nothing," she hissed, wrapping her arms around her waist.

The golden eyes narrowed. "There's a vacuum."

"What sort of vacuum?" she snapped.

"Power."

A strange chill of premonition pierced Muriel's heart.

She would chop off her tongue before she would admit that he was right, but deep inside she'd suspected that there was a storm brewing.

The precarious balance between demons and angels had started to tilt.

Unless a leader emerged who could enforce the peace, war would be inevitable.

The mere thought made her stomach twist with dread.

"I suppose you intend to be the one to end up on top?" she instead taunted.

A dangerous smile curved the Incubus's lips as he allowed his sexual energy to pulse against her, the delicious sensations nearly making her orgasm on the spot.

"With you, Mistress, I'll top or bottom. Whatever makes you happy."

She felt drenched in the heat and scent of him.

She hissed in frustration, attempting to deny the piercing need that lashed through her.

Dammit. She'd been alone for so long.

So very long.

But she wasn't an idiot.

There was no way she was going to put herself at risk to satisfy her passion with a male who used sex as a weapon.

"There's only one way you can make me happy, Incubus."

The golden eyes smoldered with invitation. "Tell me."

She released the power that had come with her gig as Warden, shuddering in revulsion as she was transported back to the outer cavern. Without giving the intruder the opportunity to react to her abrupt disappearing act, Muriel slammed shut the thick iron door, trapping him in the cramped space.

"Seeing you locked in a cell," she breathed.

The Incubus slowly turned, his smile never fading as he studied her through the narrow window cut into the door.

"Bravo." He folded his arms over his chest, his expression amused. "But do you truly think you can keep me your prisoner, sweet angel?"

# CHAPTER THREE

Jian strolled forward so he could peer out the window cut into the door.

Any other time he would have felt annoyed at being lured into the cell. Not that he couldn't get out. He could sense a number of servants roaming through the lower tunnels. With a burst of his power he could lure any or all of them to this cavern to unlock the door. Still, it was a waste of time and energy.

But Jian wasn't annoyed.

Instead he was fascinated.

It'd been centuries since the angels freely walked in the world, but there was no mistaking that beneath the Mistress of the Oubliette's hideous illusion was a female of such ethereal beauty she couldn't possibly be anything but a celestial being.

She was glorious.

Her hair was a tumble of curls the precise color of sterling silver. Her small face was heart-shaped, with delicately carved features that were dominated by a pair of deep indigo eyes.

Her body was a slender masterpiece barely hidden beneath a plain linen dress that was backless to give room for the exquisite wings that were a pure, snowy white.

And her scent…

Jian sucked in a deep, savoring breath.

She smelled of the ivory and gold orchids that bloomed in his private gardens.

Rare, exotic…delicately flawless.

It enticed him like a bee to honey.

He wanted to taste her from the top of her silvery hair to the tips of her rosy toes that were left bare despite the jagged rocks throughout the prison. He wanted to spread her across his bed and watch her ivory skin flush with the heat of passion.

A dangerous reaction. He was an Incubus. He used sex for food, for pleasure, and quite often as a weapon. Which meant he fully understood the power of desire.

This female was the first creature capable of clouding his mind with need.

Was it any wonder he was so captivated?

A wry smile curved his lips as she peered through the opening, her expression defiant despite the wariness he could sense humming through her.

"How did you know I'm an angel?"

"One of my many talents is seeing through illusions." He unleashed a small thread of power, wrapping a tendril of sexual heat around her. "Release me and I'll share my other talents."

She sucked in a sharp breath, shuddering in reaction before she narrowed her gaze and countered with her own magic.

"I have a few talents of my own," she assured him, her expression hard as the sensation of a thousand knives plunged into his body.

Jian hissed, but he managed to stay upright as he sent out another burst of energy.

"I prefer pleasure to pain, sweetheart."

She jerked backwards, her eyes dilating with an arousal she couldn't control.

Jian's smile widened. She was a pureblooded angel, not a Nephilim. Which meant she should have a small amount of resistance to his seduction.

Her reaction wasn't all magic.

At least a portion of it was raw and primal and completely natural.

Just like his.

"Stop," she breathed.

"Make me."

She gave a sharp shake of her head, wrapping her arms around her waist as she allowed her power to fade.

"Tell me why you're here."

He grimaced. Not just in relief as the pain faded, but at the timely reminder of why he was there. As much as he wanted to lose himself in his scorching reaction to this angel, he had to discover if his people were in danger.

"I told you." His pressed his hands against the iron door. "I'm looking for the Sovereign."

"I'm sure there are a lot of petitioners who want to see him," she pointed out. "Most would have waited for him to return to the fortress, not followed him through the gates of the Oubliette."

"I think he's betrayed the Incubi."

She stilled, her expression unreadable. "Why?"

"Take me to the lower dungeons and we'll discover what he's hiding."

There was a long pause. Then, with an obvious effort, she gave a dismissive wave of her hand.

"I have no interest in your world."

"Yet another lie," he countered smoothly. He hadn't missed her ease with the current vocabulary. "You've obviously studied our culture."

Her lips tightened in annoyance at his perception. "So what? Human television helps to pass the time."

He chuckled. "Let me guess. Hmm. The Real Housewives? Storage Wars? No wait...The Playboy Channel?"

A revealing blush touched her cheeks. "None of your business," she snapped.

"Ah, my naughty angel, you're pure temptation. Once I've completed my current job I intend to devote myself to fulfilling every one of your fantasies."

"There are no fantasies, Incubus. And your job has come to an end." She met his gaze squarely. "I have no stake in who sits upon the Obsidian Throne."

True. Still, he sensed that she was more interested in the Sovereign and what he was doing in her dungeons than she wanted to admit.

"But they've intruded into your realm. Can you be certain that this doesn't affect you?"

She bit her bottom lip, clearly forgetting that he could see through her illusion to witness her revealing gesture of unease.

"Why should I trust you?" she abruptly demanded. "For all I know you were sent to lead me into a trap."

It was a legitimate question. Unfortunately, he didn't have the time to convince her he could be trusted.

Instead he abruptly lashed out with his power, filling the air with his magic.

Tiny pulses of sexual compulsion swirled through the cavern and spread through the tunnels, urging the captives to escape from the cells and rush to his side.

"I could force this entire prison into revolt, but I prefer not to," he said softly.

"Don't," she rasped, a layer of sweat dampening her face as she battled to control the swelling desperation of the prisoners who were struggling to break out of their cells. At the same time she slammed him with the sensation of flames searing the flesh from his bones.

His entire body clenched with agony, his hands pressed against the door as his knees threatened to collapse.

Shit. She looked so damned fragile it was easy to forget she was an angel with immense power.

"Truce," he ground out, barely suppressing his groan of relief when the waves of pain began to recede.

"I—" Whatever she was about to say was abruptly cut short as she glanced over her shoulder. "Someone's coming."

Jian muttered a low curse as he caught the familiar scent of a Nephilim.

"Blade," he growled.

She sent him a narrow-eyed glare. "Your partner?"

"She was guarding the entrance. I knocked her out to get in here." Jian shook his head in disgust. "I should have killed the bitch."

"A convenient story."

He went rigid as an unexpected surge of fear shot through him. This female might be an angel, but she was clearly bound by her role as Warden.

What if the Blade had a weapon capable of hurting her?

Or worse...

"I can give you proof," he offered, his voice laced with compulsion.

She shivered, but her expression remained wary. "How?"

"Release me and—"

"No."

"Dammit." He grimly leashed his strange unease. The female clearly resented any attempt to try and tell her what to do. A true pain in the ass, considering Jian had no experience in having to actually use a logical argument when it came to a woman. He was an Incubus, for fuck's sake. "Can you shroud me?"

More wariness. "Why?"

He sucked in a slow breath.

*Patience, Jian. Patience.*

"If you won't allow me to question the Nephilim, then you'll have to do it."

Her lips twisted. "Or I could kill you both."

"And deprive yourself of the pleasure of torturing me?"

She paused before giving a wave of her hand, no doubt hiding the door behind a layer of illusion.

"There is that," she muttered. "Keep your mouth shut."

"Your wish is my command, pretty angel," he whispered softly.

~ ~ ~

Muriel squared her shoulders as she turned to move toward the center of the cavern.

The Incubus unsettled her. Not just because he could stir sensations that were better left unstirred. Although that was bad enough.

But he made her confront the questions that had been lurking in the back of her mind.

Why had the Conclave agreed to allow the Sovereign to enter the Oubliette without her permission as the Warden?  Why the lack of outrage that there was an open gateway into the world of mortals and demons?  Why the refusal to hear her petition to return to her family?

There was something going on...

And after years of trying to pretend that she wasn't caught in the middle, this Incubus was forcing her to accept she was being deliberately blind.

She couldn't ignore the truth any longer.

Squaring her shoulders, she conjured a long whip that she gripped in one hand. It was no more real than her façade of a red-skinned monster, but she could make her victim feel as if the leather was slicing through their flesh.

That's all that mattered.

There was barely a sound as the Nephilim

entered the chamber, her lean body dressed in black linen with a halo of curls around her too-pretty face.

The female's gaze widened as she caught sight of Muriel's gruesome illusion, a hint of fear flashing through her eyes as she came to an abrupt halt. Then, clearly annoyed that she'd revealed her unease, she made a visible attempt to regain command of her composure.

"Where is the Incubus?" she demanded, pasting an arrogant sneer onto her face.

Muriel gave a crack of her whip, smiling as the intruder flinched.

"How dare you enter this realm uninvited?"

The young female gripped the dagger in her hand, as if she thought Muriel would be intimidated by the obsidian blade. Of course, the demon couldn't know she was an angel.

The Warden was supposed to be randomly chosen.

"I'm here to retrieve an intruder."

"I deal with trespassers in the Oubliette." Her claws scraped on the stone floor as she stepped forward. "I don't need your assistance."

The Nephilim forced herself to hold her ground. "This has nothing to do with you, female," she growled. "Step aside."

Muriel spread her illusion of leathery wings. "Are you truly that stupid? No one tells me what to do in this place." She flicked a dismissive gaze over the Blade. "Especially not a mere servant."

The intruder stiffened in outrage. "I'm not a servant. I'm a Blade and protector of the

Sovereign."

She gave a sharp laugh. "Should I be impressed?"

"I have safe passage."

Muriel bared her pointed teeth, not having to pretend to be pissed at her claim.

"I was ordered to allow the Sovereign access to the lower chambers," she snarled. "Not to grant access to every Nephilim who decides to stroll through my territory."

"Ask the Sovereign—" The belligerent expression was wiped away as Muriel gave a flick of her whip, slicing a deep wound down the front of the Blade's torso. The female stumbled backward in pain. "Arrgg."

"I don't think so," Muriel informed her. "I recently lost one of my prisoners. You will do nicely as a replacement."

The female pressed a hand to her bloody chest. "The Sovereign—"

She gave another flick of the whip, snapping it a mere breath from the tip of her nose.

"Has no authority here."

The Blade took another stumbling step backward. "But he has connections with people who do."

"What connections?"

She licked her lips. "They're powerful."

"And you think they'll protect you?"

"Of course." Lick, lick, lick.

"No you don't." Muriel studied the sweat beginning to bead the female's forehead. "You might be an arrogant fool, but you can't be completely stupid. You know that once they discover you've been captured they'll leave you here to rot."

The Blade's face drained to a pasty shade of ecru. Not an attractive shade on anyone.

"No," she breathed, her brief attempt at courage shattering at Muriel's harsh reminder she was no more than expendable fodder. "Please."

"Please what?" Muriel ground home her advantage.

The Blade pressed back against the wall, blood still dripping from her wound.

"Let me go."

Muriel deliberately stepped close enough to touch her whip against the female's throat.

"Not so brave now you realize you might actually die for your cause?"

The Nephilim gave a squeak of terror. Nothing like the threat of death to gain unwavering attention.

"What do you want from me?"

Muriel pretended to give the question serious thought. "Blood. Pain. Eventual death," she at last responded.

"My family has money."

She could hear the sound of the Nephilim's pounding heart.

"And what use would I have for money?"

"There must be something I can barter."

She smiled. Now they were getting somewhere.

"There is." She assured the Blade. "The truth."

"The truth about what?"

Muriel resisted the urge to glance over her

shoulder. She didn't have to look at the door she'd concealed with illusions to feel the hot, disturbing gaze of her prisoner.

Her awareness of the male was an acute, relentless pulse deep inside.

A knowledge that unnerved her on a primal level.

With a grim effort, she forced herself to concentrate on the female regarding her with a wary gaze.

"Tell me about the Incubus you're chasing," she commanded.

A remembered anger tightened the Blade's thin face. "He attacked me and entered the gateway. He's a traitor to the Sovereign."

"A traitor?"

"Yes." The female curled her hands into tight fists. "Allow me to return him to our world and I can promise he'll be punished."

Hmm. It seemed the Incubus had told the truth about his relationship with the Blade.

Not that she was ready to trust him.

Right now, she'd be a fool to trust anyone.

"And the Sovereign?"

The demon frowned. "I don't understand."

"Why does he come to the Oubliette?"

The Nephilim sucked in a breath at the unexpected question, her expression resembling a cornered rat.

"I...I don't know."

The whip was a blur of movement as it sliced through the bitch's cheek.

"Wrong answer," she warned, her voice soft.

"Wait." The female lifted a hand to try and stem the newest flow of blood. It was a shallow cut, but the Nephilim couldn't disguise her terror. It wasn't going to take any talent to convince her to talk. It was almost a shame. Muriel was very good at her job. "He has prisoners he can't allow to be discovered."

Muriel frowned. Prisoners?

It was, of course, the obvious explanation, but somehow it still managed to catch her off guard.

"Why would he need to hide prisoners?" she demanded. "Isn't he the leader of the Incubi? He surely has his own dungeons to contain his enemies?"

"Because they—"

The words came to a shockingly abrupt end at the explosive sound of a gunshot echoing through the cavern.

Muriel flinched, and then cursed, as the silver bullet skimmed directly over the arch of her wing and slammed into the Nephilim's forehead, killing her mid-sentence.

Grimacing as the dead Blade slid to the floor with a sickening thud, she slowly turned to confront the shadowed form that filled the entrance to the cavern.

A chill inched down her spine as she studied the figure heavily shrouded in thick, woolen robes, his face hidden in the darkness of his hood.

"Forgive me," a mocking male voice drawled. "But I fear my servant was about to be indiscrete."

She spread her wings, forcing her imaginary lips into a smile that displayed her pointed teeth.

"The Sovereign, I presume?"

The gun in his hand swiveled to point directly at her heart.

"You were warned to stay out of my business."

"Don't threaten me," Muriel snapped, even as she wrinkled her nose at the peculiar odor that tainted the air.

It wasn't the rich, addictive aroma she associated with most Incubi.

This was sour...like an overripe fruit.

Was the Sovereign sick? Or perhaps it was the stench of madness.

"You think I fear you?" he drawled.

She gave a flick of her whip, more of a taunt than a threat.

The Incubus might have been given the freedom to enter the Oubliette, but she remained the Warden. To harm her would be a direct violation of the fragile peace between Incubi and angels.

"Everyone fears me."

The gun remained aimed directly at her heart. "Where's the Incubus my Blade was tracking?"

She shrugged, ignoring the growing frustration she could sense from the trapped Incubus. Instead, she added another layer of illusion to mute his sharp demand to be released from his cell.

The idiot was going to get himself killed.

"The Oubliette is vast," she murmured. "He could be anywhere."

There was an echoing blast and then the agonizing sensation of a bullet tearing through her upper chest.

Pain combined with shock to send her reeling backwards, the silver bullet that was now lodged in her shoulder blade pumping its toxin through her bloodstream.

Oh…crap.

Her lips went numb as her knees gave way and she collapsed onto the hard ground.

"I'm afraid I don't have time for games," the male informed her in cold tones, moving forward to stand over her. "Where is the Incubus?"

She blinked, her gaze fuzzy.

"You will die for this," she rasped.

"I don't think so," he said, a genuine lack of concern in his flat voice as he once again pulled the trigger. A second vicious pain ripped through her as the bullet sliced through her body to lodge in the ground beneath her. "My new partners made it clear you were expendable if you tried to poke your very ugly snout into my business."

The excruciating pain was forgotten as Muriel sucked in a harsh breath.

"You lie," she growled, even as doubt seeped through her, as venomous and agonizing as the silver that continued to poison her.

She'd already suspected that the Conclave was deliberately ignoring her petition to be returned to her family. And that they were using the Sovereign for their own nefarious purpose.

But would they truly allow an angel to be murdered by a demon?

Her mind rejected the mere thought, but her heart whispered that she'd been betrayed.

"Give me the Incubus," the Sovereign snapped,

his face still hidden in the shadow of his hood.

"I..." She lost track of her words as an urgent voice screamed through her mind, using enough compulsion to force her to listen.

"Angel, release me."

Her prisoner.

Her Incubus.

Yes...*hers.*

With the last of her strength, Muriel dropped the illusion and released the lock that held the Incubus trapped in his cell.

Then she waited to die.

# CHAPTER FOUR

Jian was slamming his body against the cell door when it abruptly popped open.

Goddammit.

He'd never felt such a helpless desperation as he'd watched his beautiful angel crumple to the floor, a scarlet stain spreading across her chest and dripping onto the pure white of her wings.

The mere thought he would be forced to watch her die had horrified him in a deep, unfamiliar place.

As if he'd known that he would be irreparably damaged if he lost this female.

Now, as the door swung open, he stumbled to regain his balance and charged toward the heavily robed figure standing over the collapsed angel.

He didn't need to see the male's face to know who he was.

The Sovereign.

The soon-to-be-dead Master of the House of Marakel.

Without hesitation, Jian was sprinting across the cavern, slashing the obsidian dagger through the male's back.

He didn't give a shit that the Incubus was his

leader. Or that he was choosing an angel over a fellow demon. He would happily destroy anyone or anything that threatened his female.

The Sovereign grunted in pain, instinctively darting to the side to avoid another strike. At the same time he twisted and fired the gun over his shoulder. Jian was forced to duck as the bullet whizzed past his face, giving the bastard an opening to run toward the entrance.

Jian cursed, telling himself to follow the retreating male.

The obsidian blade had wounded the male, but it hadn't been a killing blow. If he didn't halt the Sovereign now he would return to the fortress and surround himself with his guards.

Jian might never have another opportunity to force him to talk.

But even as logic was urging him into action, he was dropping to his knees besides the delicate angel, his heart twisting with fear.

Oh hell. He gently brushed the tangled golden curls from her cheek as he studied the blood that continued to seep from her wounds. At least one bullet still had to be inside her, blocking her ability to heal the damage.

"Stay with me, angel," he murmured softly, cupping her cheek in his palm as she released a rattling sigh.

"He shot me."

He deliberately kept his expression unreadable, disguising the fury that thundered through him.

Eventually the Sovereign would pay for his sins. For now, all that mattered was ensuring this angel wasn't permanently harmed.

"I'm going to take care of you," he assured her.

Her body spasmed, her beautiful face tight with pain.

"Silver…"

"I know."

With exquisite caution, he wiggled his arms beneath her slender form, cradling her against his chest as he rose to his feet.

She felt warm and fragile against him, the soft wings drooping so low he had to take care not to step on them.

He briefly considered returning to his world so he could take them both to the protection of his home. No one would dare to try and harm her there. But the knowledge that he couldn't be confident that the Sovereign wouldn't be waiting for him at the entrance had him instead turning toward the far side of the cavern.

He couldn't risk being attacked when his angel was so weak.

Besides, he didn't have any idea if forcing her to leave the Oubliette would harm her. She was the current Mistress, which might mean she was bound to this hellhole.

Leaving the cavern, he carried the barely conscious female through a tunnel, using his talents to see through the elaborate illusions. Still, it took a tense quarter of an hour of darting from cave to cave as he struggled to avoid the servants, as well as the prisoners who screamed in constant agony, to at last find the narrow stairs carved into stone.

With slow, carefully measured motions, he

climbed to the top, discovering a hidden cavern that was lit by torchlight.

This had to belong to his beautiful angel.

Not only was it disguised behind thick layers of illusion, but it had been furnished in an effort to ease the stark bleakness.

A handwoven carpet was spread over the stone floor, with a massive bed set in the center. The walls were covered by colorful tapestries. And in one corner there was a small dresser with a stool arranged front of the oval mirror.

His lips twitched.

So his angel had a streak of vanity beneath her illusion of a hideous monster.

The knowledge was oddly charming.

"Can you lock us in?" he demanded, kicking the door shut with his foot.

She gave a slow nod. "Yes." There was the faint sound of a click as she mentally triggered the lock, her pained gaze never wavering from his face. "How did you find my rooms? I have them hidden."

"The prison is built on illusions," he reminded her, moving directly toward the bed. "I could sense the tunnels you tried to disguise."

"Oh. I forgot." A shaky breath hissed between her lips. "It hasn't been my finest day."

Bending forward, he placed her in the center of the mattress, his chest so tight he could barely breathe as he smoothed her wings and brushed her hair from her ashen face.

Lying against the bright blue blanket she looked like a broken doll, her ivory and silver beauty marred by the garish red blood that had spread across her upper body.

With a silent pledge to make the Sovereign suffer for every second this female was in pain, he reached down to grasp the neckline of the linen shift. Then, with one careful tug, he had it split in half.

Heat sizzled in the air as he pulled off the ruined garment. His only concern was healing the angel as quickly as possible, but he was an Incubus, not a saint.

The sight of her naked body was enough to make his mouth water and his body harden with instant arousal.

Besides, his ability to heal her came from the direct source of his magic.

Skin to skin.

Pleasure to pleasure.

With a swift efficiency, Jian stripped off his clothing and cautiously stretched out beside her, his heart skipping a beat as he felt the downy softness of feathers pressed against his bare skin.

Who knew that wings would be so deliciously erotic?

"I assure you it's about to get a whole lot better," he whispered, rolling onto his side to meet her wary gaze. "Give me your name."

She licked her dry lips, the scent of orchids thick in the air.

"Why?"

His fingers brushed her cheek, his concern deepening at the growing chill of her skin.

He had to get the bullet out.

"It deepens our connection, so I can heal you," he said.

There was a split second hesitation before her name floated from her lips, as soft as a promise.

"Muriel."

It was...perfect.

"Beautiful, Muriel," he breathed, his fingers tracing the lush curve of her mouth. "My name is Jian, Master of the House of Xanthe."

"Master..." A faint smile curled her lips beneath his fingers. "Of course you would be. You're too arrogant to be anything less."

The thread of recognition that hummed between them became a tangible bond. Not from the mere sharing of her name, but the sizzling sexual awareness and intimate teasing that made him feel as if they were long-term lovers, not virtual strangers.

Perhaps they'd been mates in a former life, he inanely thought, surprised by how...*right*...she felt lying next to him.

His fingers deliberately stroked down her throat, his skin warm as he prepared to release his powers.

Muriel shivered beneath his touch, then grimaced as more blood oozed from her open wounds.

Her pain was obviously intensifying.

"Look at me, Muriel," he commanded in low but firm tones, waiting for her to gaze deep into his eyes. "I'm an Incubus."

Her brows pulled together in confusion. "Yeah, I'd figured that out."

"So you understand how my powers work."

"Ah," she breathed. "Sex."

"Yes." He wasn't sure why, but he had to be crystal clear. He usually used his powers without hesitation. To seduce, to feed, to manipulate. But not with Muriel. Never with her. "I won't force you to accept my healing. You must agree."

The indigo eyes darkened with an emotion that was far more complex than mere desire.

Pain, wariness, and a vulnerable longing for affection that he sensed she hadn't meant to share.

To him the glimpse of her heart it was like an unexpected gift.

One he intended to treat like a rare treasure.

"I accept," she at last murmured.

"Good girl," he whispered, his hand drifting down her throat until it hovered over the highest bullet wound.

Releasing his powers, he searched the torn flesh. No bullet. He moved his hand to hover over the second wound, flinching as he found the silver projectile that had lodged itself in her shoulder blade.

Shit. She had to be in agony.

Not that she was complaining. No, she remained silent as she watched him with pain-dazed eyes, so still. Unmoving. A vision of delicate, female temptation.

Fear ripped through him, twisting his gut as he gently lifted his hand to brush a silken curl from her too-pale cheek, his gaze remaining locked on the ragged holes that marred her upper chest. The sight threatened to destroy the thin leash he held on his fury.

With a fierce effort he forced himself to concentrate on the spark of hunger that smoldered deep inside her, releasing his powers to flow through her.

"Oh," she hissed.

"Are you okay?"

"Don't stop," she muttered, her glorious eyes wide as the rush of pleasure threatened to overwhelm her.

"Shh...it's okay," he assured her. "I've got you."

"It feels wonderful," she breathed, her muscles beginning to loosen as he concentrated his energy on numbing her brutal pain. "Like sunshine pouring through my blood."

When he'd done all he could to deaden the nerves, he returned his hand to lightly cover her most grievous wound.

"Muriel."

"Mmm?" she murmured, clearly struggling to focus.

A side effect of his healing was not only a sexual high, but it tended to make his partner feel intoxicated.

"Look me in the eyes." He threaded his voice with enough compulsion to force her to meet his steady gaze.

She obediently peered deep into his eyes, her lips parting as his demon magic swirled between them.

"So pretty," she said in husky tones.

"I think that should be my line," he countered,

trying to keep her distracted as he released a sharp burst of energy.

She gasped as he focused his power on the silver bullet, wrapping his magic around so he could rip it out of her flesh.

"Jian." Her body bowed off the mattress in shocked agony, the golden haze he'd used to sedate her shattering as she watched him crush the bullet in his hand before he tossed it across the cavern in disgust.

"Forgive me," he husked, pressing his lips to her temple as he stroked his hand over her chest. "There was no easy way to get it out."

His powers relaxed to a gentle pulse that offered a soothing heat.

She released a shaky sigh, her body melting back into the softness of the bed as her own powers began to return.

"Dear…heavens," she rasped.

"Is it better?"

"Yes." She gave a slow nod, her gaze still focused on his face. "I can heal myself now that the silver is removed," she said in a husky voice.

As if to prove her point her ravaged flesh began to knit back together, the wounds rapidly fading to tender pink scars that would disappear in a few hours. At the same time the blood began to dry and fleck off, revealing the ivory perfection of her breasts that were tipped with rosy crests.

Unable to resist, Jian lowered his hand to cup one lush mound, his thumb teasing the nipple to a hard peak.

"Do you want me to stop?" he demanded.

"I…" She shivered, but not from pain. Instead the scent of heated orchids suddenly filled the air. "No."

A wicked smile curved his lips. "That, sweet angel, is the right answer."

"So arrogant," she muttered, but she couldn't hide the flush of arousal that returned the color to her pale cheeks.

His fingers lightly plucked the tip of her nipple as he bent his head to place a tender kiss on her lips. She gave a small moan. A sound somewhere between pleasure and intense, desperate yearning.

Slowly he brushed his lips side to side, teasing a response rather than demanding it.

Not easy, considering that he was painfully erect.

Oh…hell.

For the first time in his very long existence the magic thundering through him wasn't about manipulation, or healing, or punishment.

It was a raw, aching male need for the woman who touched him on a primeval level.

She shifted with restless need, her body arching in a silent plea even as she tried to disguise her intense reaction.

"This doesn't mean I intend to release you," she warned.

"You think I'm your prisoner?" He nibbled at her full bottom lip, his fingers continuing to tease her breast.

His cock twitched, his balls tight. Her skin was so soft, and the feathers beneath him…

They pressed against him like the finest silk.

"You are."

He chuckled. "Before this night's over, sweet Muriel, you're going to be the one enslaved."

# CHAPTER FIVE

Muriel could barely think.

His lips were scalding hot as they tormented her with swift, too fleeting kisses, while his fingers were creating jolts of excitement as he toyed with her breasts.

"I can't be enthralled," she muttered, wanting to dismiss the delicious, addictive pleasure tingling through her as nothing more than a result of Jian's powers.

She was in bed with an Incubus. How could she not be drowning in desire?

The gorgeous male nipped her bottom lip, the tiny pain creating a startling flare of pleasure that made her shiver in response.

"Not by magic," he said, his tone smug. "But I have other methods of bewitching a female."

He did.

Her hands lifted, smoothing over the hard ridges of his chest, testing the smooth silk of his skin before she allowed her nails to dig into his flesh. She smiled at his rough groan of pleasure. Lifting her head, she allowed her lips to trace the small wounds she'd made.

He tasted of sandalwood and dark male power.

He was exotic. Mysterious. A cunning warrior who destroyed the illusions wrapped around her and left her exposed.

But she wasn't the only one feeling vulnerable, she abruptly realized. Jian was as overcome as she was by the desire that sizzled between them. She could feel it in the compulsive stroke of his hand and the rough kisses he spread over her cheek before he was burying his face in the curve of her neck with a harsh growl.

Was it possible?

An Incubus who was unable to control his sexual hunger?

The thought was oddly intoxicating. Jian was obviously a demon who was accustomed to being the master of seduction. He would demand complete obedience from his lover. But in this moment he was clearly at the mercy of his emotions.

While she...

Heaven help her, but she ached for him. With a furious need that was rapidly building to a sheer torment.

For too long she'd been a bringer of pain. Of punishment. A shadow of torment that lived in the pits of Hell.

Tonight she wanted to be a woman.

A soft, giving female who brought only pleasure.

Why not?

It was obvious she'd been betrayed by the Conclave.

Surely she deserved some measure of happiness

before she was forced to confront those who were willing to sacrifice her for their own nefarious purpose?

Craving his touch, she turned on her side and arched against his lean, glorious body. She was done fighting. She wanted to indulge in the wild excitement that coursed through her.

After years of emptiness she wanted to be saturated with sensations. She wanted to drown beneath the torrent of heat, and excitement, and sweet golden arousal.

Jian whispered her name, his head slowly lowering. His lips captured hers, parting them with a fierce hunger. Muriel moaned, feeling a dangerous fracture in the thick ice that surrounded her heart.

No. Not her heart.

This was all about lust, she grimly assured herself. An exchange of pleasure with a sex demon who could fulfill her deepest fantasies.

Something to be enjoyed and forgotten.

Nothing more.

Her heart was a barren wasteland. It had to be. She was, after all, the Mistress of the Oubliette.

Thankfully unaware of her dark thoughts, Jian lifted his head to stare down at her pale face. Then, with a fierce expression he threaded his fingers in her hair and tilted her head back.

His teeth scraped her skin as he nuzzled a hungry path down the line of her collarbone, the scorching heat of his lips making her shudder with need.

Her fingers gripped his shoulders, the breath wrenched from her lungs as he continued to press tiny kisses over the curve of her breast until he at last captured the tip of her nipple between his teeth.

Oh…yes.

Yes, yes, yes.

Her eyes squeezed shut in bliss, her hands sliding down his back as she arched forward to feel the press of his thick erection against her lower stomach.

He planted a line of kisses between her breasts. "Can I touch?" he asked in thick tones.

She felt a momentary confusion.

Wasn't he already touching?

"What do you mean?"

"Your wings," he clarified, waiting for her to force open her eyes and meet his gaze that smoldered with a golden fire.

She hesitated a second before answering. There was nothing more intimate to an angel than allowing someone to caress their wings.

"Yes," she breathed, bracing herself as he ran a hesitant hand over her feathers.

An explosion of sensations burst through her, wrenching a low moan from her lips as she dug her nails into the hard muscles of his ass.

He closely monitored the heat that stained her cheeks, his fingers moving to trace the joint where her wings met her shoulder blades.

"Are they sensitive?"

"Very," she choked out.

His sinfully gorgeous smile widened. "Good."

"You're a bad, bad man," she softly chastised, her pussy wet and aching to be filled.

"Hang on, angel," he warned, abruptly rolling

her flat on her back as he perched on top of her. "I intend to prove just how bad I can be."

"Really? I—"

She forgot how to speak as he lowered his head and sketched a path of searing kisses over her recently healed wounds.

Oh, that felt…

Indescribable.

She trembled, barely breathing as those destructive lips continued downward, briefly teasing her hardened nipples before skimming over the flat plane of her stomach.

A soft sigh was wrenched from her throat as his hands slid beneath her thighs, tugging her legs apart so he could settle between them.

She glanced down to watch the golden eyes glowing with wicked delight as he licked a slow, thorough path through her aching pussy.

A strangled shout was caught in her throat at the acute spikes of pleasure that darted through her, her back arching and her wings quivering against the bed.

"Mmm…so sweet," he said in thick tones, his tongue dipping into her wet channel. "I could spend all night tasting your sweet ambrosia."

He gave another tug on her legs, spreading her even wider as he nibbled and tormented her with a skill that would make any sex demon proud.

Pleasure pounded through her, her fingers reaching down to slide through the short strands of his satin hair.

After so long being denied even the most casual touch, she was starved for the feel of him.

"Wait, Jian." She bit her bottom lip, the exquisite sensation of his tongue stroking over her sensitive clit sending her toward a swift climax. "I want to feel you inside me."

She hissed in pleasure as she felt the tip of his cock at her entrance, the golden gaze holding her own as he slowly pressed into her slick heat.

They groaned in unison.

She'd never been so ready, but still he filled and stretched her to her limit.

It was perfect.

She cupped his face in her hands as he lowered his head to claim her lips in a searing kiss, a dark, heady desire flowing through her.

Slowly, steadily he began to stroke in and out of her, his erection pulling out to the very tip before burying deep inside her again and again.

At the same time, he allowed his golden magic to swirl around her, intensifying each sensation until the sexual arousal threatened to burn her alive.

Her fingers slid into his hair, her hips rising to meet his thrusts.

She'd never felt like this before. Not this pure, ruthless need. It was more than just lust. More than typical physical desire.

It was communication at its most basic level.

"Are you completely healed?" he rasped against her lips, his fingers trailing down her throat.

Muriel allowed her tongue to trace the sculpted lines of his mouth, refusing to dwell on her injuries. Later she would deal with the Sovereign and his implication she'd become expendable to the Conclave.

Tonight was all about pleasure.

"Yes."

"Thank God."

His strokes increased in tempo, his hands skimming her shoulders before seeking the sensitive arch of her wings.

He captured her moan of pleasure with a kiss that was edged with a savage need.

For her.

Just her.

Pressed into the mattress, Muriel gripped his shoulders as he thrust into her with a surging intensity, his head dipping down to capture the tip of her nipple between his lips. At the same time his electric energy tingled over her skin.

His teeth grazed her tender breasts, his hands lowering to grasp her hips, angling them higher so he could plunge even deeper into her welcoming body.

Muriel cried out, the pleasure threatening to overwhelm her as she hovered on the edge of a cataclysmic orgasm.

She was close.

So close.

And yet the bliss hovered just out of reach.

As if sensing her desperation, Jian lowered his hand between them, using the tip of his finger to rub against her clit.

"I've got you, angel," he assured her softly.

"Yes," she groaned, bolts of white-hot pleasure shooting through her as he surged in and out of her at a ruthless pace.

The small cavern she'd claimed as her own had

been a cold, barren place that had always been more a cell than a home. But tonight it was filled with breathless moans and the rich, exotic scent of cinnamon.

Silently memorizing each sensation, Muriel tucked them in the back of her mind.

Soon Jian would be gone, and she would once again be alone.

She had to have something to ease the bleak hours.

Kissing a path back to her neck, Jian dug his fingers into her hips as their bodies moved together with perfect harmony. He gave a strangled groan, his thick cock slamming deep inside her as his finger pressed against her clit.

Her body clenched with an unbearable tension, then for a breathtaking second she hovered at the pinnacle before bliss shattered through her with enough force to make her entire body shake.

At the same time, Jian's magic exploded around them in a dazzling display of golden light and savage sensual pleasure.

Astonishing, she acknowledged, heaving a deep sigh as Jian pressed a tender kiss to her lips.

It was no wonder females became addicted to sex demons...

# CHAPTER SIX

Jian reluctantly pulled out of Muriel's warm body and rolled to stretch out beside her.

Holy hell.

After centuries of indulging his desires with the most beautiful, talented, and experienced women in the world, he would have sworn nothing could surprise him.

But he'd been completely unprepared for his reaction to this delicate angel.

Granted, he wasn't going to complain at the stunning pleasure that continued to shudder through him. Or the compelling fascination that assured him this was far more than just another night of sex.

But she'd completely destroyed his rigid discipline, clouding his mind so he'd forgotten that she'd so recently been injured.

He grimaced, his fingers lightly pushing her silken curls off her damp forehead.

He was an Incubus, for God's sakes.

The fact that he'd been so completely at the mercy of his sexual need proved just how deeply ensnared he'd become in her feminine temptation.

"Are you okay?" he was forced to ask for the

first time in his very long existence.

She smiled, although he didn't miss the wariness that darkened the beauty of her indigo eyes.

"Trolling for compliments, Incubus?"

"No." His fingers skimmed down her cheek, lingering on the pulse that hammered just below the stubborn line of her jaw. "I can tell when a female has been thoroughly satisfied," he assured her, his smug satisfaction at her flushed cheeks and racing heart faltering as his gaze caught sight of the fading wounds that still marred the ivory skin. "I am, however, concerned that I was too rough."

Her flush deepened. Embarrassment or anticipation?

Perhaps a combination of the two.

"I told you I was healed," she breathed.

He lightly traced the diminishing scars, his gut twisting at the vivid memory of watching her collapse onto the hard stone, the blood dripping onto her white wings.

He had a feeling that particular image would be haunting him for several decades to come.

"I know, but you scared the shit out of me," he admitted in harsh tones. "I thought you were going to die."

An elusive emotion tightened her fragile features. "You stayed to save me."

He frowned. Why did she sound surprised?

"Did you expect me to abandon you when you were injured?"

"You were here to find your Sovereign," she pointed out. "Now he's gone."

"I'll find him," Jian muttered, his tone

distracted as his hand continued downward to cup the soft mound of her breast. "But nothing was more important than healing you."

Her rosy nipple hardened as a shiver of pleasure raced through her body. But he sensed that the shock on her face had nothing to do with her instant arousal.

"Jian."

"Astonishing, isn't it?" he questioned in wry tones. A part of him found it highly ironic that such a wicked demon would succumb to destiny in the arms of an angel. "How did you so easily bewitch me?"

She blinked. Then blinked again. "I have no magic."

"Lie." He lowered his head to gently brush his mouth over hers, savoring the soft temptation of her lips. "I am completely bespelled."

She stirred restlessly beneath him, but she made no effort to push him away.

"No doubt you're bespelled by a female on a nightly basis," she muttered.

"Never." He lifted his head to regard her with a somber expression. He didn't want any confusion. This was too important. "Only you."

Her tongue peeked out to dampen her dry lips. "You can't be certain."

"I'm certain enough that I should be—" He broke off with a sharp laugh.

"What?" she prompted.

"Angry. Terrified," he replied with blunt honesty. "Running away in horror."

In a heartbeat she went from enchantingly wary

to visibly annoyed by his response.

"Nice."

He stroked the tip of her nipple with his thumb. He wasn't entirely teasing her.

Like any Incubus, he'd secretly wondered what it would be like to be mated. To find the other half of his soul that would fulfill all his needs. And at the same time, he'd been horrified by the mere thought of being tied to one woman for the rest of eternity.

Surely it would feel as if he was being smothered?

Instead he felt...exhilarated.

Almost drunk on the sensations that bubbled through his blood like the finest nectar.

And the fact that she was an angel only intensified his smug pleasure.

Who knew fate could be so generous to give him a mate who was so gloriously perfect?

"Now all I can think about is how quickly I can get you to my home," he admitted in a rough voice.

The sweet scent of orchids saturated the air, assuring him that she wasn't opposed to the thought of being whisked off to his private lair.

Of course, she wasn't going to admit to her desire.

He'd already discovered that this angel was terrified of revealing any hint of vulnerability.

"That's impossible," she breathed, lifting her hands to press against his chest.

He studied the pale face that would forever be etched on his heart.

"Why?"

She frowned, as if baffled by his question. "Do you want a list?"

His hand moved from the soft temptation to the feathers that shimmered with a brilliant white glow in the torchlight.

"Give me the top three," he insisted, his lips twitching as she violently shivered as he found that sensitive spot at the very top of her wings.

"I'm an angel," she managed to choke out, a delectable color staining the perfect ivory of her face.

"Are you a snob?" He traced the graceful curve of the wing. Who knew that the sensation of feathers beneath his fingers could make an Incubus threaten to self-combust? "Do you think angels are too good to be with a mere demon?"

She sucked in a shaky breath, her lips parted in helpless desire.

A dull, aching throb settled at the base of his fully erect cock in reaction, his hunger for this female a seemingly bottomless need.

"Obviously not."

"Ah." He pressed his thigh between her legs, his arousal twitching at the feel of her warm pussy growing wet with need. "Then it's just mating an Incubus that troubles you?"

She made a strangled sound. "Mate?"

He rubbed his thigh against her swollen clit, his gaze fastened onto her flushed face.

God, she was beautiful.

"Tell me number two," he urged.

Her nails dug into his chest as she struggled to speak. "I'm the Mistress of the Oubliette."

Jian grimaced. "Yes, a far more dangerous obstacle," he grudgingly admitted. "Are you bound to this place?"

"Not physically," she said, her lashes lowering to hide her eyes. "But it's my duty."

He made a sound of disgust. He'd heard the Sovereign claim that those in charge of this hellhole had given him permission to destroy this exquisite female.

Whenever he discovered who they were and how he could get his hands on them, he intended to tear them into tiny shreds. Just as he was going to destroy his treacherous leader.

"A duty given to you by people who would willingly sacrifice you," he growled.

She flinched, as if he'd managed to strike a blow. "We don't know that for certain. You've admitted you don't trust your Sovereign," she pointed out. "He could be lying."

Jian scowled, sensing that the potential betrayal had wounded her more deeply than the bullets that had ripped through her chest.

Why? As far as he knew the Warden was chosen by a random lottery, switching from demon to angel every century to ensure that neither species managed to gain too much control over this powerful purgatory.

So why did he feel such deep sorrow through the delicate threads that were already beginning to bind them together?

Studying the brittle expression on her fragile features, Jian reluctantly accepted that this wasn't the time to press for an answer.

Instead, he returned his attention to her supposed reasons for refusing to travel to his home.

"Tell me number three," he demanded.

Her eyes abruptly narrowed, the heartbreaking look of loss thankfully being chased away by a flare of unmistakable jealousy.

"I won't become a part of any man's harem."

Jian slowly smiled, delighting in the surge of annoyance that filled the air with the scent of scorched orchids.

This was his beautiful angel.

Proud. Strong. Capable of taking on even the most arrogant Incubus.

His fingers smoothed down the snowy feathers, his leg pressing tight against her increasingly slick clit.

"Not even a harem of one?"

"One?" She gave a hesitant shake of her head. "I thought that Incubi never have sex with the same female."

"They do after they've mated."

"I can't believe you're serious."

"I've never been more serious." He wouldn't tease about something so important, even if he did enjoy the flash of jealousy in the indigo eyes when she spoke of his harem. "Not ever."

"This is madness," she muttered.

"Yes." He lowered his head, nuzzling a path of kisses over her cheek to the corner of her mouth. "But it's too late to hope for sanity."

"Jian…"

Her words were lost in a breathy sigh as Jian rolled on top of her, deepening his kiss as she instinctively spread her legs.

"My sweet angel," he husked, using the tip of his tongue to  outline the lush curve of her lips.

He groaned.

She tasted of sunshine and warm orchids.

A heady, potent combination that made his cock stiffen to the point of pain.

Grasping her face in his hands, he kissed her with an urgent need that thundered through him.

It didn't matter that he'd just enjoyed one of the best orgasms of his life.

Or that she would be the first female he'd ever had sex with more than once.

It didn't even matter that he was increasingly certain she was his mate.

This was all about heat, and need, and sweaty bodies tangled together in raw pleasure.

Plundering her mouth with savage demand, he pressed the tip of his cock to the entrance of her body, then with one thrust of his hips he was locked deep inside her, the sizzling power of his Incubus magic wrapping around them in a golden swirl of bliss.

~ ~ ~

It was several hours later when Jian reluctantly forced himself to press a final, lingering kiss on Muriel's swollen lips.

It wasn't that he feared the effects of making love to her yet again.

Granted, he'd lost track of the number of times he'd claimed her sweet, willing body. But it didn't matter if he'd reached the magical number eight that would bind them together for eternity. He'd already accepted that this exquisite angel was born to become his mate.

"As much as I would love to spend the rest of eternity with you wrapped in my arms, I can't forget what brought me here," he husked, grudgingly rolling off the bed and pulling on his clothes.

Muriel's drowsily sated expression was instantly replaced by a wary unease as she slid off the bed and headed toward a small wooden chest in a far corner.

Jian had a brief glimpse of a slender female ass before her wings were snapping together to hide the magnificent view. Then, reaching into the chest she pulled out a simple linen dress that she dropped over her head to cover her slender curves, arranging it to drape down her back without interfering with her wings.

Jian sucked in a sharp breath. Since when had a woman getting dressed been so damned sexy?

Usually his only interest was getting them *undressed*.

Shifting as his cock was once again hard and aching, he watched her turn to study him with a guarded gaze.

"You intend to track down the Sovereign?"

"Eventually." He ran his fingers through the short strands of his hair, already sensing she wasn't going to be happy with what he had to say. "First we need to discover what is hidden in the lower dungeons."

He was right.

Instantly her features tightened with an emotion he found impossible to read.

"What are you hoping to find?"

Well, that was the question, wasn't it?

When Vipera had hired him, it had been with the command to discover where the Sovereign was hiding.

His own goal was far more personal.

Especially now.

The bastard was going to pay for shooting his angel.

"Something that will prove the Sovereign is a traitor to his people," he at last said.

Her brows pulled together, forming a deep frown over the indigo beauty of her eyes.

"Do you want the Throne?"

"Not for myself," he answered without hesitation. His duty was to restore the House of Xanthe to its former glory. He would leave the role of leader to someone more suited to the task. "But I'm determined to see an Incubus of honor as our Sovereign."

"Then why don't you demand the current leader step down?" she demanded.

"Because I don't have the proof I need." He reached to grasp the obsidian dagger that'd dropped to the floor. "Not yet."

She lifted a hand to touch the silvery marks that still marred her skin from the bullet wounds.

"And it's imperative to have proof?"

"If we hope to avoid war," he admitted. He'd learned from his grandfather that it wasn't a simple matter to remove the House of Marakel from the

Throne. His burning desire to discover that evidence, however, didn't blind him to the fear that he could sense trembling through his fragile companion. "Why are you attempting to keep me from the dungeons?"

She bit her lower lip. "I've been forbidden to enter the lower dungeons."

He moved to stand directly in front of her, gently tucking a curl behind her ear.

"Aren't you in charge here?"

She gave a hesitant nod. "Yes, but that doesn't mean I don't have to obey—"

"Obey whom?" he prompted as her words were cut abruptly short.

"Those who sent me."

*Those who sent you?*

Why the hell was she being so cagey? Was there something going on with the Oubliette?

"Muriel."

With a jerky motion she was turning away from him, her wings spreading to keep him at a distance.

"I'll be punished."

Calmly, Jian walked around the feathery barrier so he could once again stand in front of her. His lovely angel was going to have to learn that he wouldn't be shut out.

Not when she so clearly needed him.

"What do you mean?"

She kept her lashes lowered, a fine tremor shaking her body.

"When Canaan escaped I was thrown into the abyss."

He winced. He'd been delighted when he'd

heard that his fellow Incubus had managed to escape from the Oubliette and regain command of his House. Now he deeply regretted the agony Muriel must have endured.

"I'm sorry."

She lifted her head, her expression grim. "I just got out. I won't go back."

# CHAPTER SEVEN

Muriel shivered as Jian ran gentle hands over her shoulders and down her arms, as if his touch could ease the memory of the flames that had burned her flesh from her bones.

And he wasn't wrong.

The feel of his light caress helped to replace the horrifying sensation of fiery pain with a golden glow of pleasure.

Not magic.

Just a female responding to her male's tender care...

"I can't bear the thought of you being hurt," he growled, his voice rough with anger.

She shrugged. "I failed in my duty."

He instantly pounced on her words, his eyes narrowing. "Duty to whom?"

"I told you," she muttered. "Those who sent me here."

"You've actually been quite careful not to name who has a claim on your loyalty," he pointed out.

She shook her head, fear arrowing down her spine.

This Incubus was so noble.

Terrifyingly noble.

Not only had he been willing to brave the pits of purgatory to help his people, but he'd stayed to save her when it would've been so much easier to leave her behind.

But he didn't understand just who he was going to have to face if he continued his search for the truth.

"Don't do this, Jian."

His fingers skimmed back up her arms and over her shoulders before tracing the upper curve of her wings in an oddly familiar gesture.

"Why?"

"It's dangerous."

His Incubi heat wrapped around her. Not to seduce, but to comfort.

"Who sent you here?"

She heaved a deep sigh. Stubborn fool.

He was going to get himself killed.

"The Conclave," she reluctantly revealed.

His eyes widened in shock. "The angels are in control of the Oubliette?"

"Yes."

"Since when?"

"I'm not sure." She licked her dry lips, unable to bear the thought of what would happen if they managed to capture Jian. "At least the past five centuries."

Demon magic blasted through the air, the sexual heat nearly sending Muriel to her knees.

Good...heavens.

She was never going to get used to that.

"The Sovereign must have known," Jian snarled, seemingly unaware that Muriel was drowning in his sensual power. "But why would he allow them to gain such power?"

She sucked in a deep breath, leashing her fierce urge to rip off his clothes and lick him from head to toe. How was she supposed to concentrate when he was arousing her to the point of insanity?

"I truly don't know," she choked out.

Turning away, Jian paced toward the middle of her private cavern, his liquid grace reminding her that while he had the sexual prowess of an Incubus, he was also a lethal warrior.

"They must have promised him something," he muttered, thankfully leashing his magic. "Power, weapons…some means to retain his Throne."

Muriel pressed a hand to her racing heart, trying to clear the fog of sex from her mind.

"They no doubt promised him any number of things," she agreed, her lips twisting into a humorless smile. "But he would be a fool to believe them."

Jian turned back to meet her wry gaze. "You think they're using him?"

"Of course." She grimaced. When she'd been called before the ultimate leaders of the angels, she'd been awestruck. Now she realized she'd allowed herself to be blinded. Not only by their unmistakable power, but by their fearsome beauty. "The Conclave have become obsessed with the desire to regain control of your world. The first step is gaining command of the Obsidian Throne."

"The idiot," he ground out, the golden eyes glowing with an inner fury. "He's become their puppet and he doesn't even realize it."

She grimaced. "He isn't the only one."

Making a visible effort to control his frustration, he moved back to cup her face in his palm.

"Why did they send you here?"

Ancient anger rushed through her. "I was told it was because I'd refused the mate chosen by my family."

His hand tightened on her face, the air prickling with a sudden danger.

"Mate?" he rasped. "Some other male tried to claim you?"

If any other male had said anything about *claiming* her, she would have made sure he understood with painful clarity she wasn't an object to be owned. Not by anyone.

With Jian, however, it sounded...perfect.

"Obviously he didn't succeed." She soothed his ruffled emotions. "I preferred to be sent to Hell rather than be forced into an eternity with an angel who viewed me as nothing more than a means to procreate."

His fingers trailed down the line of her jaw, his thumb absently brushing her lower lip.

"So you're paying the penalty for not being an obedient daughter?"

She instinctively stepped closer to his comforting warmth, oddly chilled by the unwelcomed memories of being sentenced to the Oubliette.

"That was my assumption."

"And now?"

She shuddered. For so many years she'd simply done her time as the Warden, telling herself that she would eventually be returned to her family and this would all become a distant nightmare.

Only now did she allow herself to truly consider why the Conclave had been so insistent that she be disciplined for her refusal to accept their arranged mating.

"My family isn't particularly powerful, but they have spoken out against the Conclave in their desire to expand their powerbase," she said slowly. "I'm beginning to suspect that I'm a lesson to the other families who stand against them. No one wants their children taken away from them."

Without warning he leaned down to brand her lips in a kiss that seared through her with shocking heat.

She blinked, grabbing his upper arms to keep her balance.

So that's what it felt like to be struck by lightning, she inanely acknowledged.

"You won't be their pawn any longer," he promised, lifting his head to study her with a brooding gaze.

Her fingers dug into his arms as she was overwhelmed by the urge to try and shake some sense into the stubborn male.

"You can't alter angel politics."

"No, but I can take you away from them."

Muriel hesitated. It was one thing to fantasize about a future with this gorgeous, insanely sexy Incubus. Hell, what woman wouldn't dream of having Jian as her mate?

But it was quite another to actually walk away from any possibility of returning to her home.

"My family—"

"Allowed you to be their sacrificial lamb," Jian interrupted, his voice filled with disgust. "They don't deserve you."

She couldn't argue.

She might not know exactly how the Conclave had threatened her parents, but whatever it was had obviously been worth forfeiting their only daughter.

"And you do?" she tried to tease, not wanting to dwell on the thought her family would turn their backs on her.

"Probably not." He placed a soft, lingering kiss on her lips. A silent promise of devotion. "But I intend to dedicate each day to earning the right to call you my mate."

She trembled, feeling as if she were the most important person in the world when she looked into his eyes.

"You are very good at this," she breathed.

Another long, lingering kiss. "Be mine."

How could she resist?

Even if she hadn't been abandoned by the angels and left to rot in this hideous place, she would have followed Jian to the ends of the Earth.

He was her mate.

It didn't matter that he was an Incubus. Or that her family would never, ever accept their union.

This was the male who her heart had been searching for since the beginning of time.

"My mother warned me that demons would come and steal me away if I didn't behave," she murmured, her hands stroking over the hard muscles of his chest.

359

"True." He nipped her bottom lip. "But isn't it much more fun being the bad girl?"

It wasn't just fun, it was addictive, she conceded as his fingers caressed her sensitive wings.

Still, she wasn't foolish enough to think they could waltz out of the Oubliette.

Especially not if Jian was determined to search the dungeons.

She wrinkled her nose. "That depends on if we get out of here alive."

His expression hardened with a grim determination. "I'm not going to let anything happen to you, sweetheart." With one last kiss he stepped back. "Are you ready?"

Was she?

With an effort she tilted her chin and moved toward the doorway.

She'd allowed her life to drift from day to day because she lacked the courage to stand up to those who put her in this prison.

She wasn't going to waste another second.

"This way," she murmured, leading Jian down the narrow staircase to the tunnel that wound its way through the Oubliette to the lower chambers.

They moved in silence, both focused on their surroundings.

The thick air tainted with sulfur. The screams of the prisoners. The heavy sense of doom.

All familiar to Muriel, although there was a strange vibration that was making her wings twitch.

Continuing past the rows of cells, she gave a sharp shiver.

It wasn't sympathy for the prisoners. They were

some of the most heinous in the Oubliette.

Murders. Rapists. Traitors.

But instead it was a chill of premonition.

"I feel…" Her words trailed away as her powers focused on the source of her discomfort.

Jian was instantly at her side, his hand grabbing hers in a gesture of comfort.

"What's wrong?"

"Someone's entered the Oubliette," she said, fear spreading through her like a virus.

Jian stilled, his hand reaching to grasp the obsidian dagger he'd tucked in the waistband of his jeans.

"The Sovereign?" he asked.

"No." Her mouth felt dry, her heart pounded. "The Conclave."

Jian grimaced. "Shit."

"Yeah." She squeezed his hand. "Shit."

# CHAPTER EIGHT

Jian urged his companion to continue their trek down the tunnel, smoothing his expression as he sensed her terror.

Muriel was on the edge of panic.

No surprise, considering what she'd endured over the past few hours.

He had to keep her focused if they were going to discover what was hidden in the dungeons and then escape the Oubliette.

"Can they locate you?" he asked, relieved when she managed to suck in a deep breath and once again take the lead as they hurried into an adjoining tunnel.

His brave, beautiful angel.

"No, the magic of the Oubliette will protect me for now," she said, her voice pitched so it wouldn't echo through the spiderweb of passageways. "But they'll eventually track us down."

"We'll be long gone before then," he assured her, sending a silent prayer that he could keep his promise.

"I hope so," she muttered, pressing her wings back as she squeezed through a narrow opening that led to a steep flight of stone steps. "I really,

really don't want to go back to the abyss."

"Never again," he swore, wincing as the screams from the prisoners echoed through the tunnel. "Are they always so loud?"

"Unlike you, they can't see through my illusions," she muttered. "Each of them believes that their cell is filled with whatever they fear the most."

He gave a shake of his head. "You are a dangerous female, sweet angel."

She sent him a glance over her shoulder, lowering one wing to make sure he didn't miss her warning expression.

"Don't ever forget."

He chuckled. There was nothing sexier than a strong woman who wasn't afraid to speak her mind.

"Believe me, I won't," he growled in appreciation, before his brief distraction came to an abrupt end as they entered a cavern that was shadowed in utter blackness.

For a disturbing second he was completely blind, then Muriel whispered a soft word and she was glowing with a silver light.

At any other time he would have been in awe at the sight of her ivory beauty illuminated in the soft radiance.

*This* was why angels had been worshiped throughout the centuries.

Unfortunately, he couldn't afford to bask in her loveliness. Not now.

Instead he studied the massive cave that seemed to have no end.

"Have you ever been down here?" he asked, his

gaze skimming over the jagged stalagmites and stalactites that made it impossible to see more than a few feet in any direction.

She shivered. "No."

"So there are no illusions?" he pressed.

"Not that I've created."

"Damn." He cautiously moved forward, peering behind the rock formations. "I sense—"

She moved to stand at his side. "What?"

Jian gave a frustrated shake of his head. "Nothing," he muttered. "I sense nothing."

She wrinkled her nose, allowing her silvery glow to spread further through the cavern.

"So what is the Sovereign hiding?"

That was exactly what Jian intended to discover.

Ignoring the feeling of emptiness that filled the air, he continued to search behind the stalagmites. Dammit. There had to be something here.

It took nearly a quarter of an hour before he at last stumbled on shallow trenches that had been dug into the hard stone floor.

"Muriel," he called softly.

The angel hurried to his side, her light revealing what he'd already suspected.

There were three body shapes heavily wrapped in white shrouds.

"Oh." She sent him a worried glance. "They look like mummies."

Crouching down, he tugged aside the thick material to reveal the man hidden beneath.

"Not mummies," he muttered, continuing to pull off the shroud.

Muriel made a sound of surprise. "An Incubus."

She leaned forward, her brows drawing together at the sight of the man's pale face that was surrounded by hair so dark red it appeared crimson in her silvery light. "Is he dead?"

"No, but he's been heavily wrapped in Nephilim magic," he said, struggling to accept what he was seeing.

She pointed to the other bodies that were laid side by side.

"What about the other two?"

He scooted to the shallow graves, swiftly unwrapping the Incubi from the shrouds with a growing anger.

"Watchmen," he ground out, his fingers twitching with the fierce need to wrap them around the throat of the Sovereign and squeeze...

Someday he was going to make the bastard pay.

Someday very, very soon.

"Do you recognize them?" Muriel demanded.

His gaze moved to the distinctive tattoos that circled the Watchmen's upper arms.

"Not personally, but I suspect that I know exactly who they are."

"Who?"

"The Master of House Akana and his bodyguards," he said, unable to believe he was saying the words.

For centuries they'd been told that the House had died out. And no one had ever questioned the Sovereign when he'd announced the last Master had been destroyed.

Now he struggled to accept that the poor bastard had been held in this cavern as some sort of…what?

Hostage?

Sacrifice?

It made no sense.

"A Master?" Muriel took an instinctive step backward. "Why would they be hidden in these dungeons?"

"I intend to find out," he snarled, pulling out his phone in an attempt to take pictures of the unconscious Incubi. "But not here."

Muriel frowned in confusion. "What are you doing?"

"Sending proof of the Sovereign's treachery," he muttered, hoping to upload the pictures to Taka. His bodyguard would know to take the evidence to the ruling Houses.

"I don't think that…" Muriel waved a hand toward his phone. "Technology will work here."

Jian muttered a curse. She was right. The screen remained blank.

"I'll have to try to carry them out of here," he at last conceded, slowly straightening and turning to the female standing at his side. "But not until I'm certain you're safe. We need to return to the gateway."

She bit her bottom lip, her face pale as she studied the unconscious Incubi.

"I can try to hide them with an illusion until you can come back for them."

"Will it hide them from the angels?"

She gave a slow nod. "My powers of illusion are my natural gift," she said. "I should be able to create an illusion that only I can see through." She sent him a wry glance. "And you."

Jian frowned, not needing the mating bond to realize there was something troubling her.

"You're worried," he said, reaching out to brush his fingers down the chilled skin of her cheek. "Why?"

She hesitated, as if she was going to foolishly try and deny her concern. Then, with a grimace she turned her head to glance toward the opening of the cavern. "When I weave the spell it's going to attract the attention of the Conclave. We have to be quick."

No more anxious than Muriel to give away their location to the approaching angels, Jian leaned down to slide his arms beneath the limp body of the closest Incubus, cradling him against his chest as he straightened. Then, with as much care as possible, he carried him across the cavern to tuck him behind a large stalagmite.

Swiftly he had the second Watchman and the Master placed next to him on the ground.

"Ready," he muttered.

# CHAPTER NINE

Muriel wiped her damp palms on her linen shift, struggling to ignore the prickles of magic dancing over her skin. The angels were coming closer, their power a tangible force in the air, but with a stern effort she concentrated on the three unconscious Incubi that Jian had piled next to the stalagmite.

The sooner she could finish her task, the sooner they could leave.

Or at least, she hoped they could leave.

If the Conclave managed to catch them, they would...

No. She held out her hands and released her magic. She wasn't even going to consider the varied and gruesome ways they could be tortured.

Not when she needed to concentrate.

With controlled bursts of power, she disguised the males in layers of illusion until she was certain no one would be capable of seeing more than a large rock that matched the other stones throughout the cavern.

"That should keep them hidden," she muttered.

Jian nodded, rubbing the tense muscles of his nape, as if he could sense the approaching danger.

"I don't suppose you have a secret way out of

368

this place?" he asked.

She shook her head, for once in her life wishing she weren't quite so efficient.

"No, after your friend's escape I made certain that there were no more opportunities for random gateways."

"Damn."

"There's an opening to the Sovereign's fortress as well as one to my homeland," she said. "That's it."

Reaching out, he grabbed her hand in a firm grip. "Then we go to the fortress."

Another wave of energy prickled over her skin. "We have to hurry," she breathed.

Easily sensing her fear, Jian tightened his hold on her hand and jogged toward the opening to the cavern.

Together they climbed their way out of the lower chambers, Muriel pointing the way when they came to crossroads. Around them the prisoners screamed for mercy, and those servants who'd earned her trust scurried to complete their duties, but they managed to avoid the angels as she took them through the heart of the Oubliette.

Muriel was entering the cavern that was just below the gateway when she felt as if someone had reached inside her and ripped away a vital organ.

Halting in shock, she waited to see if she'd been struck with a fatal bolt of magic.

It didn't feel as if she were dying.

Instead she felt…empty.

Oh.

"Wait," she breathed, trying to keep her balance

as her body readjusted to the sudden change.

Whirling around, Jian studied her with sharp concern. "What is it? Have you been hurt?"

She licked her dry lips. "They've taken my powers," she said.

He frowned. "You're no longer the Mistress of the Oubliette?"

Dear heavens.

It'd been so long since she'd been a simple angel with no curse to carry that she'd forgotten just how heavy a burden her position as Warden had truly been.

Now she felt free.

As light as air.

Of course, she also had no means to control this particular dimension, which was no doubt the reason the Conclave had stripped away her powers.

"No."

He ran a comforting hand over the upper curve of her wing. "Are you in pain?"

"Actually…" She gave a shaky laugh. "It's wonderful."

He pressed a swift kiss to her forehead. "How much farther to the gateway?"

She pointed toward the staircase. "It's just above us, but the Conclave is close."

He held his dagger in one hand, his features tight with grim determination.

"How close?"

She shivered, no longer capable of feeling the life forces spread throughout the prison.

"I'm not sure."

"It doesn't matter." He placed another kiss on

her forehead before tugging her toward the stairs. "Let's get the hell out of here," he muttered, taking the steps two at a time.

Muriel remained close at his side, her heart racing as they entered the large cavern above.

"There it is," she said, pointing toward the shimmering opening only a few feet away.

Jian nodded, holding tightly onto her fingers as he sprinted across the wide cavern.

A few feet from the opening, however, there was buzzing sound from behind them, and with a low curse Muriel was knocking him to the ground.

Just inches from their heads a bolt of white-hot magic sizzled past, slamming into the wall with enough power to make the entire cavern shake.

"Damn," Jian muttered, hurriedly following Muriel as she darted toward a nearby rock. "What was that?"

"Angel fire," she said, peering over the rock toward the shadows at the far end of the room.

She'd muted her illumination, making it impossible to see through the murky darkness where the Conclave was gathered.

Crap.

"I've heard about it, but I've never seen it in action," Jian rasped, his voice thick with disbelief. "Can you do that?"

"My power isn't nearly as great as the Conclave's," she said, chewing her bottom lip as she tried to judge the distance between them and the gateway. Could they make it without getting hit by the Conclave's powers? "But I do have some fire."

"You really are a dangerous female," he muttered.

"Look out," she cried as there was another loud buzz.

They both ducked behind the rock, then without thinking, Muriel lifted her hand and sent a bolt of her own magic. She hadn't lied when she said she didn't have the same power as the Conclave, but she did have an intimate knowledge of these caverns, and with unerring accuracy hit the fault line at the far end of the ceiling.

There was a momentary silence before a sharp crack echoed through the Oubliette, and with astonishing force the heavy rocks collapsed from above to bury the opposite end of the cavern in a pile of rubble.

There were screams of pain and fury from the angels who were buried beneath the avalanche of stone. Not that the cave-in would actually kill them, but it took even a powerful angel time to remove several tons of rock.

Shock jolted through her.

What had she done?

It was one thing to escape with Jian. It was quite another to actually attack the Conclave.

Of course, they had been trying to kill her, she acknowledged, a hysterical urge to laugh bubbling through her. Surely she was allowed to protect herself?

"Are you okay?"

Muriel gave a shake of her head, coughing at the thick cloud of dust that filled the air.

"I wasn't hit," she assured her companion.

Without warning, Jian grabbed her shoulders so he could gently turn her to meet his searching gaze.

"That wasn't what I meant," he murmured softly, surrounding her in the comforting warmth of his magic. "It's difficult to battle your own people."

A portion of her distress eased.

It was difficult, but she had no choice.

Not if she was going to survive.

"I'm fine," she said. And she was. The horror of attacking her leaders was already fading as she savored Jian's gentle touch. This male had stood by her and healed her, while her own people had dismissed her as collateral damage. They no longer deserved her loyalty. In fact, she would do everything in her power to protect Jian against them. "Besides, I didn't really hurt them. It only slowed them down."

"It's all we need." Rising to his feet, Jian glanced around the cavern that remained undamaged, ensuring that there were no other angels hidden among the shadows. Then, stepping around the rock he headed straight for the gateway. "I'll go first."

Muriel hurried to catch up with his long strides, easily sensing his tension.

"What are you expecting?" she demanded, belatedly realizing that escaping the Oubliette might be the beginning of their danger.

"The angels aren't the only ones who will be expecting us to use this gateway," he muttered, his steps never slowing.

"Jian." She grabbed his arm, bringing him to a

halt.

His lean body hummed with obvious impatience, but he readily turned to cup her face in his hands.

"Trust me, Muriel," he murmured, his thumb brushing her bottom lip. "I swear I'll protect you."

As if she'd ever doubt his fierce instinct to keep her safe.

She shook her head, fear twisting her gut.

Not for herself.

But for this male who would sacrifice everything for her.

"I know that. It's…" Her words trailed away as her emotions threatened to overcome her.

He frowned in concern. "Muriel?"

She gazed into his lean, painfully beautiful face before she went on her tiptoes to kiss him with a hint of desperation.

She'd just found this sexy, gorgeous, wondrous male.

She couldn't bear to lose him.

"Just don't get yourself killed," she commanded in a husky voice.

The golden eyes flared with a devotion that made her melt.

"I have no intention of dying," he promised. "Not when I have so much to live for, my sweet angel." His skimmed his fingertips over her face, as if memorizing each feature. Then he slowly stepped back and squared his shoulders. "Ready?"

She sucked in a deep breath.

"Ready."

~ ~ ~

Jian forced himself to step forward, acutely aware of the woman who followed him with complete trust.

Gods. The last thing he wanted was to lead his beautiful angel into even more danger, but it wasn't like they had any choice.

They couldn't stay in the Oubliette.

Not with the Conclave clearly determined to kill them.

Unfortunately, he didn't doubt for a second that they were jumping directly from the frying pan into the fire.

Entering the gateway, he felt a prickle of magic dance over his skin, then he was through and standing in the ornate bedchamber.

For a second he felt oddly disoriented as he adjusted to his world.

The room was shrouded in shadows, but he sensed that it was early morning. Just as he sensed that more than a day had passed since he'd last stood in this spot.

Whether it was a week or a month was impossible for him to determine.

Dammit.

Pulling out his phone, he was relieved to discover that he had enough service to send a quick text to Taka. His brothers had no doubt been preparing the House of Xanthe for war.

Now he urged his bodyguard to warn his family to wait on any plots of revenge for his disappearance.

Sliding the phone back into the pocket of his jeans, he clutched his dagger in one hand while tugging Muriel toward the silk screen that divided the room.

"Stay here," he murmured softly, his gaze locked on the doorway that led toward the outer hallway.

"This is the fortress?" Muriel whispered, her eyes wide as she took in the heavy tapestries and mosaic tiled floor.

"Yes, and we're not alone," he warned.

"Another Blade?" Muriel demanded.

"Not this time. Watchmen," he said even as two large bodyguards entered the room.

Moving to the center of the room so he would have plenty of space to fight, he covertly hid his hand holding the obsidian dagger behind his back.

Both warriors were well over six feet, with bulging muscles and shaved heads. They were heavily armed with guns as well as daggers that were sheathed across their broad chests.

The tallest of the two stepped forward, his bluntly carved features impassive.

"Xanthe."

Jian assumed an air of command. He was a better fighter than most, but he didn't like the odds.

He far preferred intimidation to actual battle.

"Where is your Master?"

The Watchman's dark eyes narrowed. "He has better things to do than deal with intruders."

*Intruders.* Not *intruder.*

Shit. The male had obviously sensed Muriel despite the fact she was hidden behind the screen.

The need to avoid a fight became even more imperative. He couldn't risk being injured and leaving his angel vulnerable.

"Better things," he sneered. "Like betraying the Incubi?"

As expected, both Incubi stiffened. There were few things more important to demons than their honor.

"We are not the ones who have tried to betray our king."

Jian made a sound of disgust. "Marakel is not a true king. He's a petty tyrant who has allowed himself to become a pawn for the angels."

The Watchman gave a betraying glance toward the open gateway, revealing he wasn't entirely comfortable with the explanations the Sovereign had been giving for his journeys into the Oubliette.

Still, he grimly held onto his loyalty. "He would never deal with the angels."

"No?" Jian stepped forward. "I have proof."

Without warning a hidden door slid open, revealing the tall, thin Incubus with a shaved head and dark eyes. With an arrogant tilt of his chin he stepped into the room.

Attired in loose pants and a white tunic that was embroidered with gold threads and a large ruby, he regarded Jian with unconcealed loathing.

"Kill him," he growled, pointing a long, slender finger in Jian's direction.

"What's wrong, Marakel?" Jian mocked, hatred twisting his gut. This male had negotiated with the angels, kidnapped and held Incubi as captives, and nearly killed Jian's beautiful mate. It was time for him to pay for his crimes. "Don't want your servants to know that you've abused their loyalty to keep yourself in power?"

There wasn't so much as a flicker of guilt on the gaunt face. In fact, there was nothing but the fanatical glitter in the dark eyes to reveal the vile corruption that had destroyed his soul.

"They understand that I am the best leader for our people," he snapped.

"You certainly have the greatest arrogance," Jian taunted.

The Master of House Marakel turned his head to glare at his Watchmen.

"What are you waiting for?" he snapped.

"Maybe they want to know why you've allowed the angels to take command of the Oubliette," Jian said, not missing the Watchmen's jerk of surprise at his revelation. Any demon with an ounce of intelligence would understand that if the Oubliette was no longer neutral ground, then an invasion by the angels couldn't be far behind. "Is it to hide the fact you've been holding the last Master of the House Akana as your prisoner?"

"Shut up," the Sovereign hissed.

"Akana," the nearest Watchman growled. "They've died out."

Jian shook his head, silently making note that the warriors clearly were unaware of their Master's treachery.

"I've seen him with my own eyes."

"Don't listen to him." Marakel released a burst of his power, attempting to compel his servants to obey. The Sovereign possessed a talent for coercing others to his will. One of the reasons he'd managed to maintain control of the Throne for so long. "He's trying to destroy your loyalty."

Jian glared at the male who had willingly betrayed his own people.

"Tell me why, Marakel."

The Sovereign waved a hand toward the two Watchmen. "What are you waiting for?"

The first of the bodyguards slowly reached for his gun, clearly torn between duty and a growing suspicion that his Master might not be worthy of his loyalty.

Before he could actually pull the weapon, however, there was a targeted bolt of energy that hit just an inch from the warrior's heavy boots.

"Don't move," Muriel warned, stepping from behind the screen and spreading her wings that glowed with a silver light.

The two Watchmen stepped back in stunned terror, their faces slack with awe as they studied Jian's exquisite mate.

"Angel," they breathed in unison.

Resisting the urge to stare at his magnificent angel, Jian launched forward, using the distraction to grab the Sovereign by the throat and slam him against the wall.

"Tell me why," he snarled, lifting his dagger to press the point of the obsidian blade beneath his chin.

The older male widened his eyes, his arrogance shattering as he realized that he was well and truly cornered.

"Because his power is to sense the birth of a

Succubus," he muttered.

Jian frowned in confusion at the mention of the female demons who'd become extinct years ago.

"There haven't been any Succubi for…" His words broke off as he recalled that they'd all thought the House of Akana had died out. "Holy shit. Have you done something to destroy the Succubi?"

Marakel hesitated, almost as if he was trying to come up with a convincing lie. Jian curled his lips into a humorless smile, allowing the sharp tip of his blade to pierce the bastard's flesh.

"Not me," the Sovereign squeaked, his frantic gaze darting toward the Watchmen who were still mesmerized by the sight of a real-life angel standing just a few feet from them.

"Then who?"

"The Nephilim priestesses," he finally snarled, accepting his guards weren't about to rush to his rescue.

Jian frowned. Nephilim? Granted, the inclusion of the priestesses in the Sovereign's nefarious plot would explain the presence of the Blade who'd been standing guard at the gateway.

But what possible interest could they have in the female demons?

"Why?" he ground out. "Why would they destroy the Succubi?"

"Because we would have no need of the Nephilim if the Succubi were allowed to return," Marakel rasped. "Their power comes from our need for their breeders."

"Damn."

Jian gave a small shake of his head.

He'd never considered what the Nephilim had gained when the last of the Succubi had disappeared.

Power. Prestige. And for some…immortality.

Hell, it was no wonder they would sacrifice anything to destroy the female demons.

Struggling to organize his chaotic thoughts, Jian nearly missed the sudden sound of running footsteps just outside the door to the bedchamber.

Jian sucked in a deep breath, catching the familiar scent.

Nephilim.

At least a dozen.

Shit.

He didn't need the relief on Marakel's thin face to warn him that these warriors were well aware of his treachery. And that they would be ready and willing to kill anyone who threatened the Sovereign.

For a crazed moment he teetered on the edge of murder. Sticking the sharpened blade deep into Marakel's heart would put an end to his current reign on the Obsidian Throne.

Unfortunately, he couldn't ignore the voice of warning that reminded him this bastard had information they might need. Not only to rescue the Master of Akana, but to defeat the Nephilim priestesses and return the Succubi.

His lust for revenge was going to have to wait until later.

Besides, now all that mattered was getting Muriel to safety.

With a swift movement, Jian slammed the blade

through the Sovereign's shoulder, pinning him to the wall.

It wouldn't kill the bastard, but it was all the distraction he needed.

Even as Marakel screamed in pain, Jian was leaping backward, grabbing Muriel's hand and releasing a burst of demon magic.

The air swirled around them like a mini tornado, the world fading away.

Jian tugged his angel close, feeling her tremble as they shifted through the darkness.

"Hold on," he whispered in her ear, breathing deep of her exotic scent of orchids.

A heartbeat later their feet were touching the icy ground and Muriel was pulling her wings in tight as they were blasted by a frigid breeze.

"Is this your home?" she demanded, shivering as she glanced around the barren shoreline bathed in the weak morning sunlight.

Jian grimaced, able to understand his mate's barely hidden distress.

"No," he assured her, glancing over his shoulder at the steep mountain that led to the fortress. "I can only carry us a short distance at a time. We'll have to hide until I can rest."

There was no fear, or censure, at his confession they were stuck on the frigid island where they might be captured at any minute.

Instead his beautiful angel gave a simple nod, her expression calm as she considered their bleak surroundings.

"I can wrap us in illusion," she assured him with a courage that made his heart swell with pride.

"They won't find us."

Jian gently cupped her chilled cheek in his hand, but before he could speak, he was stiffening as he realized they weren't alone.

Whirling around he prepared for battle, only to breathe a deep sigh of relief as he caught sight of a shallow boat being rowed toward the shore.

"Or my Watchman can take us home," he said wryly, standing at the edge of the water with his hands on his hips. "I thought I told you to return to my brothers," he growled.

The bodyguard was still dressed in his leather pants and a T-shirt, his harsh features stoic, as if he hadn't spent the past few days waiting in sub-zero temperatures for his Master to return.

"I've kept them updated, but I knew you would eventually need me," Taka said.

With a shake of his head, Jian grabbed Muriel's hand and urged her into the small boat.

"You truly are the worst-trained bodyguard," he said, his teasing words saying more to the male who was his closest companion than any amount of flattery.

Barely waiting for Jian to jump into the boat, Taka was pushing away from the shore and unfurling the small sail to send them scooting over the shallow water.

"Fortunate for you," the Watchman murmured.

"Fortunate for both of us," Jian agreed, moving to tug the silent female close to his side. "Taka, this is my mate, Muriel."

A faint smile touched the large male's lips as he cast an appreciative glance over Jian's companion.

"An angel?"

Jian pressed his lips to Muriel's temple, his heart filled with love as she wrapped her arms around his waist.

He'd gone into the Oubliette to alter the future of the Incubi, and in the end, changed his own destiny.

It felt somehow fitting.

"I always did demand the best," he said softly.

"True," Taka readily agreed, steering the boat to the larger ship that was hidden behind a massive iceberg. "Are we headed home?"

"No." Jian pulled his phone from his pocket. As much as he longed to return to his graceful mansion and spend the next century indulging his exquisite mate, he understood that until they'd neutralized the threat from Marakel and the Nephilim priestesses there could be no peace. "I need to call a meeting of the Masters," he growled. "Someplace neutral."

Taka regarded him with a somber expression. "You have the evidence you need?"

Jian turned his head to glance back at the fortress that was now lost in a fog of demon magic.

"After I share what I discovered, the Sovereign will pray the Obsidian Throne is the only thing he loses."

~ * ~

# ABOUT THE AUTHOR

**ALEXANDRA IVY** is the *New York Times* and USA Today bestselling author of the Guardians of Eternity series, as well as the Sentinels and Bayou Heat that she writes with Laura Wright.

After majoring in theatre she decided she prefers to bring her characters to life on paper rather than stage. She lives in Missouri with her family.

Visit her website at **www.AlexandraIvy.com**.

# MASTERS
# OF
# SEDUCTION

*The passion continues…*

## Winter 2014!

*For more information on the series,
please visit*

**www.MastersOfSeductionAuthors.com**

## Other books by Lara Adrian

### Midnight Breed Series

A Touch of Midnight (prequel novella)
Kiss of Midnight
Kiss of Crimson
Midnight Awakening
Midnight Rising
Veil of Midnight
Ashes of Midnight
Shades of Midnight
Taken by Midnight
Deeper Than Midnight
A Taste of Midnight (ebook novella)
Darker After Midnight
The Midnight Breed Series Companion
Edge of Dawn
Marked by Midnight (novella)
Crave the Night
Tempted by Midnight (novella, Oct 2014)
*...and more to come!*

### Phoenix Code Series

Cut and Run (Nov 2014)
Hide and Seek (Spring 2015

## LARA ADRIAN writing as TINA ST. JOHN

Dragon Chalice Series
Warrior Trilogy
Lord of Vengeance

## Other books by Donna Grant

### Dark King Series
Dark Heat
Darkest Flame
Fire Rising
Burning Desire
Hot Blooded
Night's Blaze

### Chiasson Series
Wild Fever
Wild Dream
Wild Need
Wild Flame
Wild Rapture

### Rogues of Scotland Series
The Craving
The Hunger
The Tempted
The Seduced

# Other books by Laura Wright

## Mark of the Vampire Series
Eternal Hunger
Eternal Kiss
Eternal Blood (eSpecial)
Eternal Captive
Eternal Beast
Eternal Beauty (eSpecial)
Eternal Demon
Eternal Sin

## Bayou Heat Series
Raphael & Parish (Books 1 & 2)
Bayon & Jean-Baptiste (Books 3 & 4)
Talon & Xavier (Books 5 & 6)
Sebastian & Aristide (Books 7 & 8)

## Wicked Ink Chronicles (New Adult Series)
First Ink
Shattered Ink

## Cavanaugh Brothers Series
Branded
Broken
Brash

# Other books by Alexandra Ivy

## Guardians of Eternity Series

## Sentinels Series